THE PRELUDE

A NOVEL FOR MANAGERS

THE PRELUDE

A NOVEL FOR MANAGERS

STEPHEN BRIGHT

From a concept by
Stephen Bright & Brian Thomas

Catapult Press
Austin Texas 1993

THE PRELUDE
Published by Catapult Press, Austin, Texas
First U.S. edition 1993
Copyright © Stephen Bright 1993
ISBN. 1-883860-00-8
Library of Congress No. 93-084812

All rights reserved. Without limiting the rights under copyright reserved above, no part of this publication may be reproduced in any form without the prior permission.

This book is a work of fiction. The characters and situations herein are inventions of the author.

Credits

Chapter 10 : the Pareto Chart (histogram) illustration on page 75 is taken from the work of Dr W. Edwards Deming in *Out of the Crisis* (page 3). 1986 Cambridge Mass. Institute of Technology, Centre for Advanced Engineering Study.

Chapter 22: *Changes in Latitudes, Changes in Attitudes*, Lyrics and Music by Jimmy Buffett, © 1977 Coral Reefer Music (BMI). All Rights Administered by Irving Music, Inc. (BMI). All Rights Reserved. International Copyright Secured.

Cover design

Dean Butler, Opsis Design, Melbourne, Australia, Phone 011 61 3 5103222.

> To obtain further copies of *The Prelude* or information about related materials and diagnostics see the forms at the rear of this book or contact:
> Somerset Consulting Group Inc.
> 1208A Somerset Avenue
> Austin, Texas 78758
> Phone: (512) 834 0076
> Fax: (512) 835 4998
> *Discount available for quantity purchases.*

Anna
you taught me how
you taught me why

Foreword

We talk a lot about change; about the need to raise awareness amongst managers and staff of the need to change. "Change" is a word that seems pervasive at all levels: for individuals, for groups, and for organisations.

But what does it mean? How can we explore the implications of change and present them in a way that people can understand and commit to the future development of their organisations?

Think for a moment about the film, "The Wizard of Oz". It is a film all about changing the way we see things. The beginning of the film is shot in black and white. It deals with the ordinariness of life in a world where there is restriction, and where imagination and innovation are frowned upon. But after the tornado has whisked away Dorothy to the land of Oz, a change occurs. The landscape is suddenly in brilliant colour. Where there was grey bleakness there is now colour and life. And those first words Dorothy utters could well serve most managers in contemporary business: "We're not in Kansas any more, Toto."

In her travels in Oz, Dorothy is accompanied by three odd characters: the Lion, the tin Man and the Straw man. They seek attributes which will enable them to face their futures. The Straw man seeks intelligence — the capacity to think, plan, experiment and learn. The Tin man seeks a heart — he wishes to have trust, compassion, integrity, honesty and the ability to love unreservedly. The Lion seeks courage — the strength to face the unknown, the spirit of endeavour and risk-taking that lies at the centre of good management.

In the end, these characters find the attributes they seek. They gain the skills to face the future — but not as a result of the Wizard's intervention. Rather, they realise the truth: courage, intelligence and love reside inside us. They can be nurtured and promoted, or they can be devalued and dismissed. The choice is always ours.

When I first saw this book, *The Prelude*, it reminded me of Dorothy's tale in many ways. *The Prelude* is a story about how people can learn to see things in a different way. It involves the reader in an examination of systems: the complex, interlocking, nested systems that seem all too often to interfere with the work of the change agent or manager.

It describes a world of colour, in the sense that it portrays the reality of existence inside organisation: the complexity, the opportunity, the conflict and uncertainty of management. Where most books present change as a simple linear activity consisting of a number of 'magical' steps which, if followed, will achieve instant results, *The Prelude* tries to show how results can be achieved in a complex, shifting environment. And I believe it works.

In its first printing, ten thousand copies were distributed to the top managers in Telecom, Australia's telecommunications company. It was distributed without any promotion, or any organisational injunction. It simply appeared on people's desk, and in-trays. Around three out of every ten managers read the book from cover to cover, which was a phenomenal response.

As a method for getting people on board, for creating awareness and a listening space that can be followed up by more traditional communication processes, The Prelude is proving extremely successful. It is an innovative approach to change, and it enables people to address the implications of change for themselves, their work groups and their organisation as a whole.

The Prelude breaks fresh ground in that it links the change agent's intervention to the reality of managing on a day-to-day basis.

Stephen Bright and Brian Thomas first set out to raise awareness of the issues surrounding continuous improvement in Telecom Australia. But the relevance and benefits of their work is now being shared by many other organisations. So far, *The Prelude* has also been used by Australia's largest steel producer, by mining companies, retail organisations, the military, and many government agencies. Its chain of use has spread to organisations in New Zealand, Singapore, and the United States.

Foreword

The distribution of the book is in itself, an example of nested systems: how one action can lead to another, and a complex network of discussion, opinion and endeavour can be built from a range of different sources and voices. This is how we bring colour to our world; it is how we bring courage, intelligence and love to our daily endeavours.

Stephen once told me of a little joke he'd written into *The Prelude*. The first character we meet is Albert Lapin, the embattled CEO. "Albert" is a name which derives from the Latin root, "albus" meaning "white". "Lapin" is, of course, french for "rabbit". Thus, the person who leads us into the world of *The Prelude* is the White Rabbit.

Organisational change is a lot like following the White Rabbit down a long dark tunnel, just like Alice did. At the outset of the journey, we're not sure exactly what is at the end or how long it will take to get there. But books like *The Prelude* can help managers to get a better picture of how deep the rabbit hole is, and what is on the other side.

Dr Oscar G. Mink
Professor, Adult Education and Human Resource Development Leadership
University of Texas

Contents

Foreword
Author's Preface
Map of Australia
Organisation Chart

1	Forecast	1
2	The Meeting	6
3	Newcastle	18
4	On the Beach	28
5	Meetings	34
6	Tall tales but true	47
7	All in the game	51
8	In need of repair	56
9	On the beach, part 2	65
10	Off piste	70
11	View from above	76
12	Flying high	80
13	Research	85
14	The Eagle on the Hill	91
15	Clayton's support	98
16	Twin city shuffle	107
17	Making headway	118
18	What next?	125
19	Caught napping	130
20	Natural selection	141
21	Down and out in Adelaide Hills	148
22	One-trick pony	152
23	Flight 479	160
24	Waiting	164
25	The ties that bind	169
26	Aftermath	174
27	The king must die	180
28	What future?	184
29	Wednesday morning 7 a.m.	194
30	Slow dancing	198
31	Commitment	204
32	Orpheus with his lute	210
33	The gods themselves	212
34	The song begins	220

Glossary   229

Author's Preface

The Prelude would not have been written without the help and advice of many people within Telecom Australia.

The idea of a novel written specifically for managers, and dealing with the twin themes of telecommunications and quality management, originated with Brian Thomas. Several hundred people within Telecom helped as I wandered the company over a period of several months, attempting to learn, describe and reflect the culture of a large organisation undergoing major change.

My sincere thanks particularly go to Roger Vistarini, my guide through the Telecom organisation. A finer Ariadne I could not want.

That the book has travelled as far as the United States is largely due to the foresight and support of three very helpful people, dedicated to understanding more about how organisations function: Professor Oscar Mink, Dr Barbara Mink and Ron Mundy.

And then there was Jenny Bright, my editor, proof-reader, advisor, confidant, toughest critic and greatest supporter.

Also, Anna Bright, Harry Bright, Roy Grey, Val Grey, Vincent Maskell, John McConnell, Jennifer Pattinson, David Pattinson, Ronnie and Ronnette, Loree Taylor, Roy Taylor, Bronwyn Thomas, John Thorne. And everyone at Branch 021.

Finally, I would like to thank all those people who, through their support, have encouraged the publication of *The Prelude* in America, in particular, Dr Myron Tribus, Mr Doug Campbell of Telecom Australia, and Dr Peter Ellyard, Director of Australia's Commission for the Future.

Stephen Bright
Melbourne, Australia

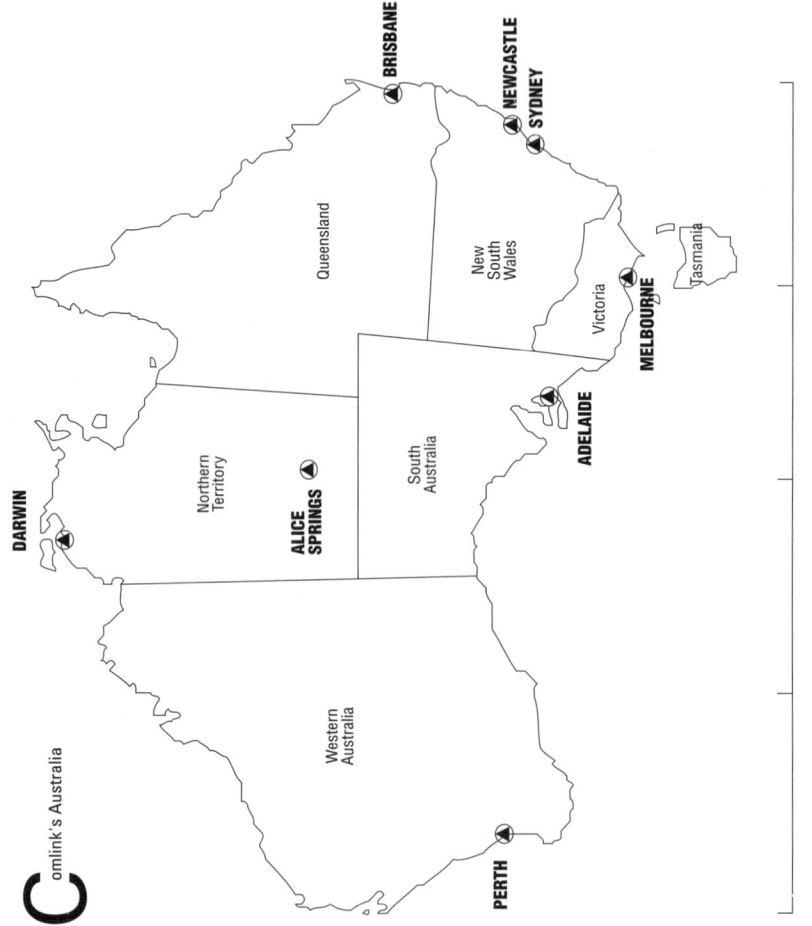

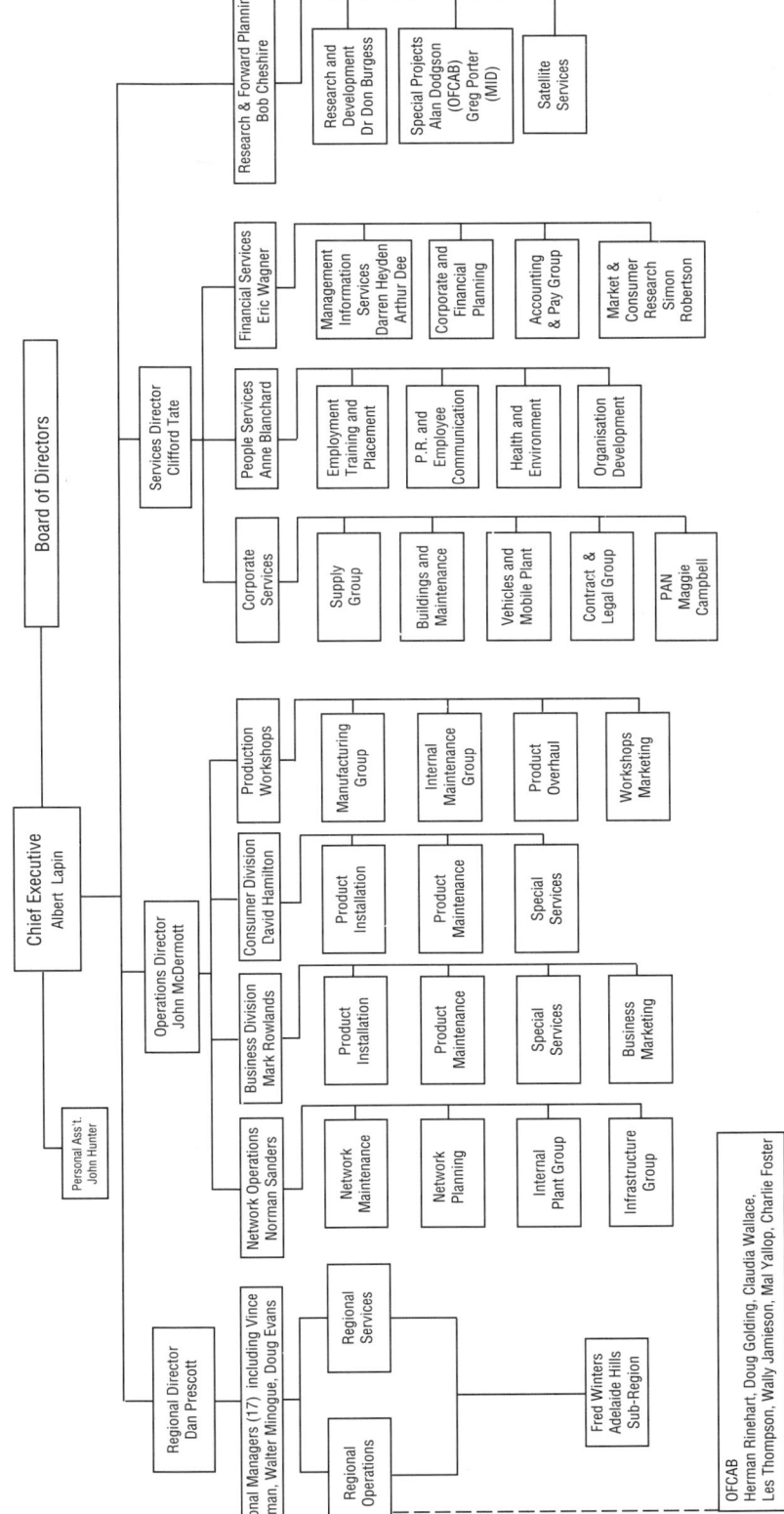

Chapter 1

Forecast

The upholstered silence of the car seemed at odds with the view through its windows. Albert lay back in the rear seat, staring out past the crowding city traffic, up into the heart of a lead-tinted thunder cloud. Somewhere behind his head the setting sun was forcing hard, pale rays of light through the grate formed by the upthrust spikes of Melbourne's office buildings. His focus drifted down to the Comlink building. Not the city's largest, it nonetheless trapped the eye this particular afternoon, standing out as shafts of light played across its mirrored facade, creating a featureless wall of blue-white radiance.

Whenever he approached the Comlink tower, Albert felt something cold and defensive about its glossy exterior. A fantasy, he told himself. Probably the result of the fascination with light, shadow and colour which had grown in him as his occasional hobby, leadlighting, developed into something of an obsession.

Albert had never been able to explain adequately the complete calmness which came to him as he fiddled with the lead trimmings and glass scraps. It was more than the attempt to capture light and transform it into patterns of meaning. There was also the smell: the heavy, earthy aroma of lead, countered by the crisp, astringent fragrance that curled upwards from crackling solder.

Solder was a link for Albert, a link to his past as a trainee electrical engineer. The scent, the glistening, molten softness, the heady blue smoke, all blended in the quiet of his small home workshop on a solitary evening. And there was texture: the faintly rough, pliable sensation of lead. Of course, there was virtually no lead in the system now, the Comlink network. But there had been once – miles of it. Hundreds of miles of smooth, curving lead,

The Prelude

snaking under the cities and between the towns and farms across Australia like the roots of an enormous tree.

Whenever he thought of all the hundreds of tasks performed by Comlink people, it was the linesman of the fifties whom Albert pictured, working in a tiny, khaki tent with PMG stencilled on the side. A tent and a pit crammed to exploding point with a hydra-headed mess of thousands of coloured wires – pairs – which had to be repaired after a foolish excavation by an unthinking council work gang.

And there was a boy of twelve, peeking in on the confusion, watching transfixed as the hard-fingered linesmen searched and picked and tested and guessed. The hundreds of pairs, each a nerve cell linking unknown places, were slowly connected, twisted together with a joint made of rough, brown paper. Each joint was a delicate operation, each a small victory. Albert watched their fingers, quick and strong, yet strangely fastidious, even as they lifted tin mugs of thick, black tea to their mouths.

Eventually, the whole incomprehensible cord of nerve cells was wrapped in its sleeve of malleable lead and the repaired cable thrust back under the ground.

The smells and sensations of that operation had stayed with Albert. Those same smells of lead, solder and earth were the central images of his leadlighting. They were the smells of Comlink to Albert Lapin.

The earthiness, the solidarity and pride in craftsmanship, came crowding into Albert's mind as he looked up at the Comlink tower. So often over the years, he had gazed at it as he journeyed to his work: initially as a harried commuter hanging grimly to a jolting tram strap; then as a junior executive with grudgingly-given access to a space in the car park, and, still later, as a senior executive with the privilege of a company car. Finally, as Chief Executive, his primacy had warranted a driver. Not something he really wanted, but something which came with the job – like the servant who rode beside a conquering Roman centurion whispering, 'Remember you are only mortal'.

The differences between Albert and the centurion were legion, but he felt them keenly whenever he thought on the role of his driver. Like so many of the trappings of his position, the actions of Luke Hughes, his driver, worked to increase his isolation, to increase the seductive vision that somehow he was not mortal like everyone else.

It was a vision which pleased Comlink. The organisation wanted heroes, legends, father figures to look after it. And Albert did not reject this role, preferring to be regarded as a father than as a hatchet wielder. He was a man who saw patterns and understood them, who read the pressures, threats and opportunities around him. The cycle of events, the play of power and the patterns of force in business were visible to Albert Lapin in the same way a tracker 'sees' his quarry in the crushed leaves and cracked twigs of a forest floor.

To read those pressures, define the patterns and guide Comlink into the future, that was why he had been given a large office on the twenty-fourth floor and a title which put him at the top of the organisation chart.

Yet now, when the need was greatest, the future-gazer was blind.

"It will take at least five minutes from here, Mr Lapin," said Luke quietly, "it would save a few minutes if I dropped you at the front."

"That's fine, Luke," Albert replied, glancing at his watch and realising he still had a few minutes to prepare for his next meeting. "Just drop me, and go home. I don't know how long this one's going to last. I'll get a taxi home and you can pick me up in the morning."

There was silence in the front seat.

Albert looked at his driver's thick neck and at the short, tough, grey hair sticking up so stiffly that Luke's head resembled a fuzzy potato. He smiled to himself at the tension in the strong, square-set shoulders as Luke gripped the wheel that little bit more tightly. It was always worth a try, but the truth was it never worked.

There was unvoiced reproach in every muscle of the driver's back. It had long become an unspoken rule that Luke would wait for Albert. The reasons were complex: some emanating from loyalty, job satisfaction and a pride in his task; others from the need for overtime rates and the belief that to allow Albert to catch a taxi was somehow to break regulations. Albert would often try to break free, but he had never succeeded, and his resolve was wearing to the point where it was easier to wander down to the car park and climb into the soft upholstery than to fight for a taxi at the end of a long day.

Albert had long ago discovered he could not re-deploy Luke, nor could he leave him idle. There were, after all, times when he did need a driver. As a result, they had settled into a relationship based on the understanding that they were both playing out roles: Albert the proconsul, and Luke the majordomo. Neither disliked their roles violently enough to want to do anything about them.

Suddenly the car was rolling to a halt at the kerbside of the Comlink tower. Albert opened the door and started to get out. He was halted as Luke turned to him solicitously.

The Prelude

"What time, Mr Lapin?"

Albert smiled slightly. Luke was deadpan. It was a battle Albert could not win. Nor was he sure he had the desire to win any more.

"Eight o'clock," he said, shaking his head.

"Good luck, Mr Lapin." It was Luke's formula goodbye. As if he felt that when Albert was roaming around outside his control there was a considerable risk that something disastrous would happen to the Chief Executive.

As the car pulled away, Albert turned to the building and looked up again for a moment. Even from this close, there was something introspective about its facade. Not for the first time, Albert wondered whether Comlink was the victim of perverse architects, or whether the designers were simply responding to the insecurities of the organisation. Wherever he went around the large, far-flung company, the same architectural styles pervaded: featureless facades of mirrored glass; massive brick walls without windows; exchanges with small windows at roof level. Buildings designed to look inwards, to keep themselves aloof from those who would be their customers.

He was reminded of the old tale about the concerned ratepayer who one day went to the local council offices where plans of a new development were on display for comment.

"Yes, of course," said the Information Clerk. "You walk out through the back of this building and find the Planning Section. Then go down to the basement of that building where you'll find the library. They'll be able to point you at the Archives Secretary who has the keys to the public comment display section."

The ratepayer started to move off on his search. "But they're at lunch right now," said the clerk.

"When will they be back?"

"Well, actually, today is a bad day. Friday would be better."

And so on the story went, with the resolute but increasingly frustrated ratepayer enduring more difficulties than Indiana Jones until finally – three months and several visits later – he found himself standing outside a bleak door at the end of a dusty, poorly-lit corridor. There was a tiny, almost illegible sign on the door:

> "In order to serve you better, your efficiency conscious council administrators have closed this office until further notice. Information about Planning Proposals can be gained from the Information Clerk in the main building."

Forecast

The ratepayer returned to the first clerk, only to be told that there was a management/union dispute over multi-skilling and that the information he required was covered by a work ban.

And so it went, until the fateful day when the ratepayer finally saw the plans, only to realise that the date specified for the closing of submissions had just passed, and there was no stopping the development anyway.

Albert checked his watch again. Ten minutes before the meeting: enough time to go over the briefing notes once more in his office. Not that he wasn't sure what the notes said. He knew very well. It was just, perhaps, that he did not want to believe it.

Chapter 2
The meeting

In the lift lobby on the twenty-fourth floor, Bob Cheshire was halted suddenly by a hefty slap on the shoulder and a raucous voice.

"How's our sun-bronzed Queenslander?" cried John McDermott, Comlink's Operations Director. "You're looking well, Bob. The rest of us Head Office wallies have been growing pale in our southern caves while you've been sunning yourself on northern shores, I hear."

John McDermott was indeed pale, but his light, freckled complexion and red hair did not give the impression of an unhealthy man. Short, bull-shouldered and thick-framed, he was in perpetual danger of bursting out of the faintly shabby tweed jackets he affected to wear. A robust renegade with a bristling orange moustache, he possessed a deft, easy style with men at all levels of Comlink.

He and Bob Cheshire had known each other for many years – since the Telecom days. Their friendship had begun at the workplace barbecues which were the vogue of the late eighties, when John had been a regional manager and Bob had just taken charge of one of the area's exchanges.

Where John McDermott was a bustling extrovert, Bob was quieter, less extravagant. He generally approached life with an easy vigour and mild irreverence.

Physically, Bob represented the conventionally depicted middle-aged man of reasonable health: forty-five, with brown hair mildly tainted by shreds of grey, and a deeply tanned face that bore the slight hardness which results from excessive time in the sun. His eyes were blue and clear, with humorous wrinkles spreading from their corners. A small crook in his nose bore witness to a short but spectacular career in Queensland's junior rugby team.

"I'm thriving," Bob replied warmly. "It's just wonderful to be back."

The meeting

They both laughed.

"Ready for the 'State of the Nation' speech?" John enquired, as they walked down the corridor to the meeting room.

"Settle down, I just got back this morning, and haven't even made it halfway through my Info-File yet. I've barely glanced through the agenda."

John caught his friend's sleeve, halting on the threshold of the room. He looked suddenly serious. "Have you spoken to the boffins this morning?"

As Divisional Manager of Research and Forward Planning, Bob was responsible for Comlink's research laboratories and workshops, product planning and development, several special projects and some of the more novel technological activities of the organisation. The 'boffins' were Bob's R & D Group.

"I spoke to Uncle Don," Bob replied, referring to Dr Don Burgess, the head of Research and Development. "He said your business marketing people had been getting a lot of info on the Dick Tracy Watch. But I didn't have time to find out what it was all about. Is there something I should know?"

John flipped through his copy of the agenda for the afternoon's meeting. He stopped and pointed out an item for Bob. "Have you had a chance to catch up with Albert yet?"

"About the item on the Dick Tracy Watch? I'll give a verbal report on the development program," Bob replied.

"Did you know that the Financial Services people have also had a good look at the Watch?"

"Yes, I did," said Bob, feeling faintly defensive. "Clifford cleared it with me before I left. They also had a good look at OFCAB, the MID Project and a number of others. What's with all the questions?" He stared at John, still unsure of the meaning within his friend's words. "And no, I haven't seen Albert yet. We were slated for a meeting this morning, but he had to cancel."

"Come on boys, some of us want to get some work done this afternoon," said a third voice.

Bob turned, and realised that he and John were blocking the entrance to the room. Anne Blanchard, the head of People Services, was standing, smiling faintly, a giant briefcase in one hand.

Anne was the only woman in the Comlink senior management group. It was no coincidence that she invariably walked into meetings armed with enormous quantities of files. She liked to be prepared. Early in her career, Anne had found that a female manager needed to be a great deal more prepared than her male counterparts.

The Prelude

Bob returned her smile and moved aside. The three moved into the room and Bob lost the opportunity to find out what John was trying to say.

Once inside the room, everything changed. The decor was neutral: grey walls, grey carpet, grey slim-line blinds on the floor-to-ceiling windows. A buffet stood to one side set with a range of coffee and tea. Beneath the buffet was a fridge, which was invariably stocked with plenty of beer and other necessities of life. Bob looked at it for a moment sensing that, somehow, at the end of this meeting, no-one would be suggesting they have a quiet drink.

The room might have been innocuous, but the atmosphere was not. Eight of the fourteen people who made up the Comlink senior management group were seated around the long table in the centre of the large room.

Anne Blanchard stood at the buffet pouring a cup of coffee. She looked up at Bob.

"Good break?"

It was an ordinary greeting, yet there was something sharp and uncertain in Anne's voice, as if she had just said something obscurely important. Bob stared at her, convinced he was missing vital signals this afternoon.

"Fine. Yeah, fine thanks, Anne." Frowning slightly, Bob reached for the back of a chair, pulled it out and sat down. He looked up and down the table. Everyone suddenly seemed to be chatting to someone else. He looked across the polished surface to where John McDermott sat facing him. The late sun slanting in through the room's blinds threw the Scotsman's face into shadow, leaving Bob guessing as to the expression in his eyes.

Bob started to say, "What's wrong?" then thought better of it. The unspoken rules which the managers had developed in this forum were strong. If he asked for an explanation someone would simply parry it, saying it was best to wait until Albert arrived.

Bob glanced at his watch. It was a couple of minutes past the appointed starting time. It was not unusual for Albert to be late by a few minutes, yet he now became aware that Clifford Tate, the head of the Services Directorate, was also absent. Clifford was punctual to extremes. A tall, thin, angular man, he had the bearing of a sober accountant and the humour of an undertaker.

Shuffling the papers before him, Bob flicked them into order and placed them fastidiously in front of him in a neat, square pile. He picked up a pen, put it down, reached out for the water jug and poured himself a glass, picked up the pen once more.

This had something to do with the Dick Tracy Watch, he thought furiously. What was wrong?

The so-called 'Dick Tracy Watch' was a new product being developed by Bob's R & D Group. It was a new-generation, highly-advanced, computerised videophone. Completely portable, small and light enough to wear strapped to the user's wrist, its revolutionary technology enabled full video, audio and data transmission. The Watch combined the application of sophisticated video design with the highly effective communication network developed from the 'cellular' net which had exploded in the early nineties.

The design achieved its remarkable portability from the use of a carrier network of small transceiver units scarcely larger than a house brick. These units could be manufactured cheaply and placed on virtually every street corner in a city, enabling the Dick Tracy unit to 'tap' into the cellular network to transmit and receive the large quantities of electronic data necessary for high quality video transmission.

The project was slated for development over a five year time span. Barely a year of that time had passed. The project was well on schedule and within its cost targets. So what was the problem?

Bob attempted to remain calm, to focus on the present rather than inventing problems for himself. He mentally catalogued the projects under his control and the items mentioned in his last status report to Albert. There was nothing substantially wrong, he felt. There were problems with OFCAB, the large-scale Optical Fibre Cabling installation project, but they had not reached a serious stage. Yet.

Bob had doubts about the OFCAB project design, and about the recommendations of the external consultants who had assessed the project six months ago when timelines really began to slip. He could not deny that things picked up a bit after the consultants went through, although he sensed they were slipping again. Still, it was hardly a cause for the massive concern he felt emanating from those around him.

He needed to concentrate on the unspoken messages. What was going on? What had he missed in the three weeks he'd been away?

It wasn't a threat: John hadn't spoken as though there was something he would be called to account for and Anne Blanchard had seemed friendly. Hardly what he would have expected if his position was in some danger. No, no-one was avoiding him as though he was about to become the hanged man. On the contrary, they were watching him as if he was going to provide something they were looking for. What had he missed? Damn the holiday.

The door at the far end of the room opened with a slight click and Albert's personal assistant slid through with a mound of papers clutched close. The door led straight from Albert's office and for a moment all the

The Prelude

managers looked around, expecting to see the Chief Executive follow his assistant into the meeting.

Yet Albert didn't appear, and the slight buzz of conversation continued after a few moments. It was several more minutes before the door opened again. Only it wasn't Albert who emerged.

The group of managers attempted to hide the upsurge of interest they collectively felt when Clifford Tate stepped through the door, to be followed immediately by Albert. Each member of the group quickly formulated a mental mantra to reduce their anxiety: 'There's nothing strange about Clifford and Albert having a meeting. Nothing at all. Nothing at all.'

* * * * *

Clifford Tate moved silently down the length of the table, taking the seat at the opposite end to Albert, a seat usually left vacant as a result of some unvoiced agreement among the managers.

After some moments, Albert cleared his throat. "This is an unusual meeting," he said softly.

"First of all, I find I need to apologise to Bob. We are going to discuss something today which involves you and your people. Unfortunately, it is something which had to be investigated while you were absent. I have had to consider it without the benefit of your advice or input."

Albert was clearly embarrassed. It was rare for him to apologise.

"I had intended to brief you this morning, Bob, but I was forced to attend another meeting. It was a meeting which has only served to make our response to the current situation even more critical."

Bob sat staring at the Chief Executive's stiff, grey moustache, his mind racing in neutral. He felt detached, unable to comment except to offer a weak smile and wait like a lobster in a restaurant fish tank.

"I want you to hear me say in front of everyone, Bob, that the fact we have had to investigate this option while you were away in no way reflects any lack of confidence in you or your management of the Research and Forward Planning Division. We have worked well together for a number of years now and there is no reason why that will not continue."

A measure of relief crept into the cold pit of Bob's stomach. But almost immediately the anxiety flooded up again as he remembered how, just last month, the Prime Minister had said much the same thing about her Treasurer. A week later, the Treasurer had departed to the dusty depths of the back benches, never to be seen again.

Albert motioned to Clifford Tate and Bob found himself staring back down the table as the tall, balding Director of Services rose. Clifford gazed around the room. His brown eyes lit on Bob for a moment and he made a slight gesture, as if to indicate he was aware of trespassing on Bob's turf, but that there was nothing he could do to avoid the intrusion.

Clifford began crisply. "In the decade since deregulation, a great deal has happened. We've had successes and some failures. Yet one thing has remained consistent: our declining share of the telecommunications market.

"The network is in excellent condition," he continued, nodding fractionally at John McDermott. "The technology is highly advanced and is deployed effectively. Large scale data processing has meant significant opportunities for us, and we have taken advantage of them. Our large corporate and government customers are significant supporters, paying for their special access facilities through the prioritisation loadings introduced in 1996.

"However, whilst we have a system which is recognised internationally as being of an extremely high standard, we have failed, time and again, to get the best out of it.

"We have a serious problem with household users. Our 'Time in Excess of Allocation' charges are a sore point with an increasingly vocal number of consumer groups. The pressure these groups have been able to marshal has been increasing recently. You have only to see the biased invective in news telecasting to see the strength of the 'anti-profit' lobby. Their complaints around a single issue have spread to take in other issues such as network access, maintenance and repair prioritisation, and community discrimination."

Clifford's clipped, humourless voice made the customer dissatisfaction sound tawdry, like a cheap betrayal by those you have laboured selflessly to sustain.

"This part of the problem is not new; I repeat it simply as background to some further comments Albert will be making. It has been compounded by the aggressive marketing of many competitors, and by the general fragmentation of the communications market in the decade following deregulation.

"We anticipated that the high infrastructure development costs associated with telecommunications would keep a good many people out of the marketplace. This did not happen."

The group was becoming restless. Clifford was not telling them anything new and Bob wondered what he was meandering towards. Another, more irreverent part of Bob's mind made comment on the attention span of executives. It often appeared to him that the higher executives rose in the company structure, the less time they were able to spend listening to someone talk before their attention drifted away. Everything had to be short, pithy, simple, and preferably visually presented. As if you were speaking to a child or a computer.

Even as Bob's thoughts formed, Clifford leant forward to the small computer console set into the desk in front of him. The room darkened with the sharp slap of closing blinds and a holographic projector above the centre of the table came into operation. A number of large, brightly coloured cubes appeared, resembling nothing so much as a carefully aligned set of child's building blocks. A complex array of statistical data, annotated with text and figures, flashed onto the small screen in front of each person present, indicating the holograph to be a representation of Comlink revenue and expenditure over the past nine years.

"This is the simple picture," Clifford rapped out. "Increases every year, largely due to increased revenue from the Customer Access Network coupled with efficiencies derived from staff reductions and sale of unused assets such as land."

The child's blocks winked out of existence, to be replaced by an even more elaborate display. A number of thick wheels with coloured and patterned segments appeared in the air above their heads. In each of the wheels a large section – like a slice from a pie – floated slightly apart from the rest, as if removed by an invisible surgeon. Several of those present sat forward, interested now in the proceedings.

"Market share," said Clifford simply. "Over the past five years Comlink has lost seventeen percent."

Clifford ran through a series of statistics. Like a reluctant conjurer, he brought into vibrant existence tumbling pie charts, bar graphs, and a pictogram of translucent telephones of various sizes which purported to show the level of installations over a five year period.

The meeting

The executives watched as Clifford trotted out the figures. Most of those present knew some of the information, but only their area of responsibility with any intimacy. It had all been there in the various reports and presentations they had viewed in the past, but they had not previously realised the inferences. Despite his austere appearance, Clifford was a capable and creative manager when it came to finding the data which gave a financial picture of Comlink.

The picture Clifford presented was insistent; it was ugly. Comlink was in serious trouble. Nothing further could be squeezed out of the organisation by reductions in personnel or sale of unwanted assets or technology.

The conclusion reached by Clifford and his planners was that Comlink needed to win back lost ground and lost confidence. The proposed remedy was to invest heavily in the development of new products already on the drawing board in order to provide some winning products for both of Comlink's major markets: business and home users. Otherwise, the long term existence of the organisation could not be guaranteed.

* * * * *

Sitting in the darkness, doodling sightlessly on the front of his notepad, Bob began to understand the concern he had felt. Whilst Clifford was adept at understanding the financial and administrative position of Comlink, Bob, as manager of the Research and Forward Planning Division, knew the position and the capability of Comlink's new generation of products.

And if these people were looking to him to supply an answer, Bob was not sure he could – at least not the one they were looking for.

The fluttering displays faded and Clifford completed his argument in the darkness.

"There are two main projects we are undertaking which need to be speeded up significantly: OFCAB – the Optical Fibre Cabling project – and the Dick Tracy Watch. These are the products we need to go into the next century. They will guarantee us a significant increase in sales, network usage and customer satisfaction.

"I'm an old-fashioned person. I am not usually an advocate of new technology where existing products will do the job. But in this case we have

The Prelude

to get these products out, and get them out quickly. The alternative is very likely a failure in terms of our financial charter. We would need to be bailed out by an injection of government funds."

"An extremely unlikely event," interrupted Albert. "We've seen enough, Clifford, let's have some lights."

The room lights came up and the blinds clicked open once more. Albert stared around the room for a moment before beginning.

"This morning I had a meeting which convinced me that the government will not provide funds if we go to them. Nearly ten years ago deregulation became a reality. We cannot turn back the clock. If we are in financial difficulties it might be possible to put together a proposition for the government, but why should they accept such a proposal? What's in it for them? All we'll be saying is that after ten years of brave talk and poor results we can't make money out of telecommunications. Well, you saw the figures. In case you don't realise, there are plenty of people out there who can."

Albert paused, his uncharacteristic anger draining away as he passed one hand over his eyes in a gesture of frustration. To Bob, he looked for a moment like a tired man; a man who had fought too many battles for a cause he was finding difficult to recall. Yet Albert's voice was firm when he continued.

"Given current trends, the most pleasant scenario is that Comlink continues to exist as it has for perhaps another ten years, slowly losing ground until we end up with a giant network which no-one wants to use because they can get better results by using our competitors.

"The worst scenario is that, within three years, our most profitable corporate areas will be put out of business by competition. This would throw enormous pressure on our consumer network. To maintain our infrastructure we would be forced to raise charges. The result of that would be our customers switching to alternative suppliers: to the extended ISDN and microwave transmission networks of our competitors.

"These networks exist already, as you're well aware. They have not yet been able to make significant inroads into Comlink's market share because to date we've been able to provide a relatively cheap service. Once that fails, we are into an ever-worsening spiral of contraction which will end only when Comlink is bankrupt.

"But it doesn't have to be like that," Albert continued strongly. The doubt and confusion he had felt earlier sloughed off his shoulders like a receding tide. The plan he had formulated was action. It was certainty.

The meeting

"We've got some great products in development. In addition, the OFCAB project will be something special: something this country will be able to recognise as a major benefit well into the next century. What we need to do is to ensure these projects are successful.

"OFCAB will be completed by the end of 1999. Next year's deadline can stay, but it has to be met. There can be no delays. The main effort we need is to bring the time horizon of the Dick Tracy Watch forward by at least three years, to the beginning of 2001."

Albert waited. Most of those in the room were receptive, willing to accept what had to be done. John McDermott had the massive resources of the Operations Directorate. He could probably manage to put extra groups into the projects as needed. His Business and Consumer division managers appeared confident. For them, the task was a major marketing and advertising activity, little more. The others seemed to have been lifted by Albert's apparent determination to face the difficulties of the future squarely. Clifford was looking directly at Bob Cheshire. Bob was still staring down at the paper in front of him, doodling, his pen making thick, dark slashes on the paper.

"We're pretty stretched, Albert. The development of the Watch will not be easy to alter," Bob said quietly.

"We need it, Bob. We've had a look at your resources. It can be done."

Albert punched a couple of buttons on his console and the overhead lights dimmed. He did not bother to close the blinds, allowing diffuse, striped bands of sun to play across the table.

In the dimness, a timetable model appeared in the middle of the room, about an arm's length above the table.

"This is your current timeline," Albert said. The model was green, its undulating line curving slowly upwards through a series of dates into the early part of the next century, like the rolling hills of a pastoral landscape.

"If we bring forward development and production by three years, this is what you will have to achieve."

Albert pressed another button. Superimposed on the green hills was a rough, angular construction of steep lines.

"It's a tall mountain, Bob, but we can climb it. The figures say we can achieve the target by early 2001," Albert finished.

Bob dropped his pen. His voice was tight as he gripped the edge of the table with his left hand.

"We can do it, Albert. We can do it if we have to. But it's not going to work. You'll destroy the product if you force it out too early."

15

The Prelude

Clifford stirred in his seat. "Look, Bob, I know you weren't consulted before planning this thing, but there wasn't time. You were away. We needed answers for a recommendation today."

"It's got nothing to do with whether I am offended," Bob said, his anger surfacing. "We've spent several years developing the ground rules for this project and I don't want to see that effort thrown away by a premature release. This is not the first time we've advanced deadlines to cope with our economic problems. It's the traditional response of this organisation: to rectify its problems by a quick technology fix."

"This isn't a technology fix, Bob. We need to get an excellent product out as quickly as we can. You've seen the projections. It will provide enormous revenue from business customers."

Bob glared at the Services Director, wanting to convince Clifford of the rightness of his argument, but hopelessly aware that he was sounding like a petulant dissenter.

"It's a quick fix that is going to blow up when it reaches the customers," he said, before turning once more to Albert. "We are the people who are supposed to plan the way Comlink delivers its products and services. If we bring out the Watch too early it won't change anything. We'll just be dumping problems on the technicians, counter-staff and installers and asking them to fix what should have been fixed in the development phase."

"There's nothing wrong with our techs, Bob," said John McDermott, bristling visibly. "You should know that, you were one once."

"The old problems about service delivery, maintenance and customer satisfaction won't go away simply because we have a new product," Bob responded.

"Why not?" asked Mark Rowlands, the Business Division manager. "If it's a product people want, and we market it correctly, we'll be delivering a good service and satisfying our customers."

"That's not enough," Bob urged, knowing that he was failing to keep the argument in perspective. "You're asking the customers to take the responsibility for uncovering our own product shortcomings. It's nonsense. If we're having trouble supplying a decent service on existing products – and some of Clifford's figures show we are – why introduce yet another product without adequate support, and risk even greater dissatisfaction when we haven't got the systems to maintain and service the thing properly?"

"Steady, Bob," Albert intervened. "It's John's job to provide the service and back-up for a product. Our internal indicators show we are doing that fairly well. It's not perfect, I agree, but we are regularly meeting the targets set on all maintenance and customer service indicators."

"Then why are the customers themselves saying they aren't getting the service they need?"

"That's a matter for me, Bob," said Clifford. "We've been trying some new methods of assessing customer response and we believe we are asking them the wrong questions. We still haven't got away from our image as a government body yet. People like to complain about us as a way of saying they're unhappy with the economy or the government."

"Alright, Bob," said Albert. "Suppose you are right, and customer service is a larger problem than we consider it at the moment. Just suppose – although you have no quantitative evidence – that you are right. The Dick Tracy Watch is the perfect way of getting improved service. It opens up the network, provides better access for businesses, and will take some of the heat off our standard network. It's a superior product.

"Our job is to develop technological solutions to communications problems. It's how we stay ahead of our competition, and we happen to be very good at it. You, Bob, more than anyone, know Comlink has a proud history of technological innovation. If we don't introduce the Watch soon, we'll lose a march on the opposition. Someone will get hold of the technology and we'll lose any advantage we've got. Do you want that?"

Bob shook his head. He felt as tired as Albert looked, although he was more than ten years his junior. "If the product is not ready, nothing changes, except the demands on our staff who have to work within a deficient system and cope with the fallout from disappointed customers. No wonder we've got morale problems," he said.

Albert stared at Bob. "It's your job to make the product ready. Can you do it?"

Bob nodded slowly. The unspoken threat was there. *Can you do it, or do I have to find someone who will?*

Chapter 3
Newcastle

The city ranged below them in a wide bowl of morning sunlight. From their vantage point on a clearing above the Blackbutt Reserve, Bob Cheshire and his Project Manager, Alan Dodgson, looked out over the sprawling anomaly that was Newcastle. An enormously tall, thin man with a jutting chin and a shock of sandy hair, Alan had been born and raised in Newcastle. He had studied at the local university, where he had gained an engineering degree and a confused bitterness against his home town.

On the one hand, the Newcastle landscape was breathtaking: a gracious sweep of bay stretching around to the north in an arc which built from wide beaches and towering sand dunes before marching away into the blue distance beyond the Stockton Bridge at the other end of the scale was the city itself, particularly the clustering brown mass of heavy industry around the port and the southern curve of the bay. Newcastle had been a steel and coal town since its infancy. The legacy of that industry was a scene of cluttered, ugly buildings, filthy coils of brown smoke and upthrust chimneys which blasted out burning clouds of waste gas at irregular intervals.

The view summed up the confusion and enigma which made OFCAB – the Optical Fibre Cabling project – so important to Newcastle. The city was dying; it had been dying from a wasting disease for nearly half a century. The days of the steel towns and coal mining centres were over. The cost of wresting the remnants of coal from the tortuous underground circuits snaking beneath the Newcastle region had become prohibitive, and the local industry could not compete with the giant steel mills of south-east Asia. The past decade had seen a massive restructuring of the twin industries supporting the people of the Hunter Valley. 'Restructuring' was a dirty word in this part of the country. From where the Novocastrians stood, it seemed like nothing more than bloody-minded retrenchment.

The Blackbutt Reserve was a rugged forest area at the edge of the vast plain which led down to the Pacific Ocean. While the city crawled in a cluttered quilt across the plain, the reserve was a protected enclave of rich bushland rising several hundred metres above sea level.

"The main point of the reserve," Alan was saying, "is to protect the koalas."

"Koalas?" said Bob without removing the binoculars he was using to scan the city.

"This has been here forever," Alan said proudly, "as a wildlife reserve, I mean. It had the last colony of disease-free koalas in the country, outside of the zoos. But that's changed now. They found a koala with the disease – a sort of meningitis – about two years ago. It's been killing them fast since then."

Bob grunted. Then the seriousness in Alan's tone caused him to turn and look sharply at his companion.

"Last in the country, did you say?"

Alan was silent.

They stood for a moment looking out at the city.

"Let's go down and see some of the worksites. I've got a good enough grasp of the geography."

* * * * *

OFCAB was one of the main jobs managed by Bob Cheshire's group. The Special Projects Department provided specialist management skills for anyone in Comlink involved in a project which presented difficulties as a result of size, logistic problems, technical and engineering complexity, or 'political' importance.

Optical fibre had been around for twenty years or more. The effort which Comlink had produced in the early nineties to complete a 'glass ring' around Australia had taken on the status of legend as an engineering feat. At the time, the proposal to provide a high-technology, large capacity carrier-cable linking all the capital cities of the country had caught the public imagination. With its blend of sophisticated laser optics and old-fashioned

The Prelude

pick and shovel labour, the project was regarded as the industrial achievement of the decade.

More than the engineering or industrial aspects of the glass ring project, it was the human endeavour and commitment which had really fired community endorsement. Stories emerged of opposing teams of workers striving to beat their mates across the wide expanses of desert. The nightly news featured gaudy graphics depicting their progress as, over the months, the two lines struggled towards each other.

The glass ring became a high point in the history of Comlink. The OFCAB project, aside from its economic importance, was also an attempt to follow up the glass ring success with something which could equally catch the excitement of the moment. With OFCAB, Comlink was building the communications environment of the future.

From the late eighties, in a developing experiment, optical fibre had been taken from the exchanges to the streets, and finally into houses. In early 1996 Comlink had selected the target site for a bold, large-scale field test. The target city was Newcastle, and the project aim was to have all homes and businesses on the optical fibre network by the turn of the century.

OFCAB was to give the people of Newcastle a high-powered, completely flexible communication system in their own home or business: shopping and banking would be possible without leaving home; video banks and pay-TV would provide entertainment and access to live sporting events; simple home computers would link to mainframes and databases carrying an enormous array of information services such as health, law and finances; access to the electronic library of the local university – and hence all educational institutions in the world – would be available. In addition, videophones with high-definition sound and pictures were to be installed in every home and office. These would link with the computers to provide instant communication in any medium or blend of media: voice, pictures, text, data.

From Bob Cheshire's viewpoint, the project was a nightmare of organisation, although he took comfort in the way Alan Dodgson was coping as Project Manager. The major difficulty with OFCAB lay in the need to co-ordinate activities as diverse as cable engineering, computer programming, public relations, product marketing, installation and maintenance, industrial relations and customer research.

Despite that, Bob enjoyed working on the project. It was an exciting challenge and one which was politically, economically and socially worthwhile. On its completion, Newcastle would possess the most modern communications infrastructure in the country. Such a system would act as a major carrot in luring business back to the depressed city. It would provide jobs, careers and economic growth where they were most needed.

Bob also saw it as an important project for Comlink's collective mentality. He knew and loved the organisation, having committed the bulk of his working life to it. Comlink people were proud of their record of turning tough engineering projects into a reality. Since the hard days of the last century, when the thin copper wire of the telegraph was stretched from coast to coast, Comlink – or its ancestors – had come through for the community when the need was high. That knowledge was a cornerstone of the confidence Comlink people felt in their abilities.

* * * * *

They drove down from the clean air of the encircling hills into the hot, wind-sheltered bowl of the plain. Alan provided Bob with an update of OFCAB's progress as they drove towards the depot.

Almost six months ago the project had been slipping badly. Work was chronically behind schedule, costs were way over budget and increasing. As a result (and partially in response to the concern of the Regional Director, who had felt his Regional Managers were not equipped to handle a review of their own project) Bob had agreed to a review of the project by a firm of external management consultants.

The firm of Murchison Smart and Falk was reputed to be one of the best in the world. The review had recommended sweeping changes to functions, titles and job descriptions. Project design was partially altered to allow for greater control and supervision of work groups. The effect was considerable. Quotas were achieved with regularity, targets were met and work settled down into a smooth pattern. Although Bob did not have the confidence in consultants which many in Comlink had, he would gladly have admitted he was wrong about MSF and their work on the OFCAB project – that is, he would have, if the wheels hadn't started to fall off again after barely six months.

Alan turned the car into the cluttered compound of the central maintenance depot in West Newcastle. The building itself was crammed with people in every corner, since it still had its normal complement of technical and clerical staff as well as the OFCAB work teams who were using it as a base.

He led Bob through a tight maze of permanent and semi-permanent dividers until they reached the Regional Manager's office, a sort of plywood and glass box which had clearly remained unaltered since the sixties. Vince Penmann, the Regional Manager, was chatting to a man whom Bob assumed to be the OFCAB sector supervisor.

This assumption proved incorrect. "Charlie Foster's down at the main cable site. We'll be going down there in a while. This is Barry Todd, our UCWU man," advised Vince, a black-haired, laconic character of medium-height with a fuzzy beard which always looked as though he had been growing it for only about three weeks.

Barry Todd could almost be Vince Penmann's brother. A fraction shorter, skinny and angular, with a beard which was somewhat thicker and more riotous than the Regional Manager's, he was very similar in appearance. Yet, whilst there was a marked physical similarity between the two men, Bob suspected there was little or no ideological common ground for these two. He sighed mentally: there was another problem to resolve.

The UCWU – United Communication Workers' Union – had grown out of a number of consolidations, amalgamations, power struggles and out-and-out brawls which had taken place between the fifteen or so union groups which had been representing Comlink workers by the mid-nineties. The result was a remarkably strong, tightly-knit union executive, able to focus on the needs of their members without the distractions faced by interest groups in other industries.

While the new union grouping was powerful, it was inclined to be conservative, due to the need which sometimes existed to find a policy solution to satisfy divergent interests. This had created a strong awareness among union officials of the importance of political groupings in an organisation such as Comlink. Bob had often heard Anne Blanchard express the view that UCWU officials had a far better understanding of how things happened than their management counterparts, most of whom had not ventured out of their offices and onto the worksites for many a long year.

Bob could not help reflecting on this as the small group chatted for a moment prior to leaving for the work site. Vince was a good manager; it was well known that he could get results quickly. But did he get out of his office often enough to get a feel for what people needed in order to do their work? This was probably his first site visit for many months.

Bob was painfully aware that he could be accused of the same. There always seemed to be something more important: a meeting or briefing, forms, reports, any number of things which he usually ended up spending his time on, instead of talking to the people who were actually doing the work of installation, maintenance, development.

"Tell me about the delays," said Bob, when they were in the car. He deliberately didn't address the question to anyone in particular.

Vince Penmann spoke first. As Regional Manager, he provided the functional management team which enabled the work groups to operate. While Alan was the Project Manager, Vince supplied management resources and administrative support for jobs which were based in his region.

"Three months behind and getting worse. We need more resources, Bob. This is a bloody big job."

Bob had expected something like that. It could well be true, and if Albert wanted this done on time it might be necessary to put in more people. But Bob wasn't convinced at this stage.

"We put more people onto the job prior to the MSF review. Manpower levels have increased by twenty percent, and overall cost by fifty percent in the past eighteen months."

"More people won't help a bit," chimed in Barry Todd. "All your precious review did was put in two more levels of managers to look over our shoulders.

"We need materials. My people are doing their damnedest to make this thing work, but no-one can get anything done if there aren't supplies or materials when you need them. We've got continual problems getting plant and equipment, materials, parts, everything. One day there's a million of them, the next it's all been shipped into oblivion."

"We've been through that, Barry," Vince said, his voice rising. "I can't control it, it's caused by –"

"Yeah, yeah, Supply Branch, or workshops, or the contractor, or any convenient bloke who can step in and catch the blame. Spare me," Barry interrupted.

Vince scowled. "Anyway, the inventory sheets show supply isn't that bad. It's not perfect, but if we could cut down on losses, we'd be in a much better position."

"What does that mean?" demanded Barry.

Vince turned to the back seat. A minor glaring match ensued.

"Look, you two, I can do without the bitching," said Bob. "We'll look at all aspects of the problem. You may well be right, Vince, about more resources. I don't know yet. Are you suggesting pilfering is a serious problem?"

The Regional Manager looked blankly at him and shrugged.

"And you, Barry, might have a point about supply. We'll see. But they're not your people any more than they are mine. They're men and women who work for Comlink. Got it? The main job is to get this project back on the rails, and fast."

Alan started laughing. "You know, Boss, I think I'm inclined to believe both these guys have got a point. I've been working on a new analysis over the past few days. I'll show you when we get back. My main concern is that we don't really know what the problem is. Sure, we've all got some ideas, but no-one really *knows*. Everything has been changed so quickly and so randomly that we don't know where the problems are."

"You'll soon see where the problems are when you see men standing around for hours because there's nothing for them to do, and then having to charge in like maniacs to do a job in half the time when the equipment or parts finally arrive," responded Barry, unwilling to be mollified.

"One thing's sure, an external review didn't change any of the root problems," Alan said. Vince and Barry nodded agreement.

* * * * *

They found the 'Mole' a few minutes later. It was located in a field on the north-eastern edge of the city where the tightly-packed, old terrace houses gave way to sprawling suburbia and eventually to hobby farms and paddocks.

The 'Mole' was the name given to the large combination ripper/trench digger which walked across open ground, simultaneously digging a trench and laying the optical fibre cable. It was used in open ground to lay the cable which linked all the outer exchanges in the OFCAB network. These joined to form a rough circle, like the rim of a stage coach wheel. At the hub of the wheel was the major regional exchange in the centre of Newcastle. This, in turn, was linked by an underground fibre cable to the larger ring which encircled Australia.

Weighing in at around forty tonnes, the Mole was a five-metre high, yellow steel monster, begrimed by the dust it raised as it tramped across the land. Between its rear legs was a four-metre steel claw which ripped the earth in its passage, forming a deep trench into which rolled the delicate optical fibre encased in a shiny, black covering.

Alan parked the car at the roadside and they began to walk across the field to the Mole, where a couple of dozen men were grouped. This was the support crew: the 'navvies', bronzed, blue-overalled labourers who dug the trench in the tight sections where the Mole could not go; the jointers and 'pit men', who installed the plastic underground junction boxes at given periods, and the crew of the Mole itself.

The Mole had a crew of eight. Only one driver was needed, but a group of assistants fed the cable from a huge, two-tonne, alloy drum attached to the machine's front. The crew followed in the Mole's tracks to ensure the cable fed smoothly into the trench, and that the robot shovels which trailed behind the claw piled the earth back into place after its passage.

As they drew near, Charlie Foster, the sector supervisor, hallooed to them. He was a big, beer-bellied man with a larrikin touch that served him well in dealing with the boisterous work gangs. These were the real characters of Comlink, the people who kept the faith when it came to hard work for the community combined with unrelenting insubordination to senior management. Many turned away swiftly when the staff magazine came looking for stories, and it was a popular myth that there were those who would rather the police, or their ex-spouses, did not know their exact whereabouts.

Bob watched as the Mole approached a fence between two paddocks, turned with a ponderous movement and headed for a wide gate further up the line of the barbed wire fence. The work gang spread out and the navvies hurriedly went to work on the last ten metres where the Mole had been unable to get close to the fence because of a row of trees.

Charlie bustled up, shaking hands with everyone. They got down to business quickly.

"We've got a daily quota on that monster," he said, pointing to the Mole. "As a result of this silly, bloody cost-accounting business, I have to pay John McDermott for the use of his equipment.

"I can't keep track of all the mythical money if we can't get cable. That lot just arrived an hour ago. We didn't even take it to the depot, I just got the driver to drop it straight out here," Charlie indicated a flatbed truck which was edging across the paddock towards the cable trench. On the back of the truck were several large drums of cable, ready to be off-loaded by a compact hydraulic crane attachment.

Charlie broke off speaking for a moment to yell across to the gang.

"Tell that bloke to give the Mole plenty of room".

A blue-overalled figure waved in response and trotted off towards the truck.

"Bloody idiot," muttered Charlie, "driver's probably never been anywhere before except the concrete apron of a depot. We shouldn't have to drag them out here, Bob, they're not used to it."

The Mole had edged through the gate and back up the other side of the fence to the cable trench. The driver manoeuvred carefully around a couple of large gum trees and backed into position against the fence, ready to start digging. He shut down the Mole and waited for the cable truck to arrive and unload.

"I suppose we're not doing so bad," Charlie continued, with half an eye on the unloading operation. "Although I don't like having to give the men such tight deadlines. They'll gladly respond once or twice, but not every day."

Suddenly, he broke off the conversation and stepped back several paces to give himself waving room. "Get that thing away from there, you dopey bastard," he yelled to the truck driver. "Not there!"

Charlie began to stride towards the work group. After a few seconds, he broke into a trot, still waving his arms. He had barely taken a dozen paces when the hydraulic arm on the back of the truck swung across with its heavy load of cable. The arm crashed into an overhanging branch of the gum tree. Branches and leaves tumbled down. The driver instantly stopped the hydraulic arm, leaving the drum suspended, swaying slightly.

After a cry of alarm everyone fell silent, looking up at the creaking chain and its two-tonne load of cable. With a flat crack Bob could hear easily over a hundred metres, the chain parted and the cable drum dropped. Catching the back of the truck, it hung for a second, pivoted and then careered off the side.

Shouts of pain and shock erupted. The drum smashed across one man, demolishing his hip and legs before rolling onto another, who screamed in outrage. His scream turned into a strangled cry of terror as the drum continued to roll tortuously forward, crushing him wholly beneath its vast weight.

The drum rolled over the fence, snapping the taut barbed wire, which flew apart, wrapping itself around a third man, who thrashed and shrieked as the highly-tensioned wire curled and bit into his flesh, gripping ever tighter as he writhed.

Bob found himself running with the others, shouting something wordless, as his mind repeated the litany he had always feared: *Oh God, what do I do, I'm supposed to be in charge? This is real. What do I do?*

Chapter 4
On the beach

"It was a disaster. I couldn't believe it was happening," Bob said softly into the telephone. The ambulance, the police, the news teams, the instant conferences with legal, welfare, industrial relations; it had seemed to go on forever.

"And to top it all, Barry Todd has pulled the plug. The union's shut down the project until a full investigation's been held. They even want representation."

"I wish I could help," Janice Cheshire said. "Can't you come home tonight?"

"No, I don't know how much more talking I'll have to do tonight. I've got to go down to the hospital and see Theo. They're still operating on Les Thompson. God, his legs were like a broken windscreen," Bob paused, resting his ear against the receiver. He could feel the reassurance, the strength in the silence between them.

"I've never seen a dead man, Janice. I was scared."

"You did well, Bob. I've seen all the news reports. No-one's been critical of how you coped."

"I guess it was lucky a couple of us knew some first aid. I never thought I'd ever have to use it."

"It was more than that," said his wife. "You grew up in the bush, you've seen wounds from barbed wire."

"Yeah, they were trying to unravel Theo at first. I had to tell them to cut the wire into smaller bits, otherwise they'd have torn him apart just getting him loose.

"It shouldn't have happened, Janice. They were in too much of a hurry. There's no reason why it had to happen. We've got all these bloody slogans and stickers around the place saying nothing's more important than safety, and then we put these guys under so much pressure they have to take short cuts. Now Wally Jamieson's dead."

"Try to relax, darling," Janice Cheshire said. She was worried by the rising note of anger in her husband's voice. "It wasn't your fault. You did what you could in a difficult situation. I'm proud of you. I only wish I could be there with you now."

"I wish you could be too."

He rang off a few minutes later. Janice had made him feel better, but there was one thing she'd said which just wasn't true. It was his fault. It was his job to make sure things like this didn't happen. If it wasn't his job, whose was it?

* * * * *

Alan shared dinner with him that evening in the motel restaurant. The visit to the hospital had been bad, but less draining than Bob had expected. Theo was glad to be alive.

"Even though I was yelling, I heard you telling them what to do with the wire. It was hurting so much. But it came through to me somehow, what you were saying, and I prayed they'd listen. Thanks, Mr Cheshire," the short, heavy-set man had said.

Bob felt he had not been able to offer anything to the injured man. He felt that instead of offering sympathy and strength he was drawing it from someone who had little to spare. "It shouldn't have happened," was all he could say.

"Hey, I know that, but you can't be responsible for every little thing. It was just chance that you were there at the time. A lucky chance for me."

Bob stared at the deeply-tanned face, at the criss-cross tracks of ugly black stitches patterning his cheeks and neck. He couldn't agree with Theo's definition of luck.

Les Thompson was still in the operating theatre: compound fractures, both legs crushed. Too much damage to repair. The surgeons had been forced to replace all the bone in his left leg with stainless steel; his hip joint had been replaced with ceramic and his fractured pelvis was being pulled back together with wires, screws and bolts. It would be at least three hours before they were finished. Les's right leg had been past saving. It had already been amputated at mid-thigh.

"I doubt he'll walk again, Mr Cheshire," said the doctor, "even with prosthetics. We don't know. At least it was something that you kept him immobile until the chopper got there."

Bob grunted. He had caught sight of the small, pale woman sitting on one of the hard hospital benches. She was surrounded by three children in their teens. One of the girls, blonde, pretty and dressed in an impossibly baggy jumper and jeans, reminded him of his own daughter, Emma. She would be asleep now, after having had her daily tilt at her mother over the issue of a pony. It was an on-going campaign, waged with all the bitter resolution of a Russian general facing a winter engagement.

It was the hardest thing in a long, hard day to go over and talk to Martha Thompson. It was one of those conversations composed of mumbling, pain and bleak stares, where both parties are conscious of the social theatre intruding on their shock, forcing them to play out the stylised lines of public tragedy.

The day had probably been worse for Alan. While Bob was busy with the police and in trying to report the events to Albert Lapin, Alan had been the one to take the news to Wally Jamieson's wife.

Thus they sat in the motel restaurant eating little, drinking too much.

The more he talked, the more Bob felt all his problems were somehow tied together in a bizarre Gordian knot. OFCAB was running behind time: that meant more pressure on timelines and for quick results. Yet the system did not alter: you did everything the same way you always had, just a little faster, and faster, as the tune from up the line played quicker and louder. Eventually you fed more people into the cycle: more people, more supervision, should equal more results. Only it didn't. All that happened was that the pressure on each individual increased. The music played faster and louder as pressures increased all over the organisation. The response? Speed up the Dick Tracy Watch, speed up OFCAB, speed up everything.

Bob had met a crazy Dutchman once. He had joined forces with Bob for a few days in the mid-seventies, when Bob was having his small rebellion hitchhiking around England. It was a time of laughter and tension, living on the edge without enough food and money.

There was only one thing Bob could remember clearly. They were smoking marijuana and swigging cheap wine in the back of someone's beat-up Ford Transit, arguing about something long gone from Bob's memory while the van bounced along the highway to Manchester. 'Dutch' had dragged on the joint and passed it to Bob, peering at him through the drifting smoke. Letting his breath out slowly, he had fixed Bob with a look which would have done the Ancient Mariner credit.

"People don't change," he said. "They just learn to cope."

Bob gaped for a moment. Dutch stared harder, nodding slightly, as if willing Bob to accept the truth of this homespun wisdom. Then the moment of seriousness passed and they burst out laughing, relieved to be able to step back before anything even more earnest was said.

Now, twenty years later, Bob found himself telling Alan the story. He'd never been sure just why that little message had stuck so tightly to his consciousness through the years, yet it had. And now, surprisingly, Alan was nodding sagely, very like the Dutchman. Perhaps, thought Bob, it was one of those universal truths which were crystal clear only when the hearer is under the influence. Such truths were invariably elusive in the morning.

He stood up, laughing at the serious expression on Alan's face. "Let's take it easy tonight. There's a lot on tomorrow."

Alan was in no mood to go home. He lived on his own, having separated from his wife some years ago. He dragged Bob through the city on an after-dinner walk. They wound through streets cluttered with terrace houses of locally quarried sandstone which had once been soft shades of clay, but which were now a grim reddish-black.

"It's an ugly town," muttered Alan, "but it could have been beautiful. Parts of it still are. Whoever discovered coal here made a big mistake when he gave away the news."

After some minutes, they emerged from the narrow streets onto a wide lawn area which led down to the stone esplanade fronting a broad, sandy beach. Bob realised they had walked over the spine of a point thrust out into the bay. On the other side, now hidden from view, were the steelworks, working three shifts, continually smelting ore and passing the refuse into the atmosphere.

A strong on-shore breeze blew in their faces as they walked down to the beach. The night was cool and clear with a small sickle moon drifting high in the western sky. Away from the ambient light of the city streets, the stars shone bright and clear.

It was a surprise to Bob to find a beach such as this in a place he had characterised as industrial wasteland. They sat on the stone wall and removed their shoes and socks. As Bob's feet touched the cold sand he felt some of the tension leaving his body. The gritty particles massaged the soles of his feet as he walked down to the water's edge and let the foamy water run around and

The Prelude

over his feet, wetting his ankles and the cuffs of his trousers.

Alan picked up a flat, round shell and flicked it across the crests of the surf, watching it bounce once, twice, before being taken by the water.

"Your Dutch pal was right," he said. "It's easier to make people adapt than it is to adapt the systems they work with. People learn to cope with the demands we put on them. What we should be doing is making a system that can adapt so that you don't end up testing people to destruction.

"Look at what we did with the typewriter."

"What are you talking about?" Bob asked.

"The typewriter was invented by a bloke who couldn't type. Once the device proved successful we trained people to type faster and faster. No-one wanted to redesign the keyboard. It was easier to make the people cope with the pressure. They typed faster and faster, until they got sick. So then we just got more people in and trained them to type even quicker. Besides, most of them were just 'silly women' who were talking nonsense when they said there was something wrong with their wrists, their arms. For generations we said the only problem was their minds, their 'feeble' female minds. We might have saved a lot of bother by redesigning the keyboard."

Alan flicked another shell into the water.

"Today was different," Bob said. "They weren't watching what was happening, they were hurrying too much. As managers, we should have been aware of the danger."

"Why were they hurrying?" Alan asked, looking sideways at Bob.

"Because we've got a deadline," Bob answered. "I don't like it any more than you, Alan, but this is a worthwhile job. This country needs the best communication system we can give it. This city does too. You ought to be able to see that. Alright, people get killed and they shouldn't. That doesn't mean the job's not worth doing."

"That's just the point. The system isn't working. So, instead of changing it, we just ask them for a bigger effort. We make them cope with the deficiencies we've built into the way we work. Just like the typist working with a badly designed keyboard. Today they made mistakes, but we put them in a situation which was so unstable anything could happen. It's just surprising we don't get more accidents," Alan said bitterly.

"Well, what can we do about it?" demanded Bob. "This organisation is in serious trouble. OFCAB is just part of it. We need to improve our products and services drastically. Our credibility, our market share are both going out the door backwards. We need to work faster and better. This is no longer a government sinecure, we're in a world where we've got to compete if we're going to stay around."

"You sound like an annual report," Alan accused. "You also said you don't believe we should be racing to speed things up. You said it was the wrong decision to rush the Dick Tracy Watch."

"That's just my personal opinion. A decision's been taken. I have to support it."

"The only way anything will ever change is if people back their personal opinions. All that we're doing now is asking people to cope with the increasing demands we put on them. That's not going to solve our problem or get the job done. We saw the proof of that today," Alan said. He was standing very close to Bob now, facing him directly.

"Look I'd like to think we could do something–" Bob began.

"Would you? Would you really?"

The two men felt the tension boiling up between them as a result of the day's frustration and fear. They glared at each other, conscious that it was easy to go too far. The high wind and clear air seemed to have focused the problem for them. Bob felt the challenge in Alan's voice, but as well as that there was a rising excitement.

"Yes. I would," he replied.

"Fine. Then come with me," Alan said. A smile played across his lips for the first time that night.

Chapter 5

Meetings

Anne Blanchard stepped off the plane at Pelican. She had never been to Newcastle before and would not have come here now had it not been for Albert's command.

Still, the airport wasn't too bad, located as it was on the narrow neck of land where Lake Macquarie poured into the sea. The morning sight of ocean, lake and palm trees together with the large flock of apparently dozing pelicans lifted some of the apprehension she had felt ever since her briefing with Albert at six that morning.

An enormously tall, blonde man was bobbing about in the crowd, waving frantically in her direction. Anne checked if there was someone following behind and realised that the waver was obviously aiming at her. This was a shame, she thought, a great shame. His suit looked as though he'd slept in it, he had a grimy shadow across his chin and from a distance of several metres she could see his bloodshot eyes glowing with the intensity of an overboiled frankfurter. His trousers bore a dark line halfway up the calf, as though he'd been standing in water half the night. As he bustled up, grinning, Anne attempted to keep her distance, offering her most detached fish handshake.

In fact, Alan had not slept. He and Bob had been poring over the results of the information he had been getting together before the accident occurred. Alan had been gathering intelligence about what were the perceived problems of OFCAB, and what were the real ones he could deal with as Project Manager.

The list of issues had interested Bob from the first. It had evolved from discussions with the line managers and supervisors, and the people in the work gangs. The list had become something of a fixture in Alan's flat, where it resided, taped to the lounge room wall. Alan had been surprised when Bob had taken to it quickly, racing ahead of his own thoughts. They had agreed that the first thing was to look at the processes which people were involved in: to look at what work was done and how it was done. An alarmingly simple thing, but one which was rarely ever undertaken.

Bob had driven himself and Alan all night, questioning the issues on Alan's list, trying to identify the root problems they wanted to address. When he finally laid down his pen at six-thirty and stared around at the metres of 'butcher's paper' scattered around Alan's flat, Bob was satisfied that they at least had a plan of action to put to the project team and union officials when the round of meetings started later in the morning.

The first meeting was scheduled for eight o'clock at Bob's hotel with the OFCAB management team. Bob had asked Alan to pick up Anne Blanchard and bring her to the meeting. "I'd prefer you to be there from the start, but Anne will be handling the IR side of this and I need you to brief her on the proposal we've put together, so she doesn't come into this unprepared. Besides, she'll have talked with Albert this morning or late last night. I want to know what they've worked out. She won't talk to just anyone."

"Are you saying I should use my well-known charm?" Alan asked, rubbing his stubbled chin.

"No," laughed Bob. "I'm saying you should use your lesser-known brain. It's not much, but it's all we've got at this stage."

Standing in the airport mob, waving at the tall, elegant woman, Alan reflected it was a shame that this was a job requiring brains. He would have much rather preferred to use charm.

It was almost eight-fifteen by the time they got Anne's bags into the car. Alan started to relate the story of the previous night.

By the time they'd reached the point where he and Bob were standing in the surf shouting at each other, Anne's expression of repugnance had changed to a reluctant smile. She had always liked Bob Cheshire, regarding him as an ally and a capable and intelligent manager. She hoped Alan would be able to help him through a difficult time.

"Pull over, I'll drive. I don't want you putting us through a shop front if you haven't slept all night," she said.

Alan gladly complied. Once in the passenger seat he gave some directions, then pulled out a mildly crumpled notebook from his jacket pocket.

The Prelude

"This is the reasoning we've used so far. You know what systems theory is?"

"Come on, Alan. I've been to school too," Anne replied. Adopting a stilted voice, she recited, "A system is a group of related processes organised for a purpose. To identify a system it is necessary to distinguish its boundaries, to be aware of its purposes, to know what happens inside it, and to be aware of what goes in and what comes out."

"Inputs and outputs," Alan said.

"What goes in and what comes out," Anne repeated. "Don't confuse it with jargon."

"Point taken. OK. The OFCAB system is out of control. It's unstable."

"What's that got to do with one man dead and two more maimed?" Anne demanded sharply.

"Plenty!"

"Alright, take it easy. I'm just asking the same questions you'll hear from other, less sympathetic groups soon enough."

Alan subsided, "Yeah, you're right. I need to be ready for it."

"*We* need to be ready, Alan. Now tell me more."

* * * * *

While Alan and Anne were making their way from the airport, Bob Cheshire was standing in front of a whiteboard in the hotel conference room. Tension in the room was high. Charlie Foster and Vince Penmann were present, both looking as though they hadn't slept either. All the other sector managers, the supervisors who reported to them, and several of Alan's staff were also present.

Bob began with a description of the meeting in Melbourne which had precipitated his visit.

"We're under pressure. Not just this project, but our whole organisation.

"The problem is one of slow erosion of customer confidence. Access to the network is poor, maintenance is often ineffective, we can't get or guarantee parts and supplies; I could continue. It's enough to say the end result is that people don't trust us to deliver an efficient service.

"We're attempting to change this perception. One way is through the Dick Tracy Watch. It's a new, exciting product, one which can really change the service we offer to people. Another key element in the strategy to gain back customer confidence is OFCAB."

Bob took time to look around the room: some of the managers were listening; a few seemed indifferent, as though they couldn't see any possible reason for being in the room; others were angry, eyeing him with expressions of rebellion. Fine, he thought. It'll be good for them to get a little angry, we'll find out what their real problems are.

"Yesterday's accident wasn't an accident. Wally Jamieson was as good as murdered," Bob said. The attention was focused now, but the hostility had not diminished.

"Wally was killed because we had to rush; because we were disorganised. For the past few months we've done nothing except run around fighting flash fires, looking after the small day-to-day emergencies instead of getting on with what we're supposed to do – manage the project."

"We wouldn't be running round like blue-assed flies if it wasn't for the balls-up MSF created," growled Mal Yallop, a tough, heavy-set supervisor. "We don't need external consultants crawling all over us like mud crabs."

"I take your point, Mal," Bob responded, "and I won't argue the toss over the consultancy exercise. The point is that it's been taking virtually all our energy to keep the systems running. That's left no time or energy for fixing the problems which we all recognise are there.

"As a result, we're concentrating on the wrong things. We're working all the time to maintain the status quo when we should be able to look at what we're doing and improve it."

"You said it yourself – there's no time," interrupted Herman 'Bear' Rinehart, the Lines Installation Manager. The tall, greying man spoke with a slight accent, throwing his words out in a direct challenge. "We're already behind and every bugger in the world is after us. You expect me to slow down for this? I've got better things to do."

"Well, we have to make time," responded Bob too quickly. There was an edge in his voice despite his desire to keep everything calm and in perspective.

"Just like that, I suppose?" Bear Rinehart said thickly, clicking his fingers.

"We can't make time out of nowhere, and I'm not suggesting that anyone in this room isn't doing enough already," Bob replied, aware that he was breathing too hard. He took a short moment to relax before continuing. "But we need to make some time. At the moment we've got a project which is so out of balance that people are starting to get killed because we are pushing them too hard."

Several managers grumbled agreement. Wally Jamieson had been a long-time employee, known personally to most of those in the room. His death had been a hard and ugly shock for all of them.

"The thing we've got to do is fix the system so that people don't have to work with unnecessary pressures. And we're not going to change anything by managing the same way we've done in the past."

Vince Penmann spoke up. "I don't think that's necessarily right, Bob," he said. "Industrial accidents happen. They just happen, and there's not a lot you can do about it. It doesn't mean we're doing everything wrong."

"Not everything, Vince. But we have to look at the way we manage. We are responsible for what happens to people."

Bob paused, aware of both the tension in the room and the reluctance to consider anything except the grim death less than twenty-four hours earlier. The last thing he wanted was to end this meeting in acrimony. He needed to find a way to concentrate on solutions for the future rather than failures in the past. But as he closed his eyes, trying to think for a moment, all he could see was the large cable drum swinging down in a deadly arc.

He felt tired, too tired. Neither he nor Alan had slept for a full day. Maybe there was something in all the reams of paper from last night: a sketch, an idea, a concept. So often understanding – and support – seemed to flow not from ideas themselves, but in the way they were presented.

He turned to the board, "Have a look at this, and what I've been saying might make some sense."

In one corner of the whiteboard he drew a quick sketch, a rectangle with a high curve running across it almost cutting the corner angles.

"This is how we work." He shaded the upper left section of the rectangle.

Actual

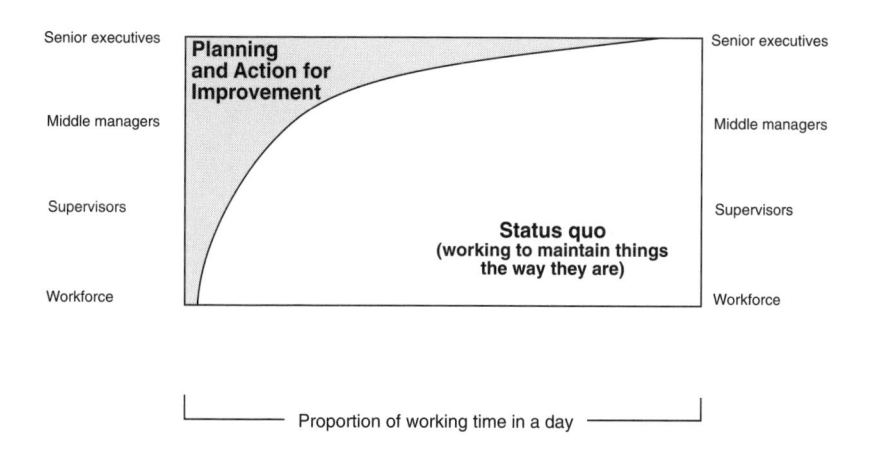

```
Senior executives    ┌─────────────────────────────┐   Senior executives
                     │Planning                      │
                     │and Action for                │
                     │Improvement                   │
Middle managers      │                              │   Middle managers
                     │                              │
                     │                              │
Supervisors          │         Status quo           │   Supervisors
                     │   (working to maintain things│
                     │        the way they are)     │
Workforce            └─────────────────────────────┘   Workforce

         ├──── Proportion of working time in a day ────┤
```

"Think about what you did yesterday, or the day before. How much of your work was dedicated to fighting fires, and how much to working out if things could be done better?"

The question prompted a ripple of ironic murmurs.

"Sounds like very little," continued Bob. "This is where we are: most managers spending most of their time keeping current work processes patched up and running, and very little on planned management." He indicated the large segment of unshaded space.

"The rectangle represents a working day. The way it is shown here, it's difficult for anyone – especially middle managers and supervisors – to spend time on improving the work systems. As a result, things never change, except for the increasing demands placed on the system by those outside it."

He quickly scrubbed out the curved line and drew another, a straight slash, almost bisecting the corner angles. He filled in the shading so that the two halves were roughly equal.

The Prelude

```
                    ┌─────────────┐
                    │  Desirable  │
                    └─────────────┘
Senior executives   ┌─────────────────────────┐  Senior executives
                    │Planning                 │
                    │and Action for           │
                    │Improvement              │
Middle managers     │                         │  Middle managers
                    │                         │
                    │           Status quo    │
Supervisors         │      (working to maintain things  Supervisors
                    │           the way they are)
                    │                         │
Workforce           └─────────────────────────┘  Workforce

                    └─── Proportion of working time in a day ───┘
```

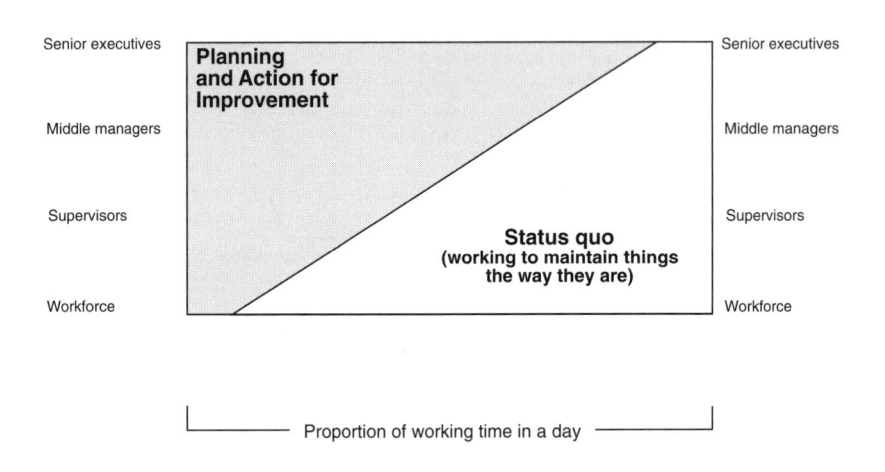

"This is what should happen: managers planning – rather than responding to daily crises." He indicated the re-arranged proportions.

"We wouldn't have to spend so much time fire fighting if we had enough people," Vince persisted.

"Alright, let's accept that tentatively as one of the issues," said Bob. He scrawled the comment on the board beside the diagram. "What are some of the others? Come on, you've all been working on the project long enough, tell me what your experiences are. I'm not looking for solutions at this stage, just your understanding of what is stopping you doing your job."

"Bloody consultants," Mal Yallop growled distastefully. The mood lightened as most people grinned at the irascible supervisor sitting stolidly in a too-small chair, bare arms folded tightly across his chest.

Again Bob wrote the comment on the board. "What about supply? I've heard plenty of people saying they can't get materials."

The group grumbled assent and Bob wrote the comment on the board. Even Bear Rinehart nodded at the mention of supply problems.

"Hang on, Bob. It's not so much we can't get materials, we just can't get a decent response from the supply department about when orders are coming through to the depots," Charlie Foster said.

"And half the time the suppliers are our bloody competitors," Colin Campbell, a sector supervisor, pronounced with a sour grin.

It went slowly at first, but gradually the managers found confidence and began to feel able to speak out without being shot down. By the time Alan and Anne walked in a little after nine o'clock, a list of 'issues' was flagged on the board.

- Need more staff
- Don't need external consultants
- Can't get materials
- No inter-department communication
- Suppliers are often competitors
- Unrealistic targets
- Morale low
- Parts and fittings are incompatible
- Lack of communication
- Management skills poor
- Other sections stuffing us up
- No leadership
- Need more supervision
- We don't know what's going on
- Project doesn't meet customer needs
- Information on targets is rigged to show success and hide problems

The Prelude

Anne glanced at the board as she settled quietly at the back of the room. This wasn't her show. She was due for involvement with the industrial relations side of things later that morning. Anne grabbed Alan's sleeve as he moved to the front of the gathering.

"How did you know? That list is almost identical to the one you described from last night," she whispered.

Alan winked, "It's surprising what people will tell you if you ask them."

* * * * *

Bob handed over to Alan. The younger man was still the Project Manager and there was no reason why he should be replaced. It was important for Bob to show that he supported Alan. When something went wrong, Comlink often looked for scapegoats. It was part of the company mythology that if you stuck your head up someone would kick it off.

Alan was painfully aware of the invidious position he occupied. As Project Manager he held ultimate responsibility, under Bob, for the well-being of OFCAB. That sounded fine in practice, however the reality was different.

On occasions such as this Alan felt clearly the thin line between tolerance and rejection. Many of these men were older than him; most had many more years experience in the telecommunications industry. They were experts in their specific skill in a way which Alan could never hope to emulate.

For Alan, the past few months had been a long, slow effort to develop support and networks within the management group he was controlling. As he looked over the group, he realised the time had come to test that support and commitment.

"The list you have generated today is very much like one I've been developing over the past couple of weeks." Arms were folded, legs were crossed. This wasn't going to be easy.

"There is a common thread in many of these things and it is an ironic one for Comlink. The issues you've identified relate broadly to communication, the thing we claim to be expert at achieving for others.

"Our communication is bad: between departments and suppliers, managers and staff, head office and regional office. The result is, we don't know what's going on.

"Let's see what we can do to alter that. Let's start with this thing about rigged information." Alan gestured at an item on the white-board. "What did you have in mind?"

He paused, looking enquiringly at the group. As the silence lengthened, Alan pondered wryly on the old legal maxim about never asking a question to which you don't know the answer yourself.

Claudia Wallace, the Customer Services Manager, finally spoke up. She was a small, wide, forthright woman in her late forties. It was the function of her department to provide customer service and accounts.

"Somebody's been fixing the figures for months," she said brusquely. "They're rubbish." Her imperious gaze swept over the sector managers in a matriarchal accusation.

The charge created an uproar of claims and counter-claims.

Claudia was undaunted. She stood up and pointed to the Installation Manager, Doug Golding. "Doug, what's the status with homes in the western sector, do you know?"

"Yeah," he replied cautiously. "We've completed installation of videophone terminals and computers in about seventy percent of houses."

"Alright, how about you, Bear?" Claudia turned to Herman Rinehart.

He stirred and growled heavily, "We're behind, I'll admit that, because we're getting problems with the Fibre Encoder Units. But we've run glass into about fifty percent of the homes."

"Well my figures from the exchange monitoring system tell me that only thirty percent of people are hooked up and paying revenue in that area." Claudia completed her argument triumphantly.

Alan jumped in before any further uproar ensued. "Alright, this is just the kind of problem I want to uncover. I don't want anyone carrying on that it's all someone else's fault. We're all working on a system that's been set up to do a job. We've got to find out how it's working before we can try to change anything."

"Doug?" he invited.

The Product Installation Manager shifted in his seat. "Well, the techs have been installing videophones at a great rate. That's what they're supposed to do."

"Yes, but do they work?" Alan asked.

"Bloody hard, Alan. You know that!"

"Not your staff, the equipment they install. Is it working?"

"Most of it doesn't," Bear muttered, buying into the discussion.

"Because of the FEUs?" Alan queried, referring to the Fibre Encoder Units which linked the cables from a group of houses into the main circuit. The task of jointing their cables was tricky and time consuming.

"Because Bear's linies can't keep up to our schedules."

Doug Golding and Bear Rinehart glowered at each other, their normally placid relationship showing the strain of the morning.

"If your techs could make an appointment once in a while, instead of wasting our time..."

"Calm down you guys. I want to hear this but we're not going to get anywhere swapping recriminations. Doug, does this mean we've been installing phones in houses without being able to commission them?" Alan asked.

Doug nodded.

"How long is it before people get their phones commissioned?" Alan feared the answer he would hear.

"Less than a week on average."

"On average," mused Alan. "What about the worst possible scenario, how long might some people wait?"

"An estate over towards the lake has been queued for ten weeks now," said Bear Rinehart in an aggrieved voice. "We've made appointments to commission areas with the techs, but they just don't turn up. If they aren't there, we have to get on with our schedule and the estate has to wait until we get some spare time – which looks like never, the way we're going."

"We've got a schedule too, mate. Since the MSF review our targets have been increased."

"Hold it," Alan said. "Does that mean that some customers might have a fantastic, state-of-the-art, does-everything, bells-and-whistles videophone bolted to their wall for up to ten weeks before they can use it?"

Nods.

"How would you feel about that? Imagine it. You've got this magic piece of equipment, one of the first videophones in a private house in Australia, and all it does is stare at you like the useless lump of plastic, glass and steel it is. How would you feel?"

"I'd feel pretty pissed off," Doug Golding admitted after a moment. His statement brought a round of chuckles from the group, and a wry grin from the Bear.

"Well it's not really the objective of this project to see how many Newcastle citizens we can piss off," said Alan. "Unless the consultants changed the project description without telling me.

"Claudia's got a point," he continued. "If Doug's returns say his group has installed seventy percent of videophones, we should be able to receive the appropriate amount of revenue. Perhaps it's a case of faults with the FEUs, or the way we're scheduling the work. Maybe the techs have an installation target which puts too much stress on other sections, or we're hurrying too much and getting nothing done. The essential point is, we don't know what's wrong with the system we've got, so how can we improve it?"

The question was intended to be rhetorical, so Alan was both surprised and gratified when a response was forthcoming.

"Map it," said Mal Yallop. He had been sitting quietly, leaning back in his chair while the storm had raged between the installation managers.

"Map it," Mal repeated in response to the questioning looks.

"I've been worried for some time that we were getting behind in my sector. I got talking to some of the gang foremen," he continued, nodding towards Doug Golding and Bear Rinehart. "The only reason we've got to have both the tech and liney there to commission the cable is because of faults with the FEUs. If we could ensure the FEUs were working correctly when they were installed, then a good deal of the pressure on your blokes would be removed."

"Thanks, Mal," said Alan, "I'd like you to follow that up with Doug and Bear, and list all the steps involved in the installation and commissioning process."

A disgruntled stirring sound caught his attention. "You're right, Claudia. You started this and we should be working for a solution for you too. How about you map out the process which involves your people and see where the links are to Doug and Bear's work?"

The Customer Service Manager looked at him uncertainly.

"Sorry, that's jargon isn't it?" Alan apologised. "What I mean is for you to look at what happens once the commissioning is done. The linies and techs fill out a return which goes through the exchange and eventually to your billing section. Maybe that paperwork is getting hung up somewhere; maybe we can devise some better way of getting information – correct information – to you."

"There's the OSP 813s which come from the exchanges when a circuit's on line. My staff are always complaining that they're not filled in properly," said Claudia.

"Alright, check it out. Perhaps they need to be clearer, or maybe we don't even need them at all. Perhaps we need something entirely different."

The Prelude

At the back of the room, Bob signalled quietly to Anne Blanchard to follow him outside. A glance passed quickly between Alan and Anne, a smile and a nod of encouragement. Alan felt he was on the right track. What he was suggesting was not a great departure from established management principles, all it meant was that a manager should take the time to understand the systems he or she was trying to manage.

But then again, maybe it was a radical departure. To understand the systems and processes you managed it was necessary to ask your staff how they worked.

Not a strange idea, yet Comlink tended to manage using a military model – everyone was part of the line of command in which the manager told staff what to do and how to do it. For a manager to ask the staff, 'how do we do this?' or 'how can we improve it?' might be to risk the relationship between supervisor and staff. The Comlink environment did not encourage risk-taking.

Chapter 6
Tall tales but true

Sunshine greeted Anne and Bob as they stepped out into the street and headed in the direction of their meeting with the union.

"Where did you find the hairy stick insect? He's amazing," laughed Anne, jerking a thumb back towards the hotel.

Bob looked at her closely, "He's earnest, I'll give you that," he replied. "You know, Anne, I think we've got the right approach with this problem. For once, we don't deny or defend. The union will try and blame the accident on management and this time they're right. We're responsible, all of us, because we force people into situations where they have to either take risks in their work or lie about the results."

"What are you saying, Bob? My brief is to negotiate nothing," Anne said with a flat certainty.

"You heard them. We had a review six months ago and all we did was up the work quotas. We didn't change the way anyone did anything, just forced people to take short cuts. When Alan gets some results from that crew I'll be very interested. I'll bet we find Doug Golding's people have got an unreasonable quota to fill and as a result they're just bolting the phones to the wall and not bothering to connect them."

"Why on earth would they do that? It just means they've got to make another trip back later."

Bob laughed. "It's an old lurk," he explained. "I'm the son of a dyed-in-the-wool country tech. I've lost count of the number of times I went out on the road with my old man during school holidays.

"Dad would be given a number of jobs to do in a day. Always more than he could handle. That was the way the system worked: if a bloke could do ten in a day, you gave him twelve. Just in case. So, of course, you were always behind; always looking for a way to get ahead.

"Take fault reports as an example. You got a call to Mrs Smith's place: there was a fault on the line. If, as sometimes happened, the fault was intermittent and when you got there the line was working, that was great, because you could clear the fault. It counted towards your tally. And the beauty of it was you didn't actually have to spend time fixing it. Sounds great, huh?"

"Yes," Anne responded cautiously, eyeing a group of people walking across the concrete plaza towards them. They were carrying what looked suspiciously like television cameras.

"So, when a tech was dispatched on a job where the fault was reported as intermittent, he hoped like hell that it was working when he got there.

"On one occasion, we'd been to a house where the fault had been undetectable when we did our stuff. No fault, no work. As I was carrying the toolbox back to the car, I looked up at the overhead wire where it joined the eaves of the house. The junction box was stuffed, wires chaffed. Even a twelve year old kid could tell the fault was probably caused by the wires making occasional contact.

"Of course I blurted this out to the old man, pleased with my initiative. The householder was still in earshot, so there was nothing for it but for Dad to get out the ladder, clamber up and do the repair. Hell, he gave me a good kick later."

"Yes, but that was when you were in short trousers, Bob. There isn't much of that sort of thing any more," Anne said.

"Don't be too certain," Bob replied. "There's another example from only a couple of years ago. So far as I know, no-one's come to grips with the problem yet.

"A few years ago, one of the administration groups was researching patterns in new phone connections. At that time, the system for new connections was for Corporate Planning and Sales to give each region a target for the number of new services to be connected in the coming year.

"Over the years, regional managers found they'd receive a 'please explain' letter if the number of new connections in their area was not up to target. When that happened, they'd let their sales and ops managers know what was expected of them. The sales and ops managers, in turn, would inform their staff of the expected result, and so on down the line. After that, the figures would improve dramatically.

"Figures showing the number of new connections were forwarded to Head Office on a quarterly basis. When they took a look at several regions in the research, they realised that what was happening to provide the required improvements in figures was that enterprising young clerks – in response to the explicit or implicit instructions of their supervisors – were taking it upon themselves to fix the problem of the targets. On the final day of each quarter they would raise orders for the required number of new connections. If a region was two hundred short, then two hundred mythical orders would be raised and entered into the computer, which would then show that the target was being met. A couple of days later they'd cancel the false orders. No problem. Head Office was happy, regional management was happy, the clerical supervisors were happy, Sales was happy.

"It came as a shock to the researchers when they realised that an unofficial habit of providing corrupt figures was being sanctioned by the demands of the Head Office structure. Each of the people concerned would have been astonished to realise they were part of an organisation-wide farce. But, equally, all felt that a little fiddling with figures at the local level would certainly do no harm – in fact, it would do some good, since it kept Head Office at bay and allowed staff to get on with the work they were being paid to do.

"The message was clear. If the next person up the ladder was interested in good news, then you gave that person the news they wanted to hear. So for years we were getting corrupt data and making decisions on the basis of fabricated figures."

The TV crew had almost reached them. For all his apparent confidence and the feeling that they were on to something in the meeting, Bob could not help fixing his gaze on the snout of the camera pointed towards him. It looked like a stubby rocket launcher.

The news journalist was a slim, neat woman in her early thirties. She had a professionally cold smile and perfectly painted fingernails, which looked as if they had been freshly dipped in the blood of her previous interviewee.

"The Secretary of the UCWU has gone on record as saying his men will not go back to work until the safety issue is resolved," she smiled.

"That's possible," Bob replied cautiously," I haven't spoken to the Secretary this morning. I was actually on the way to a meeting with the UCWU when you stopped me."

"Is your meeting going to achieve anything, Mr Cheshire? There have been a lot of meetings over the past few months. Yet nothing seems to change."

Bob stared momentarily at the reflective blue sheen of the camera lens. This was only marginally a safety issue. Writing safety commitment statements or issuing hardhats wasn't going to make a difference. For Bob, this was an issue of trust and communication. Every bit of research from Alan's notes had shown somewhere a failure in trust or communication. People either did not know how, or did not feel safe enough, to comment on the processes in which they found themselves working. It was easier for both managers and staff to go on as they had always done, until something like yesterday's accident happened. Then they would all rush around for a period like disturbed ants, waiting for the confusion to die down so they could rebuild their nests in the same pattern they had always used.

Yet Bob knew if he tried to explain how he felt it would come out wrong, or be twisted into an indictment of him, his work and his organisation.

"Maybe we'll be able to change something this time," he muttered, moving away from the camera crew.

As they moved off across the square, Bob looked at his watch. "OK, Blanchard, this is where we earn our keep. Let's see if we can't sort out the union's problems. "

"I'm ready, Bob."

He paused, measuring her willingness to accept his arguments before speaking his thoughts.

"I don't want any hatchet-work done on this, Anne. I want to solve this problem by working with these people instead of against them."

"New approach, eh?" she laughed. "You'll put me out of a job, Bob. Didn't you know that industrial relations is based on argument and confrontation? Once you start to actually solve problems, IR becomes a meaningless pastime!"

Chapter 7
All in the game

Albert barely heard Luke's ritual "Good luck, Mr Lapin," as he walked quickly away from his car towards the candy-striped tent on the grassy rise behind the eighteenth green.

People were milling about everywhere in the hot, clear air. A stiff breeze from the south-west provided only minor relief from the unseasonable heat.

Unseasonable? he reflected, gazing at the blue Comlink flags topping the marquee. What *was* seasonable? There seemed to be no rhyme or reason to the weather any more. It was as if the confusion and uncertainty which had characterised life over the past three decades had somehow permeated the atmosphere itself, disturbing the diurnal rhythms of the globe.

Golf. He hated it! Whose idea had it been for Comlink to play corporate sponsor to the biggest golf tournament on the calendar? Worse than that, who was the creature who'd suggested a meeting of the Comlink Board in this, of all places? Sometimes Albert suspected it was the sole aim of public relations departments in companies all over the country to pass their time in finding new and allegedly exciting venues for their jaded executives to meet.

Walking into the marquee, Albert was greeted by a number of managers and the various members of the Comlink Board who were present. The purpose of this exercise was to promote informal discussion between Board members and the Comlink managers who worked under them. At the back of the tent a table had been set up for the formal Board meeting which would occur in private later.

The members of the Board were a mixed bunch. The unusual position of Comlink in the nation's affairs meant that its Board of Directors was

The Prelude

necessarily a compromise organism. It included business and commercial power, community involvement and union participation.

Amongst those present was Paula Murchison, the UCWU member. As the union expert on Health and Safety issues, she had a large stake in what was happening in Newcastle.

Paula broke off her conversation and turned to Albert.

"Well?" she said.

"I don't know, Paula. Not yet. I've spoken to Bob Cheshire this morning," he replied, referring to a hurried video conference with Bob and Anne Blanchard following their meeting with the union.

Bob had asked for leeway in his discussions. To Albert's surprise, Anne had expressed her support. "The issues are complex here, Albert," she had said, "I think we can solve it at a local level, but we need your support in keeping this a local issue."

Albert had consented to their request. Now he attempted to convince Paula Murchison.

"They're going to try for a resolution at the local level. I agree with them: the problem was caused by local issues."

"Employee safety is not a local issue, Albert," she replied coldly.

"You know how good our safety record's been in recent years, Paula. We've done a lot, most of it through work with the unions. But I'm not convinced that this is entirely a health and safety matter."

Paula raised her thin eyebrows. "You'll need to convince us of that," she warned.

"Bob has been working with the local Project Manager, Alan Dodgson. Together they've come up with something which they've asked I support. We can talk about it later." He glanced at his watch. "They'll be putting it to your Newcastle operative right now."

He pulled a small, electronic diary out of his suit pocket and consulted it.

"Bob will be back on Monday. After I've talked it through with him, I'll contact you and we'll meet to discuss his proposal. In the meantime, talk to your people in Newcastle."

* * * * *

There was a large number of people in the tent now, far more than the number slated to attend the Directors' meeting. Some were obviously guests, invited to the sporting function as a result of their business relationships with Comlink. Others appeared to be professional freeloaders — probably from the public relations department, Albert thought moodily.

At that moment, his eye caught someone in the crowd who had no right to be there. Two men were on the verandah where the tent opened up to provide a view of the final fairway. Albert could see the unwelcome guest talking to Leo Carnic, one of the industry lobby members of the Comlink Board.

Carnic was the Managing Director of a vast investment management business. He controlled a large slice of the funds available to Australian business with a firm, unforgiving ruthlessness which earned his supporters spectacular results and his opponents early graves. Together with Neale Kale, another Comlink Board member, he had set up and financed some of the largest deals to shape the economic face of Australia in the past decade.

Albert thought of Neale Kale, wondering where he was. As head of the Australian operations of an international banking concern and an expert in the rough realm of international finance and investment, Kale held even greater influence in the business community than Leo Carnic.

The image of the dark-suited, fussy businessman with a face as white as milk never failed to bring a wry grimace to Albert's lips. It was unusual for Kale to be absent from a Board meeting. But that was not what had disturbed Albert's equilibrium. Rather, it was the man who stood with Leo Carnic: Hugh Britten, the Managing Director of NetWork, Comlink's main competitor.

NetWork was the local subsidiary of a multi-national communications corporation. Since deregulation, it had moved into the Australian marketplace with a swift and savage aggression. Under Hugh Britten, NetWork had become a considerable strength in a relatively short period. Recent successes with several public housing projects, where NetWork had been awarded the contract for large-scale outer-urban developments, had given the company the bonafides necessary for a sympathetic hearing from some quarters of the industry.

NetWork had been extremely clever in its lobbying and promotional activities, playing initially on its smallness and the way it faced unfair competition from the monolithic Comlink. It was a classic David and Goliath argument, presented slickly by Hugh Britten's publicists. Unfortunately, Comlink had not responded quickly enough to the potential threat, believing

The Prelude

its own myth that the huge capital cost of network development would effectively keep competition out of the marketplace. As a result, NetWork had been making advances, both in market share and – perhaps more importantly – in terms of customer perception of its ability to provide good service.

Now the advertising had begun to change. NetWork was claiming it could run a complete customer access network more efficiently than Comlink. And people were starting to listen: government, business and even ordinary consumers.

Overseas, NetWork's parent company had a history of moving into the marketing vacuum opened up by deregulation. In a number of countries, its aggressive stance had severely damaged the prospects of those former state bodies who had once been solely responsible for telecommunications. Their actions in Britain and on the Continent had been fast, brutal and effective. Their major concern was with high profits and shareholder satisfaction.

Many of the local 'experts' had said, "Don't worry, it won't happen here. Australia's too large, the tyranny of distance will stop them replicating their overseas strategies." That was true to some extent, but it hadn't worked out like many of the pundits had prophesied.

NetWork's attempts to demonstrate it could run a complete system for a lower cost than Comlink had not originally been taken very seriously within the industry. Albert, and many others, saw such statements as ambit claims. Once the multi-national company controlled any large network it would begin slicing off the least profitable areas like a corporate vivisectionist. High-paying, easily-serviced business customers, based for the most part in the eastern capitals, would be wooed at the expense of low-paying home consumers in isolated rural and outback areas.

But lately, both the commercial and private sectors of the market were giving increased credence to NetWork's claims.

It was clear that Hugh Britten had been invited as a corporate guest to watch the golf from the Comlink marquee, although he had certainly not been on Albert's invitation list. Still, Albert mused, he couldn't simply whistle up Luke and a couple of his burly acquaintances to toss Hugh off the verandah and onto the eighteenth green. Instead, he approached the NetWork executive with his heartiest smile planted firmly on his face.

"Hello Hugh, glad you could make it."

Albert extended his hand to the NetWork chief. Hugh Britten grabbed it with the classic, double-handed action of a salesman, closing his left hand over his grip in a display intended to emphasise his intense joy at seeing the individual involved, but which left Albert unimpressed.

"Sorry to hear about the accident in Newcastle, Al," Hugh Britten said sweetly.

Albert shrugged and took back his hand.

"How's business for you then, Hugh? You're not here touting are you?"

They all laughed at the joke that wasn't.

"Just a pleasant afternoon at the golf," Hugh replied. "You've supplied the communications set-up for this tournament, haven't you?"

"Yes, this is the first Major Event in which the PGA has used our transmitter ball. If the system works out as we hope, the applications will be immense. The tough part was the design of an impact-resistant transmitter able to handle the incredible forces applied to a standard golf ball. We've got Don Burgess to thank for the design."

"Nice toy," Hugh said, smiling.

"It's more than a toy," Albert responded. "It has enormous potential for our satellite communications program."

"You certainly stole a march on us there, Al. Congratulations. I hope it works for you."

The groups behind Albert were breaking up now, moving towards the meeting table.

"Looks like you're ready to go, boys," Hugh Britten said, placing a hand on the shoulders of Albert and Leo Carnic. "I'd better get out of here before I get caught and hung for a spy."

He moved off to the exit, waving once with a hearty gesture of encouragement.

Albert was concerned. He moved off toward the table, thinking deeply about Hugh Britten's appearance at the tournament. The NetWork executive's pleasant smile had rung warning bells for Albert. It occurred to him that it was quite within Britten's character to appear as a gesture; to indulge himself in the game of alerting his competitor to something he did not intend to reveal openly yet.

As he took his seat, Albert thought intensely about the possibilities which the NetWork executive's inconclusive appearance presented. Had he looked down the length of the table, he might have seen a small, tight smile on Leo Carnic's lips.

Chapter 8
In need of repair

"Darren, I'm not telling you to drag the whole project to a halt. I just want to be sure we're going to be measuring and reporting on the right things."

It was Monday morning, and after an intensive weekend of meetings with Alan and the other Newcastle managers Bob Cheshire was back in his Melbourne office, on the phone to Darren Heyden, head of Comlink's Management Information Group.

Darren and Bob were involved in a project which had been set up almost a year earlier, largely at Albert Lapin's instigation. The Management Information Database program was designed to enable Comlink managers to get daily access to the information in the various databases of the organisation.

It was just as well, thought Bob, that he didn't have a videophone yet. His voice might sound calm and relaxed, but the picture of him leaning forward, elbows on the desk, running his fingers through his hair would be a give-away to anyone at the other end of the line who could see him.

Before Bob could respond to Darren's refusal to entertain the possibility of changing anything about the 'MID' program, his door burst open and the figure of Dr Don Burgess strode into the office.

The chief of Comlink's Research and Development Laboratories was a white-coated bundle of energy, whose brilliance was renowned throughout the telecommunications world. He stood hopping from one foot to the other, nervously approaching Bob's desk with a couple of bustling, energetic steps, then stepping backward reluctantly with his arms spread wide and his shoulders tensed, like a loose-limbed sailor pushing against a wind-filled sheet.

In need of repair

Bob waved to him and attempted to continue the conversation with Darren.

"One of the issues that came up in Newcastle was the lack of reliable information," he explained. "Yes... I know that's what we're trying to rectify with MID. The point I want to look at is whether we're going to use the databases to give us sensible answers. If we ask the wrong questions, we'll get the wrong answers."

Bob felt uncomfortable. The objections Darren Heyden was raising were quite legitimate. They had spent almost six months looking at all this already. It was all there in the project specs. What was he carrying on about now, after the project was already underway?

Yet there was something deeper that Bob needed to address: the discussion which followed the OFCAB accident had highlighted something fundamentally wrong in the way Comlink gathered and interpreted its information.

"We uncovered an example in Newcastle, where all the performance figures appeared to be under control, but the result was that customers had a useless phone bolted to their wall for anything up to ten weeks. I'm concerned that what we are doing with MID is simply transferring the current reporting systems we've got into a more elaborate electronic framework. The faults that are in our current system will remain there, and they'll be harder to eliminate because we'll have institutionalised them."

Bob glanced at Don Burgess. The man was bobbing slightly, his face pink with emotion.

At the other end of the phone, Darren Heyden was defending his team of experts, claiming that, as management information specialists, they knew their job well enough to be able to design a system without faults.

The awkwardness of it from Bob's viewpoint was that everything Darren was saying was absolutely true. His team were the experts, and it was a rigid rule in Comlink that you did not make unwanted suggestions about the operation of someone else's business. That wasn't the way to make friends. Besides, Bob didn't know exactly what it was he wanted Darren to do. He just had a vague notion that the way Comlink gathered its information caused people to look after themselves and their jobs, rather than expend their efforts trying to look after their customers.

But what to do about it? How could you change that? Perhaps it was a necessity of work that you asked people to concentrate on the physical

57

The Prelude

aspects of their tasks rather than on the outcome of those tasks – which was surely supposed to be customer satisfaction?

Bob had believed for a long time that a manager's job was to direct people so that they could achieve their allotted tasks. Simple. And it worked.

Yet there was something not quite right about that assumption. It hinged on the definition of what a customer was.

He had seen the result in a field in Newcastle and had been thinking about it ever since. The supply people and the depot people had not given their customers — the Mole crew — good service. The goods were late arriving, the job was hurried, the driver was in unfamiliar circumstances, and a man was dead.

But if you'd asked any of those people involved whether they had been giving customer satisfaction, they would have said 'Sure, what do you think? The customers want this line working as soon as possible'.

Who were the customers? The people in the houses and businesses who wanted the videophones? They wanted the service, that much was true. But it wasn't crucial to them that it happen instantly, since the old audio system was working adequately. The consumers would not be fussed about a reasonable delay, provided the system worked when it was connected.

Yes, the consumer was the customer, Bob decided. But so, too, were the people you were doing the job for. The supply people were doing a job for the depot people. The depot people were doing a job for the Mole team. The Mole team was doing a job for the 'pit and pipe' men, and so on, until the long daisy chain was completed. And it was not completed until the consumer was given a phone that worked, and kept working.

Bob was surprised to realise he had been doodling his thoughts as he attempted to listen to Darren Heyden. A rough collection of linked shapes had spread themselves across the pad on his desk and he was blocking in the letters of the various sections involved in the daisy chain.

Maybe, he speculated, attempting to draw the daisy chain analogy to its final conclusion, the job of the manager was to ensure that all those links in the chain held strong; so that each link understood and fulfilled the needs of the next link in the chain, leading to the final product and a satisfied consumer.

In need of repair

System

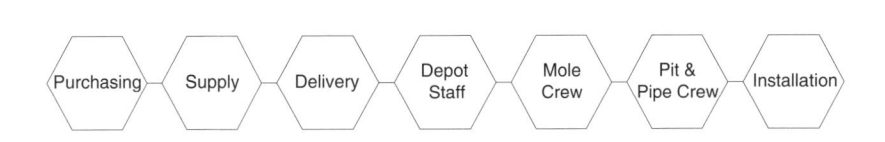

Purchasing → Supply → Delivery → Depot Staff → Mole Crew → Pit & Pipe Crew → Installation

**Who is the customer? The manager?
The consumer?
The next in line?**

Bob thought about this definition. He wasn't sure it was right, but it was more useful than the cruel indictment which emerged from the customer definition he had seen in Newcastle.

There, the 'customer' had not been the next work group in the line, nor the consumer who would eventually pick up the phone. The 'customer' in Newcastle had somehow come to mean the project managers: the people who told you what to do, imposed the timelines, then demanded more performance without attempting to change the work systems.

The Mole crew had been working to provide satisfaction to their managers, not to the people who mattered: the ones who formed the next link in the chain, or the consumers who would eventually use the phones.

Bob was endeavouring to explain these concerns to Darren Heyden, but without success. He shouldn't really be surprised, he thought, that Darren wasn't buying it. After all, for so long he, himself, had been sure that he knew exactly how his people were working.

His people? He remembered telling Barry Todd that they weren't anybody's personal possession.

59

"Darren, I don't think it's necessary to stop the development we're working on at the moment. But I do want you to give me some assistance with the tack Alan is taking in Newcastle. He's trying to analyse the work systems at the local level. I'm betting that such an analysis will show major differences when compared with the systems documented in MID."

Darren was not impressed.

"I know we've done the exercise in a significant number of work sites to gain a correlation," Bob acknowledged. "But I'd still like to have a look at OFCAB. I think we'd find the existing manual and computer information systems are providing a completely false picture of what is happening ....Arthur Dee? Who's he?"

"Alright," Bob said after the explanation. "I'd be more than happy to have him help us with an analysis of OFCAB. He's a statistician? OK, thanks for your help, Darren. Please have Arthur call me when you've filled him in."

It was something, at least.

Bob hung up and turned to his unrequested visitor. Don Burgess was hunched moodily in one of the corner armchairs.

"Yes, Don?" he enquired sweetly.

The scientist's face was still as pink as when he had burst into the office. He opened his large mouth to speak, sucking in a final gasp of air before commencing. Bob held up a hand to forestall him.

"You look as though you're seriously disturbed, Don. Hold on a moment." He turned to the answering service on his desk, selected a message from its gallery of recordings and flicked it on.

"We won't be disturbed now. Perhaps you could close the door too?"

Don Burgess, apparently continuing to hold his breath, walked stiffly over to the door and pushed it shut.

Bob settled himself in his chair, smiled bleakly at the scientist's refusal to do the same, and waited for him to begin.

It all came out in an undirected rush as the man walked briskly back and forth in front of Bob's desk, flapping his arms with agitation.

"I'm sick of my work suffering at the hands of bureaucratic expediency. My staff are sick and tired of wasting their efforts on ill-conceived, half-assed projects that are rushed out into the marketplace before they're ready. It's impossible to maintain an effective research program in this place if every time you or the sales people have a problem you want us to come up with some wonderful little toy that is going to sell like pies at the football, cost less than a litre of milk and make us all millionaires. We can't do it time and time again. There are limits to the amount of extra effort we can put into a product to speed up its development. Beyond that it's simply not worthwhile. We can't speed something up just because you, Albert, Clifford or anyone else wants it. If you want our products to work when people get their hands on them, you must allow us the time to develop them properly. Otherwise, we may as well not bother.

"Honestly, Bob, it's a sickening thing to have to rush through everything all the time, working our bloody hardest to make some arbitrary goal that has been put on us for no other reason than that the competition is getting close or the exchange rate is bad or the month has a full moon in it. Those things have got nothing to do with us, and changing the development times in some silly report is not going to help get the thing done any faster."

"Don, I sympathise, and I agree."

"What?" said the scientist, narrowing his eyes slightly.

"It's the Dick Tracy Watch, that's the problem isn't it?"

"Of course it is. And for that matter, why didn't you tell me what was going on? It's bloody marvellous to hear what's happening through the minutes of a management meeting. We're supposed to be working together and I hear everything second-hand. How am I supposed to have any credibility with my team if I'm not even consulted about the work we are doing?"

Before Bob had a chance to argue, his phone rang. They both looked at it in annoyance. After several rings, Bob picked up the handpiece.

"Hello, John....Well thanks. Look, can I call you back? I'm in a conference at the moment.....I did, the damn thing doesn't appear to be working."

He hung up and looked enquiringly at Don.

Momentarily deflected, the scientist came around the side of Bob's desk and tapped the offending answering machine.

"It's perfectly simple. We should be making these things ourselves instead of buying them from other people."

He flicked the machine, stared at the flickering lights on its control panel then pulled a screwdriver out of his top pocket.

"I know it's not a good decision to speed up development of the Dick Tracy Watch. I fought against the decision myself. But now it's been taken I have to support it," Bob said.

"Solidarity, eh?" murmured the scientist. He had removed the cover of the answering machine and was probing gingerly inside, his long, thin nose almost buried in the machine.

The Prelude

"That's not it, and you know it, Don. We've got serious problems and we need a winning new product like the Watch to boost sales and consumer loyalty," replied Bob, his hands tightly gripped on the arms of his chair. Any second now, he half expected a flash of blue lightning to emerge from the answering machine's carcass as a result of the Doctor's surgical poking.

"Relax, Bob," said the scientist, "after all, who fixed your coffee machine?"

He waved loosely at the solar-powered expresso machine which had been a gift from one of the kids. Emma or Sandie? Bob wasn't quite sure. Anyway, the thing had never worked properly – at least not until Don got hold of it.

"I realise there are difficulties from where you sit, Bob. But there are limits to what I can achieve. Besides, I heard what you were saying to Darren before." He looked up from the machine long enough to tap the scrawled doodle on Bob's pad. "Who are *we* working for?"

Bob shrugged.

"You know how hard this business is getting, Don. There just isn't the time any more. Years of leisurely development and testing is a luxury we just can't afford any more. I don't like it, but that's how it has to be."

With a crack, Don succeeded in separating a small circuit module from its motherboard. He harried it with the edge of a knife as he spoke to Bob.

"I'm not asking for years," said the scientist, "I just want enough time to be sure our product is a good one when we release it. You know what happened with the CD Data Phone. We released it before it was ready. As a result, we've had to do the testing and product development in the field. Now the thing's got a reputation for being just one bit less reliable than a British Leyland P - 76.

"I designed that phone, Bob. It was a bloody good unit and we allowed it to fail. That hurts. I'm getting to the point where I don't trust this company. If I had some marvellous invention, I doubt I'd even bring it along to show you. I've seen too many go down the drain because of lousy policy.

"How is a Dick Tracy Watch that we can't guarantee going to help the customers one bit?" he finished bitterly, emphasising his disappointment by slapping the cover of the answering machine and screwing it back into place. "It'll work now."

Bob looked sideways at the thin, white-coated man. It was true. He'd told the people in Newcastle that the rush had caused the death of Wally

Jamieson. Had the lesson worn off so quickly? He had hardly been back at Head Office for a day before he was telling his chief scientist to hurry up with another project.

If he was honest with himself, Bob realised, he had no idea whether Don and his staff could hurry the Watch. He'd just assumed they could: everybody knew there was always some slack you can pull in if you have to.

The trouble was that pulling in the slack had caused a death on OFCAB. What was he asking Don Burgess to do now? Kill the Dick Tracy Watch? What about all that stuff he and Alan had talked about: systems, processes, change? It seemed a long way away now.

You couldn't have it both ways, Bob thought. Either you took the time and did the job properly, or you hurried it and did the best you could, praying it would work well enough to generate the necessary sales and revenue. There wasn't a third option he knew about.

The Dick Tracy Watch could possibly make the difference between long-term profitability and going annually to an increasingly hostile government cap-in-hand. The ramifications of success and failure were enormous for all those people employed by Comlink. How, then, could he justify squandering vital time in possibly unnecessary testing and development? If the thing worked, it should be out in the market earning revenue.

Don Burgess tucked the screwdriver back into his pocket and looked at Bob sadly.

"We'll never change anything unless we make a decision to put in the effort needed to produce a quality product which meets the needs of the market. If we don't take that time – to plan what we're doing and see it through decently – then we'll be locked into a cycle of expediency forever.

"...Aw, what's the use? I shouldn't be talking to you like some bloody marketing bozo. I'm a researcher."

Bob took a deep breath.

"You're right, Don. I've been so concerned with solving one problem, I can't focus on the others. In Newcastle I told the managers that we needed information about the processes we're involved in. The first thing is to look at how your groups are working at present. Do they have any problems with equipment, supply, personnel, access, anything? I want you to do something for me. Draw up a detailed plan of the existing timelines on the project. Then draw up another showing what would have to be the case if you are to achieve the new deadlines. Then we'll compare them and see what's possible."

"What for? We've done the scenarios by computer a dozen times. It can be done. We know that, but the cost will be terrible – and the result? Well, I wouldn't guarantee it for more than about three-quarters of an hour."

"This time ask your people what they are doing, what they need to achieve their tasks, and what they aren't getting. Talk to them," said Bob.

"Yeah, sure. The way you're talking to me. What can I say? We've got instructions to achieve the target. How can I turn around and say we can't do it. How can any of my staff? They'll just tell you what they think you want to hear. Of course they'll say they can do it. If they argue they'll get shafted."

"No," said Bob harshly. "I'll go bail. If this project can't be achieved properly within the current working procedures I want to know about it *now*, not when we get halfway down the track and find we're six months behind schedule and everyone's saying 'Well, we told you it'd be difficult'. I want to know what you are capable of. If I've got to go to Albert or Clifford with this, I want a clear understanding of what we should be asking from your people."

How could he have asked for more effort from the R & D people, thought Bob, without first knowing exactly what they were involved in and how they were achieving it? At the moment he had no idea – and he suspected that most Comlink managers would be in a similar situation if called on to provide improved performance. He had fallen into the trap of simply demanding a greater effort. It was an insult, now he thought about it, a deliberate insult from a manager to those who work for him. To demand a greater output without changing the work systems was to say nothing more than that the people involved were bludging, deliberately avoiding a full day's work.

But how could he change the way the systems worked: OFCAB, MID, the Dick Tracy Watch? Already there had been an army of consultants through the OFCAB project and the nett effect of their presence had been no more than if they had been a group of deckhands aboard the Titanic, straightening up the deckchairs as she slid sorrowfully beneath the waves.

Chapter 9
On the beach, part 2

Monday night in Newcastle. And if you didn't particularly enjoy pumping credits into a poker machine or cruising up and down Hunter Street at a hundred kilometres an hour, there was arguably not much left to do.

The last of the meetings had been held and the semblance of an agreement thrashed out between Comlink and the UCWU. Barry Todd had agreed to recommend his members return to work.

The deal was a complete review of work systems, no cutbacks, a review of safety issues and a look at increased budgets for the project. A good result, as far as Anne Blanchard was concerned, who saw it as a major victory that both managers and union representatives had been prepared to take on board the proposition that improvements to processes – the way people were involved in the chain of work tasks – would result in improved safety, reduced pressure for deadlines, and better work practices.

They might have accepted the argument, thought Anne, but they didn't believe in it. No way. Still, that might come if Alan could demonstrate some success soon.

She looked across the table at her dinner companion. He was a curious mixture, a blend of boyish desperation and healthy cynicism. Watching him over the past four days, Anne had come to the conclusion that Alan's strength lay in his direct and inelastic honesty. People were willing to believe he would try to fix the problems, not just sweep them under the carpet. He would have a good chance of bringing something positive out of this whole mess.

It was different for her. Industrial relations seemed to be a rearguard action fought between groups whose main interest was preservation of the status quo. Her role was to frustrate and withhold, to make sure nothing

The Prelude

changed. And the union executives acted in much the same way. Who then was winning? Who were they fighting? There was a rough honesty in her work, yet somehow it had become distorted over the years of confrontation and futile aggression. It had been a long time since she had seen things through the eyes of simplicity.

Anne sighed softly to herself and smiled at Alan, who lifted his glass in salutation.

"You did some pretty fast negotiating there," he said.

Anne nodded, staring at his eyes which were hooded with tiredness.

"You're beginning to look like this city."

"How's that?"

She paused, looking closely at him, the way a gardener looks at a rose bush just prior to a serious pruning job.

"Seedy. Definitely seedy. And tired. Washed out......In need of rest," she said finally.

Alan watched her slow, thoughtful scrutiny with an odd blend of curiosity and uncertainty. It was two years since Michelle had left him – or he had left Michelle, he was never very sure of the sequence of events now – and in that time Alan could not remember a woman whose company he had enjoyed so much as Anne's over the last few days.

He finished his wine. "It's tough to be a saint in this place."

"It's tough to be a saint anywhere," she responded. "But you did well, we both did. You've won some time to do what you wanted."

A waiter drifted listlessly past their table and Alan ordered a brace of ports to finish their meal. "There's never the time," he said, "never enough to do what you want."

"And what do you want?" Anne asked, toying with her glass. For once she would not meet his eyes.

"What do I want?" he echoed her question. "Ease of life, peace, love amongst all humanity. Not much," he smiled, gazing lazily at Anne through a slightly mellow haze.

She was definitely an attractive woman, he thought, somewhat in surprise. Tall and elegant, with sleek, shoulder length hair and a cool, slightly remote air, her attraction had not been apparent to him at first, but he was beginning to feel it quite strongly. Alan shook his head lightly, bemused at his own thoughts.

They chatted amicably for a time, until eventually a waiter explained that the restaurant was closing. Grinning foolishly, they wandered outside.

"Let's walk down to the beach for a minute," Alan said. "It's not far."

He threw an arm around Anne's shoulder and guided her across the street in the direction of the nearby ocean. The casual physical contact between them sparked an acute, emotional response in Alan. He was almost relieved when they reached the sandy beach which he and Bob had visited some nights before, and Anne drew away to perch on the narrow wall which ran along its edge.

They sat for some time, gazing silently at the water and the stars, feeling the pressure of the past days draining away. After a while, Anne shook her head vigorously. Pulling off her shoes, she jumped down from the parapet onto the coarse sand. Her hair flew about her face as she danced lightly away from Alan, shrugging off her jacket and tossing it to him before racing down the beach to the sea.

Alan followed her actions, somewhat bewildered by the transformation in Anne who, in the space of twenty metres, had changed from a friendly and attractive businesswoman to an elemental shape, her white blouse and blonde hair billowing in the breeze, blending into the glowing, white surf.

She was standing ankle deep in the foaming water when he came up to her, one hand holding her skirt clear of the swell and an expression of girlish pleasure on her face. Alan's gaze flickered over Anne's slim frame before meeting her eyes. She smiled back at him as he stepped tentatively towards her. Their lips touched in a faint experiment, and then they were kissing deeply, sliding into a deep embrace and twining their arms around each other's bodies, pressing close. Anne's body was warm and smooth against his as Alan ran his hands over the contours of her flesh, holding her tightly with desire and the need for closeness.

They parted, laughing: in part at the release of tension; in part at the happiness they felt. Alan grabbed Anne's hand and ran with her down the beach, away from the lights of the main esplanade. They veered away from the surf, up onto the dry sand and tussocks of the beach dunes.

"What next?" Anne smiled wickedly, as they threw themselves down in a sheltered hollow, collapsing in a welter of arms and legs.

Alan stared at her face, its chin thrust slightly forward, lips parted, nose up-tilted. Such a lovely nose, he thought, and bent to kiss her again, lingeringly, until their bodies trembled hungrily and their hands roamed freely, exploring each other.

When the embrace broke Alan looked at Anne, her expression smiling and open, her elegant reserve shed with an ease he could never have suspected. He wondered if he was the same – glowing, grinning foolishly, optimistic.

The Prelude

"Are you prepared?" she asked in a husky voice.

"Mmmm?" said Alan from somewhere in her thick hair, nuzzling the satin softness of her skin and inhaling the scent of her body.

"Protection!" she laughed. "Have you got a condom? Or three preferably!"

Alan flapped futilely at the back pocket where his wallet lay, thinking for a moment that there may, by some miracle, be one hidden in its dark recesses. No, that was a fantasy. It had been months since he'd had plans along the lines of what was happening.

"Have you?" he enquired, hopefully.

"Of course not, Silly," she said, stroking his cheek softly.

"Well, I didn't exactly come prepared either."

Anne groaned.

"Come on, Anne. It'll be alright, I haven't got anything."

Anne turned towards him, her face partially obscured by the darkness. Alan was unsure whether she was upset or thought their situation was amusing.

"You don't know where I've been?" Alan tried to keep his voice light, to pass it off as a joke, something they could laugh about later. But there was a sudden defensiveness in his tone.

"It's not like that, Alan." Anne shook her head as if to clear it.

"Sorry," he said bitterly, "I just wasn't expecting to get seduced tonight."

"Seduced!"

"Anyway," he continued recklessly. "You're the liberated lady executive, didn't you come prepared either?"

"Do you think I do this sort of thing all the time?" Anne replied quietly. She passed a hand across her head, pressing the furrows on her forehead.

"Well, I ..."

Without waiting to hear further, Anne batted his hands away and stood up, glaring at Alan as though he had just crawled out from under a rock.

"I think we'd better go back now," she said frostily, gathering her dignity around her and dusting the sand off her blouse.

They made their way in silence back to the esplanade wall. Collecting their belongings, they walked the short distance back to Anne's hotel. In the lobby, Anne turned to Alan, brushing the hair from her eyes with one hand. The free-moving elemental had disappeared, to be replaced once more by the elegant businesswoman.

"Good night," she said formally. "I'll be returning to Melbourne tomorrow, so I won't have a chance to see you again. Thank you for a pleasant evening."

Equally formal in his own anger and frustration, Alan shook her hand. He stood stiffly as Anne disappeared into the lift and the doors whispered shut behind her, leaving him staring bleakly at his own image, distorted hugely in the polished surface of the stainless steel.

In the privacy of the lift, Anne felt tears of rage pricking the back of her eyes. What was wrong with her, to have allowed a minor problem to get so completely out of hand? Could she no longer bear to be vulnerable, emotional? All the directness she practised in dealing with work problems seemed to evaporate when she was personally involved in the equation. Damn her stupidity. And Alan Dodgson too, she thought fiercely.

Chapter 10
Off piste

"Get off me, Gus!" cried Arthur Dee, swiping feebly at the mop-shaped head of his exuberant Old English sheepdog. "Good dog! Sit, Gus," he sputtered through clenched teeth as the animal bounced, grinning, from the bed to lollop ostentatiously on the carpet.

The statistician, kindly donated to Bob Cheshire's cause by Darren Heyden, lay back on the bed which had been placed in his study. He wriggled painfully, trying to ease the position of his leg, which was propped up on pillows and encased from heel to knee in a plaster cast.

Arthur looked up at Bob apologetically. "He's usually obedient. He just gets excited by visitors."

Bob could not help staring. The statistician didn't look at all well. His eyes were surrounded by raccoon circles of purple bruising and his nose – or what Bob could see of it protruding from the large square of white bandage – seemed inordinately flat. Arthur's condition, as he had warned Bob on the phone, was the result of an intimate embrace with a remarkably solid tree on the ski slopes in New Zealand a week earlier.

Well, at least it wasn't all that bad, thought Bob. Like most managers within Comlink, he had a preconception that all statisticians were pale, wiry, nervous and be-spectacled. Maybe there were some out there who fitted the mental picture which had been created by too many low-budget, science-fiction films, but clearly Arthur Dee wasn't one of them. He was a strong, athletic man in his late thirties, with dark hair and clear brown eyes. Granted, his nose was a bit wider than most, and he would not be moving very quickly with a broken ankle, but apart from these relatively minor faults, he appeared to be a sturdy creature: deeply tanned, robust and likely to be quite energetic once he got off his back.

"Don't worry," Arthur said. "I'll be up and about in a few days. It's good of you to come out and see me here."

"You were right when you said we may as well get started now, so that as soon as you're up you can come over to help us on the MID project."

At that moment, two children flashed past the open doorway of Arthur's study in a blur of brown hair, arms and screams. The sheepdog heaved itself to its feet and with a single, deep bark gave chase, gallumphing heavily out into the hallway.

Arthur shrugged expressively. "The twins. Working at home isn't all it's cracked up to be. I think I'll be glad to get back to an office."

"You've got no objection to coming to work with Forward Planning?" Bob asked. "As I said, we'll be looking at MID, and you've already done a lot of work on the project. It might mean being in the position of finding that some of that effort has been wasted."

"I'd like to help, even though I think it's fair to say that no-one – especially in Management Information Services – will be very interested in reviewing the specifications of a project which is already underway. I think you've got a point when you say there'll be problems with data collection; it's difficult to change direction on anything as big as this. Particularly without evidence," Arthur replied.

The two had spoken at length earlier that afternoon. Arthur, Bob had learned, was one of the few remnants of a failed internal consultancy program which had run in Comlink in the early nineties.

There had been nothing wrong with the program or its concepts; everybody had agreed at the time it was a worthwhile enterprise to improve the way Comlink delivered its products and services to customers. Yet the program had failed, for reasons similar to those which had been uncovered in OFCAB: poor communication, indifference, inability to accept change, confused messages to middle management about what was the right thing to do, lack of support. You couldn't just tell people to change, Arthur contended. Change was not a single event, it was a progression, a series of slow developments.

So, with a combination of poor salesmanship, premature release, misunderstanding of the degree of change required from people within the organisation and lack of resources, the project had eventually withered away. Arthur Dee's position had been transferred to Darren Heyden's area, where his work became less concerned with people and more wrapped up with the statistical analysis of raw data for which there was always a ready market in Comlink.

The Prelude

It had been a difficult period for the normally exuberant Arthur, to whom data analysis was merely the commencement point for enquiry – a tool for opening up questions and providing a platform for exploration. Too often, in his work now, he saw statistics used in the opposite way: as a substitute for enquiry, a method of restricting or foreshortening debate on issues of importance.

"It's a weird thing, but people will do almost anything to avoid looking at a difficult issue. Statistics is one of the things which can either hinder or help societies to look at their problems and keep a perspective on them."

Bob looked quizzical. "Is that what we're doing with the MID specs?"

"Maybe. I'm not sure. We'll have to find out," replied Arthur. "I'll give you an example of the way we avoid decisions, and you see whether it fits the way things happen in some parts of Comlink. Remember back in the late eighties, there was a commission into police corruption in Queensland under that bloke, Fitzgerald?"

"Yeah. That was the beginning of the end of the local National Party wasn't it?"

"Right. But before that, remember how there were disputes, a planned referendum, leadership coups, public fighting and all that? The effect of it was that the government committed suicide rather than face up to the need for a decision.

"The decision was whether to do something about the Fitzgerald enquiry recommendations. They wanted to avoid that decision so badly they were prepared to kill themselves. The whole argument there was bound up in statistical analysis – right from counting numbers in the party room, through to analysis of the gerrymander and surveys of public opinion. At every step, for every reason imaginable, the figures and trends were used to restrict debate and avoid making a decision. The party itself couldn't see what it was doing until it was too late."

"Yes, but were they suicides or scapegoats?"

"I'm not sure," Arthur replied. "But the point for Comlink is that often we get so wrapped up in how we want the world to be, we completely ignore the way it is. And for any group that ignores reality there is only one fate."

He looked at Bob mischievously, as if weighing him up.

"I'll give you another example. One you can test for yourself."

Bob nodded, "I'm game."

"OK. Imagine the time you are at work as a circle, like a pie chart. Within the circle there are various sorts of things you do while you're at work:

real work, make-work, coffee and chatting time, re-work of mistakes, unnecessary work and so on."

Arthur reached behind his head and pulled out a folder from the bookshelf next to his bed.

"I haven't used this for years," he said shyly.

He opened the folder to a simple chart divided into five uneven slices.

"There've been enough studies done to give a representative idea of what happens in any business. This may or may not apply to you as an individual, I'll tell you how to measure that later. But we can be sure that in any large organisation, the amount of *value-added work* – work on the right things, productive work that customers will pay for – is only about 25%. The other 75% of effort is dissipated through a variety of things: *re-work* – fixing errors, checking, responding to complaints and so on; *unnecessary work* – like writing reports that no-one ever reads, attending meetings of no use and so on; *necessary but unproductive work* – such as filling in expenses sheets, taking inventories, travelling between offices, and a final category of *not working time* – waiting time, idle time, holidays, coffee breaks and so on."

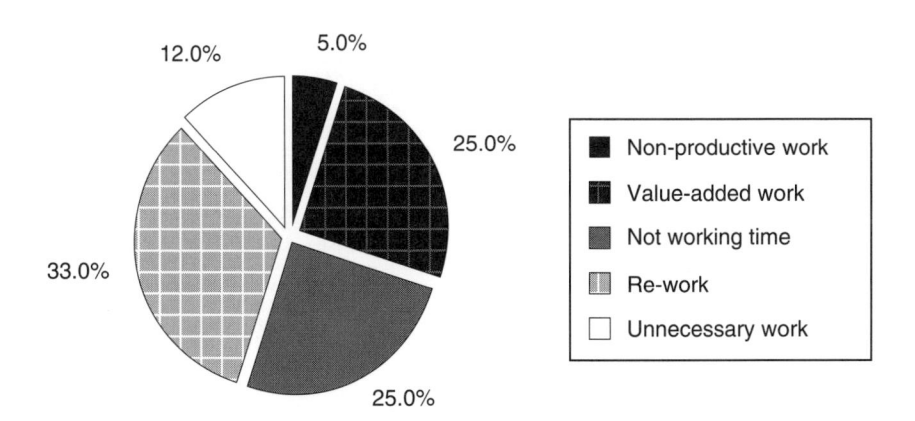

The Prelude

"Are you telling me we need to cut down on our coffee breaks?" Bob asked.

"No, certainly not. Some of the time spent not working is essential for building good relationships between people in the organisation.

"Re-work and unnecessary work are the two things that kill us. We spend a third of our time finding errors, checking things and people, inspecting, re-designing, attending to complaints, making mistakes because of the complexity of things we do. About another 12% is wasted on unprofitable meetings, calls, report writing and the rest. It's a simple concept, easy to demonstrate, but bloody hard to change."

Bob looked at the pretty little pie chart. It looked great in principle, but he couldn't believe that it would apply to him or to people like Alan Dodgson, Darren Heyden, or Clifford Tate. He thought about the last few days. It was ludicrous to say that almost half of his time had been spent chasing his tail.

"Try it yourself," Arthur said, reading the incredulity in Bob's face. "All you need is a piece of paper with five columns representing the five categories. Then tomorrow, while you're at work, try to remember to stop every thirty minutes and make a tick in the column that approximates what you are doing at the time – it might be easier if you use a timer or something. It'll only take a moment. Try it for three days in a row and see what comes out. You don't have to make a fancy pie chart, all you do is draw up the data as a simple Pareto Chart."

"A what?"

"A Pareto. It's a basic sort of graph used for presenting data simply and visually. It's also called a 'histogram'. At the end of three days, you just add up the number of ticks in each column, then draw a graph. Say you have thirty-four ticks in the *Re-work* column and twenty-seven in the *Value-added work* column, graph them like this, going from the biggest category to the smallest," Arthur said, pulling a pad from the bookcase and drawing a simple graph.

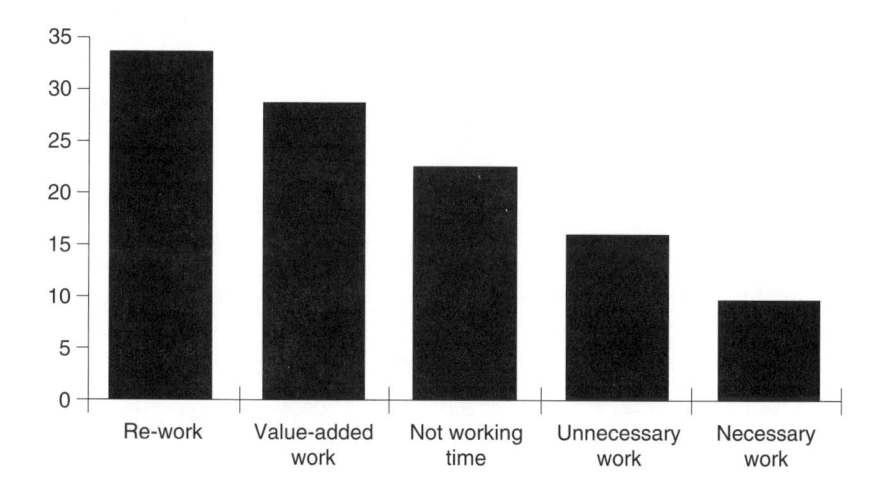

[Bar chart showing: Re-work ~34, Value-added work ~29, Not working time ~22, Unnecessary work ~16, Necessary work ~10]

"Looks easy enough."

"It is. But remember, it's just a starting point. Using this example it's easy to see you spend a large amount of time on re-work and unnecessary work. The next thing is to start asking questions like, 'Why do I spend this amount of time on unnecessary work?', or 'How can I change the amount of effort expended on non-productive work?' Try it with some of the people you work with. The results will surprise you."

Chapter 11
View from above

Hugh Britten stood at the window of his Sydney office, looking down at the evening lights shimmering in the city below, and at the small Comlink van parked on a corner of the street. Near it, two men in their distinctive Comlink overalls were in the process of removing the steel cover of a 'pit', the concrete cavity which housed the joints for the telephone cables in the area.

A fault? Routine maintenance? Who knew. Comlink people always seemed to be about their business at odd times, as if they were struggling to maintain a rotting system; one which needed to be tied up in plastic bags to stop it spilling out everywhere.

It was pathetic, thought the NetWork chief, that these men were pottering about down there, working in an antiquated fashion for an organisation which, as far as he was concerned, was too large, too unwieldy to look after its own.

Hugh Britten was a man who understood about looking after one's own. It was what he did best, and why he was in charge of NetWork, the most virile and pugnacious competitor Comlink had known. The shareholders loved someone who could look after himself, because he would also look after them.

"Comlink," he said dismissively, turning from the window. "I've no time for dinosaurs."

The visitor sitting in shadow in one of the leather armchairs across the room made no response. He was a small, neat man of less than medium height, with the fastidious appearance and practised blandness of a professional politician. His face, almost hidden in shadow, was slightly tanned with a strong nose and small black eyes which regarded his host with mild disdain.

View from above

"They can have their base network," Britten continued. "I won't be getting NetWork involved in that area, it's too unprofitable. But there are a lot of rich fruits hanging on the Comlink tree. I'm going to slice those fruits off, one by one. What's left can fend for itself.

"I think you'll be glad you came tonight, Minister. My proposal has a lot to offer you."

"I wonder," the other responded flatly. He tugged at one protruding cuff, extending his hand in a faintly feminine gesture.

Over the next few minutes, the Minister for Transport and Technology listened passively as the NetWork chief explained his vision for the future of telecommunications on the eastern seaboard.

"Fascinating, Britten," the Minister responded at the conclusion of Hugh's remarks, "But I fail to see what any of this has got to do with me."

For reply, the NetWork chief picked up a small remote-control and squeezed a couple of buttons. The large picture window through which he had been looking a few minutes earlier blackened and instantly came alive, as a colourful map of the state appeared a few inches in front of the glass. A spider-web of light spread out from the capital city, tracing the existing railway routes.

"NetWork is going to put together an integrated business network. I want every railway station in every town in the state to carry a microwave dish on its roof. That will enable the fast, cheap transfer of data, fax and telephone calls.

"To link up the system over a larger area, I want access to a corridor beside every railway track in the state. In this corridor, NetWork will lay an optical fibre cable to transfer information between population centres.

"With access granted by your ministry, we'll be able to put in a glass fibre network for a fraction of the amount Comlink has had to invest in their system, and to charge significantly reduced rates. We'll reserve the network for business customers: better service and maintenance contracts, higher returns from large-scale data transfers. We'll take the market from under Comlink's nose.

"In order to accomplish this, I need you to arrange for NetWork to lease those sites at a reasonable price."

The Minister for Transport and Technology regarded his host impassively. "Very interesting, Hugh. I wish you well. But why should I bother to help you? Nothing you've told me so far has convinced me of the benefits of doing so."

The Prelude

Hugh Britten smiled tightly. "I'm sure you're aware, Peter, that the Premier is widely perceived as ineffectual."

The Minister nodded warily.

"It's obvious from the polls that if your party is to retain power at the next election a change of leadership is needed. A new leader needs an issue which will catch the public imagination; an issue which will provide a quick result and show the electorate why your government should stay in office. I can supply you with that issue, Minister."

He paused.

"Go on," the politician said cautiously.

"What's the biggest loss-making area in your portfolio?"

"Railways. Two billion a year, recurrent losses."

"If you were to take up my proposal, you could almost guarantee to eliminate that loss within five years."

The NetWork chief pressed the remote-control and another slide appeared. This one depicted the Sydney metropolitan area. Dozens of lights flared to highlight patches of railway-owned land, most of it stations in heavily congested business districts.

"Real estate. The railways department is going to change its land-holding policy. So far, precious little has been done with the land they own."

"Think of it. In every city there are dozens of prime business sites wasted on nothing better than a handful of tracks and platforms. Here in Sydney alone, we've identified sixty-five sites with a value of seven billion dollars."

"Talk sense," the other interrupted, "those sites are occupied. Are you suggesting we close down the bloody rail system for you?"

"We build *over* those stations. Last year NetWork acquired a construction company. It's a small outfit, but with the correct financing deals I can turn it into something larger. That's where my associates come in. I have the necessary financial guarantees from my backers."

He turned back to the hologram control. A typical suburban railway station appeared before them. In quick stages, pylons and heavy supports appeared, until a gleaming office building stood complete with tiny computer-animated figures bustling about and trains moving in and out of the station that still operated below the building.

"Intelligent buildings. All telecommunications and data equipment will have been built and installed by NetWork – the latest ISDN equipment.

Obviously, the tenants of the buildings will be locked into long term service deals which provide them with access to our microwave network.

"Benefits all around, Minister. A profitable enterprise for us both."

The politician nodded thoughtfully. He could see the implications for himself and his party. With a carefully thought-out game plan he could announce a series of profit-generating initiatives. The plan had everything: jobs in a depressed building environment; reduction of the public deficit; growth for the city area, plus a great slap in the face for the Feds.

As a state Premier sitting on the other side of the political fence to the federal government, he would enjoy nothing better than to see their faces when the last remaining advantages of the federal telecommunications business evaporated as a result of intervention by a state government eager to reduce its own deficit and ease the burden on its taxpayers.

"You'll assist us, of course?" Britten said, attempting to keep the tension from his voice. "It will be more than worth your while."

"Leave it with me for a couple of days. I'll have someone contact your office on Thursday," the Minister replied. He would make the NetWork chief sweat a little; make it clear who was the senior partner in this deal.

All that he needed to do was to speak to the permanent head of his department, go through the motions of discussing and altering policy. It would be easy. And the prospect of the deal's effect on his future status in the party was glittering.

Chapter 12
Flying high

"God, I hate flying," muttered Don Burgess. He wrenched at the seatbelt, hauling it as tight as he could. Unclipping the front of his laptop computer, he lifted the screen to the operating position. His long nose thrust forward like a hound's when the scent of prey is rich in the air and his fingers began to tread a diffident pattern across the keyboard.

Bob Cheshire glanced sideways. The scientist was well known around Comlink for his eccentricities, one of which was an almost pathological dislike of airplanes. The two of them were about to fly over to the research laboratories in Adelaide to inspect some of the prototype support systems which would be part of the Dick Tracy package.

For the Watch to function effectively, a high-quality interface was needed to link the portable wrist-carried communicator to the transmission network. This was necessary as the two elements – the Watch and the network – operated with independent (and usually exclusive) technologies, namely microwave transmission and laser-optical transmission. Don's research team had developed the interface technology which would allow the Watch to handle the scale of transmissions required for video and data, but the means of enabling it to operate in an unrestricted environment had not yet been mastered.

"The Watch technology is really going to free up the way we communicate," Bob said, in an effort to take his companion's mind off the forthcoming flight.

"I'm not so sure," replied the scientist. "We rarely deal in true technological innovation. In fact, we try to avoid it whenever we can. Just look at the way we train people so that they'll reject any radically new technology."

"Come on, Don. That's a bit hard. People have to feel comfortable with new technology. That's part of why you're claiming we'll have difficulty with the Watch. You've been saying the techs and installers won't have the familiarity they should have with the product. You can't have it both ways."

"I'm saying we've become stuck with a scientific and engineering ethic in this organisation; one which restricts our ability to accept any change." Don spoke quickly, trying to give himself something to think about other than that the plane was beginning its journey to the main strip.

As the plane moved forward gathering speed, he leaned towards Bob, speaking louder in an effort to counter the rising noise level.

"A hundred years ago, the basic need was to provide a network. It was an engineering task and we did it bloody well. But that task is over; the objectives have to change, and we've been slow to accept that."

"How does that fit in with a rejection of new technology?" Bob countered. "It's just the opposite. Our delight in new technology is a large part of our problem. We love technology so much we regard customers as a hindrance. How many times have you heard some tech in a brick-walled exchange say, 'We don't get paid to worry about customers'. All they want to do is get back to their fabulous network. And the less customers there are fouling up the network by insisting on using it, the better."

Don leaned back in his seat. The plane was in the air now, so he felt he could almost relax for a time.

"For a bloke who's poured half his life into knowing every widget in every piece of equipment in his exchange, there's no choice. He has to support the status quo. For years, he's been told that those widgets are the most important thing in his life. You can't just turn around to people and tell them it's all changed. If you do, they won't believe you. And they'll do everything in their power to resist your innovation. The best you can hope to do is sneak change through increments."

"That's what the unions are always accusing us of doing," said Bob. "Whenever there's an attempt to change something, they carry on that it's the thin end of the wedge. I'd hate to think that was true."

Don shrugged. "It's how we do things. We train people so that they'll resist change. Then we act surprised when they do."

"But we're in an environment where everything is changing so rapidly. There's no way any of us can ignore the changes we need."

"You'll be surprised at the human ability to resist the pressures of the environment. I sometimes think it's what we do best," Don murmured, stifling a wave of airsickness.

The Prelude

"Look at what we've managed to do to our natural environment. We've stuffed it up so badly you can't even rely on the weather any more. The environment is changing: the world's heating up; seas will start to rise appreciably in about ten years; the weather's going berserk. Already we've got cyclones as far south as Sydney.

"And what is the human reaction? We just ignore it. Pretend it doesn't exist. It's what we do best. Here, look at this," Don turned to the screen of his laptop and pushed a sequence of buttons.

Bob leaned over. Instead of the words and figures he had been expecting to see, a graphic image resolved itself on the slate-coloured screen.

"It's a tree," said Bob, unsure of what he was supposed to be seeing.

"It's a special tree, Bob Cheshire." Don's eyes shone as he gazed at the screen, his great nose quivered, as if he could smell and hear the image as well as see it.

"This is a radical change," he said emphatically.

"What is it?"

A brief expression of uncertainty crossed Don's features.

"A tree. I can't talk too much about it yet. It's something I've been working on at home for a long time now. I just wanted to show it to you because it represents a radical leap in technology – perhaps the most radical thing that has happened since the development of the telegraph. But it's going to stay in there for a while," he said, patting the casing of the computer. "It's going to stay there because I want to be sure that whoever takes it up can really do something to develop it. I don't want it stifled, destroyed."

"A tree?" Bob repeated.

Don Burgess nodded conspiratorially.

They lapsed into silence as a stewardess hove into view with the obligatory cups of coffee and squishy sandwiches which were somehow meant to make flying a comfortable experience. Bob could sympathise with Don. You either loved flying or you didn't. Certainly, sandwiches weren't the thing that was going to change your mind.

He thought over Don's statements. Was that the way Comlink worked? People wanted the world to change; they wanted the chemical pollution to end, something to be done about the depleted ozone layer. They had wanted that change for a long time now, at least a decade.

But nothing ever happened.

What stopped the change? People were all for the change. So what was stopping it?

As the plane sped over the pale brown dustbowl of eastern South Australia with its pattern of rising salt, over-cultivation and poor pasture etched across the face of the land, Bob could not rid himself of the feeling that perhaps it was the organisations – the governments, businesses and bureaucracies which created the environments in which people lived and worked – that might be inhibiting change. If that was the case, then Comlink was a victim of its own organisational structures, tottering along a path dictated by rules and procedures rather than human needs.

* * * * *

An hour later they were in a car, heading out to the northern suburbs of Adelaide where the Comlink research labs were located. Since the introduction of more flexible computer links, intelligent modems and database access, it had become less important to maintain centralised facilities around the country. This arrangement was probably not the most sensible, but it was one which Bob favoured. Coming as he did from outback Queensland, Bob knew how important geographical location was to Comlink employees. Nobody wanted to commute large distances to work. It was just one of Comlink's strange cultural phenomena: you could get people to do anything in the way of overtime – they'd crawl around in muddy pits and black, cockroach-infested tunnels at three in the morning – but ask them to travel an extra ten minutes to get to work and they'd tense up like a sheep at a Butchers' Picnic.

The South Australian labs were a group of flat, single-story, pre-fab buildings with an air of permanent temporary accommodation. The Adelaide Hills, a giant amphitheatre which encircled the city itself, formed a haze-shrouded backdrop to the scene.

Don pulled the car into a spot marked 'Chief Scientist' in a lonely corner of the large car park.

"Why are these reserved spots so far away? Is it some new executive exercise program?" Bob asked.

"Jim Kurtz's idea," Don explained, as they began the long walk over to the main building. "When he took over here there was a row of reserved parking places for all the big wigs right over near the main door. The assumption was they were busier, more important than the plebs, so they

The Prelude

deserved a place where they could rush in, park their company cars and get inside easier than the rest. And it was an added bonus that they wouldn't have to get wet when they arrived late and it was raining."

"Stopped it, did he? How did the execs handle that?"

"With ill grace, but Jim stuck to his guns, and I applaud him for that. He insisted that if you couldn't get up early enough to get in for one of the nearest spots, you didn't deserve it.

"Jim Kurtz is my resident iconoclast," the scientist laughed. "He maintains that everyone is equally important for the operation of this place. If they aren't, it's the fault of the supervisor, not the worker. Any way you look at it, there's no reason why the worker should be penalised because their manager needs special treatment to do the job.

"It's a bit hard in some ways; you can't make the manager responsible for everything. But I think Jim wanted them to accept this change as a symbol of what he sees as the shared responsibility of both manager and worker. I agree with him on that. It's very easy to accept the idea of upward accountability. But many people, once they are put into a senior position, tend to ignore any downward responsibility.

"Come on, you can meet him yourself. But if I was you, I'd at least loosen my tie. You look like you come from Head Office."

"Bullshit Castle? I do," Bob laughed.

Chapter 13
Research

By three o'clock that afternoon it was clear to Bob that the Dick Tracy interface equipment was everything its designers claimed it to be. It was equally clear that the research team, headed by Jim Kurtz, had really put their hearts and souls into this one.

But a worrying problem had been brought up by Jim: the failure rate in the optical splitters used to carry the signal from the portable Watch to the optical fibre networks. This was the one area of development with which he was unhappy. Optical splitters were not a radical new development; similar splitters had been in use for several years now, and the new ones were simply an enlarged version capable of handling many more channels.

Yet in the several hundred prototype transmitter units which had been constructed for the initial field trials, there had been a recurrent and unacceptable rate of failure in the optical splitters.

A variety of reasons for these failures had been advanced, ranging from poor specifications to poor design, manufacture or installation. The prevailing view was that the Comlink workshop technicians who were putting the things together were doing a sloppy job.

They had talked around the problem for about ten minutes before a thought came into Bob's mind. It related to something Arthur Dee had said and which was being borne out by the work Alan Dodgson was doing in Newcastle.

"Is there a new supplier for the splitters?" Bob asked.

"Yes," replied Jim Kurtz, "we awarded the contract to a new company this year. They're working to the same specs as previous suppliers. The design has changed, but the tolerances have remained the same."

"Is that appropriate?"

"Yes," Don Burgess said, "the splitters are just larger versions of previous ones used. They're a piggy-back arrangement, modules linked together."

Bob accepted Don's verdict. He tried another tack.

"Why a new supplier?"

"Cost," explained Jim.

"Any other reason?"

"No. The old supplier was usually on time and could deliver when we wanted. It was just a commercial decision. You know how tight budgets are."

"A large margin?"

"Significant. We went back to the original supplier but he couldn't match the new one."

"What does the new company say about the failures?"

Jim shrugged, "They're certified correct when they leave the factory. We've even tested sample loads. They check out alright. It has to be poor installation."

"Are they tested under load in the factory? In conditions similar to those under which they'll eventually function?" enquired Bob, wondering to himself when someone was going to accuse him of whistling in the dark. He was following a lead which had proved useful in Newcastle, but ultimately he was just testing a theory — a theory which might mean nothing in this instance.

"No, they can't replicate our conditions," Jim said, beginning to sense where Bob's questions were leading. He looked over to his construction supervisor. "Were the batches we tested under load?"

The supervisor shook his head and proceeded to swap jargon, serial numbers and load ratings with the two scientists in a conversation which Bob was quite unable to follow.

After a few moments, Jim Kurtz gestured at Bob. "He's not so dumb for a manager. It's worth a try."

"Under a loaded situation," he explained, "the micro-processors might be caught in a feedback loop when the volume of encoded information is high, especially when some overlap interference is encountered as a result of low shielding."

"Does that mean other nearby sources of electro-magnetic radiation might be causing the failures?" Bob asked, trying to clarify what he had heard.

Jim nodded. "Shielding isn't part of the specs, but the old splitters had a built-in circuit shielding arrangement which the new supplier doesn't include. Where did you learn so much about optical splitters, Bob?"

"I don't know anything about them, but we've been doing some work on contracted suppliers recently and one thing we've learned, and which has panned out in every case, is that if you award your business on the basis of price alone you'll end up with a worse product every time.

"I'll bet that when you go back to your new supplier and tell him what you need the price will rise to about that of your previous supplier."

Jim Kurtz wasn't altogether happy with the explanation. "But if you don't go to tender how can you keep your prices down?" he demanded. "The sub-contractors and suppliers will just gorge you every time."

"There's nothing wrong with tendering," Bob replied. "It can improve competition and give you a clear idea of the market price and conditions. And it may turn up unexpected and unplanned for refinements. But think about the main point of tendering. Is it to cut your costs, or to ensure you get a quality product?"

"Well, it can be both, but I suppose it's no good getting a better price if your quality drops. People won't buy your product if it doesn't work."

"Worse than that," Bob said, "if you force your suppliers into a bidding situation, they've got no option but to reduce quality. You're effectively saying to them, 'We want it cheap, not good'.

"Besides, the research we're doing indicates that if you stick with a supplier you develop a lot more leverage for improving service and delivery. After all, the long-term supplier is geared to your needs. He needs your continued business a lot more than a bloke who got the contract because he undercut the opposition. You can't ask such a bloke for improved service, and he can't give it even if he wants to, because your tendering practices have forced him to cut his margins to the bone. There's no way for him to give you what you need."

"I can see that," said Jim Kurtz slowly, "but all the same, it's not our job to keep other people in beer and skittles. If they can't afford to be in the business, they shouldn't be in it."

"True," replied Bob, "but only up to a certain extent. If you build up a long-term relationship with your suppliers you can reduce costs significantly. They will know your needs and be working to fulfil them. As a result, there'll be less rejects and re-work, so total supply costs should drop.

"Think about it. Supplier A has worked with you for ten years. His foremen know what you want and his production line people know as well. They're familiar with your equipment and there'll be less mistakes in construction. Less rejects, lower overall production costs. On top of that,

The Prelude

your costs will be less because your people don't have to spend so much time checking, re-checking and measuring everything in sight.

"Supplier B, on the other hand, has just come in and won the contract on the basis of his low price. His people know nothing about your product. They'll make mistakes in production, supply, billing – all over the place. To avoid those mistakes he either has to spend extra money training his people – something he hasn't got the leeway to do – or try to absorb the waste. He can't charge you more than the contract price, so he'll manufacture the product to the lowest possible specifications you gave him. You get only what you ask for, nothing more. You haven't asked for quality, you've asked for cheap, basic equipment, so that's what you'll get. Plus, you end up with a whole heap of hidden costs from the work your people have to do in checking, monitoring, returning defects and so forth."

Bob paused and looked around the table. "Is that a fair assessment of the problem you've got at the moment?"

"Pretty fair," Jim Kurtz said ruefully.

"Will you do something for me?" Bob asked. "I want you to review your tender processes, say, for the past five years. Look at which contracts have changed hands and for what reasons. I want to know if there's any correlation between price-based tendering and equipment performance. I suspect it's there, but I can't prove it at this stage."

"Sure, I can arrange that, especially since it sounds like we could end up saving some money in the long run. I like that part of it," Jim grinned.

"And I'll get the workshops to check their tender operations," he added, gesturing in the direction of the production and maintenance workshops which abutted the research compound. "They're as anxious as we are to lower their costs and improve performance."

*   *   *   *   *

It was four o'clock when the meeting finished. Bob was pleased with the progress of the Watch and with the discussions over the tendering process. Supply of materials seemed to be at the heart of a good many problems, but Bob wondered if it was a symptom of a deeper, more widespread problem.

He was sharing some of these thoughts with Don Burgess as they threaded their way through the corridors of the research building towards the main entrance.

Suddenly a deep voice boomed out from the far end of the passageway. "Cheshire, you bastard!"

Both men turned towards the sound. A giant frame stood silhouetted in the glow from the windows about forty metres away. It raised a thick paw and pointed at Bob.

"Stay right there. I want a word with you!"

Bob shook his head sadly, "Oh no. Not me," he said.

Don Burgess took a nervous step away from his boss, trying to distance himself from what was about to happen.

The big man strode towards them, his massive paw thrust out in greeting. He was as tall as Alan Dodgson, possibly even taller. But where Alan was thin and craggy, this man was built like a two-story telephone exchange. In another age, thought Don, he would probably have been a blacksmith, or perhaps a draught horse.

"Don, this is Fred Winters. We've long been pals – in fact we went through tech school together. What are you doing here, Fred? I didn't know you were operating in this neck of the woods."

"It's a long story, mate. I tell you what, when are you planning on going back?"

"We're booked on the five o'clock."

"Aw, that's no good. Look, I've got a bit of business with a couple of boffins, but that won't take long. You re-book your flight. There's one for Melbourne about nine. We'll go and have a couple at the Eagle." He stood grinning at Bob like a long-lost brother.

"I can't stay overnight, Fred. You have to understand that from the outset. I have to get back to Melbourne tonight," Bob said, a faint note of despair in his voice.

"Janice will understand. You just ring her, Bob. Tell her Fred'll look after you."

"Nine o'clock, Fred. That's it."

The big man looked down at them with the air of an injured innocent. With a laugh that seemed to rumble up from his size thirteen shoes, he slapped Bob on the shoulder.

"Well, get to it fellers. What are you waiting for?" he stormed back down the corridor once more. "Meet you there at five-thirty!" He yelled disappearing around the corner like a Viking into a time tunnel.

The passage seemed smaller and quieter when he had gone.

"Is he normally like that?" Don murmured.

"You're just lucky I didn't tell him you were a damn boffin. He eats them for breakfast."

"Bob, I'm sorry, but I've got to get back for a late meeting. I'd love to stay, but....."

"Coward," Bob said in mock bitterness.

"I've heard of Fred Winters, that's all!" said Don, smiling weakly.

Chapter 14
The Eagle on the Hill

Everybody had heard of Fred Winters, Bob reflected, as the taxi snaked its way high into the Adelaide Hills. He was something of a legend in Comlink, renowned for his ability to get a region running like a Swiss clock and to work with people at all levels in the organisation – except senior management. Fred had no desire for the politicking which seemed to form a small but essential part of the senior management day and had deliberately chosen to remain at regional management level.

It was no surprise to Bob that Fred had chosen The Eagle on the Hill as their meeting venue. The pub had been a favourite rendezvous for drinkers for nearly a hundred and fifty years, ever since the days when it had served as the last staging post before the long and hazardous journey down to the plains of Adelaide. Since that time it had been destroyed by fire at least twice, most recently in the early nineties as a result, of all things, of a lightning strike. Miraculously, no-one had been injured. But there were those who swore they'd seen the Eagle's stove blasted high into the afternoon sky, like a rocket bound for nowhere.

Bob smiled as he paid the taxi-fare and made his way into the public bar, taking in the smells, sights and feelings of a happy place. He ordered a pint, which in South Australia wasn't a pint but was something more like three-quarters of a pint.

He had called Janice to let her know he would not be back in Melbourne until later than expected. She had sounded rather dubious when he'd mentioned, as casually as possible, that he would be having a social drink with Fred Winters.

"Take care, darling," she had said, as if he was a soldier in the trenches about to go over the top.

The Prelude

He didn't have to wait long for Fred. The big man bustled into the pub a few minutes later. A number of the patrons hailed him as he strode up to Bob.

Fred had just been transferred to the Adelaide Hills region, of which the Eagle was a part. One of the few Comlink people who had opted for regular transfer in his career, Fred had taken over as Regional Manager.

"I just started a few weeks ago. It's not really a region, more of a sub-region if the truth be known. It's small, but it's a great place. The Hills are fantastic."

"How's it going? Are you settling in?"

Fred shrugged expressively and gestured up another couple of beers. "The place is in a bit of a mess, mate. I've got five small exchanges, a fault-finding centre, some linesmen and installers, a couple of labouring gangs, a handful of clerical and admin folk. You know the set-up, a couple of hundred people."

"What's the problem?" asked Bob. It was unusual to hear Fred Winters voicing his difficulties aloud.

"Recurrent equipment faults, bad maintenance, complaints from the customers. People are pissed off." Fred sighed. "Remember the good old days, when you went in to work and you did your job? Everybody knew what they had to do. You did it, and if there was any time left you could have some fun and nobody would give you a hard time. It's all changed now. I spend three-quarters of my time in bloody meetings."

He paused reminiscently. "Hey! How about that firecracker trick? Got ya there, feller."

"Bastard," Bob muttered, recalling the incident in one of the mechanical exchanges where they had served their apprenticeships. He had been alone at the test desk around three o'clock one morning, in the drowsy state of half-wakefulness which seemed to come on late in that shift. A fault had shown up in one of the rear racks, so he had strolled down sleepily to examine the old cross-bar equipment.

The exchange had been a maze of ceiling-high racks containing thousands of clicking, snuffling relays and switches. Bob had located the fault at the back of the switch room, where the unforgettable smell so unique to telephone exchanges, the aroma of light machine oil mingling with ozone created by the clattering electrical circuits, hung thickly in the air.

Suddenly a series of explosions had shattered the early morning calm, filling the narrow space with blue smoke and scaring Bob half out of his wits.

The line on the test desk had begun to ring frantically. Picking up the handset, he had been greeted by Fred inquiring solicitously whether he had heard the alarm clock?

It was an old trick, as Bob eventually found out. Put a couple of jumpers across the relay of a disused line and when you rang the number given to that line the wires sparked. With a twopenny bunger tied in the right way, the spark would set off the fuse with startling results. Repeat the process with four unused lines and you could frighten ten years out of a young technician. Fred's added refinement had been to rig a fault which showed up only when he rang a specific number. That way, Bob had been guaranteed to be as close as possible to the exploding bungers.

Bob had been surprised that evening to realise he knew so many swear words. But the incorrigible Fred had simply laughed at each new insult.

"Still, in all fairness, you had your revenge," Fred mourned, "I might have married that girl if it wasn't for you."

They toasted each other, grinning like recalcitrant schoolboys.

* * * * *

"I suppose things have changed a bit," mused Bob after a few more drinks. "One thing I know, those old brick exchanges aren't as cannon-proof as we thought they were. Reality has started to knock down the old walls."

Fred shook his head mournfully. "There's always too much to do, too many people looking over your shoulder. When we were kids it was somehow discretionary whether you fixed a problem. You got to be a good worker by fixing lots of problems; by fixing the problems other blokes couldn't be bothered with. And there was always someone who recognised what you were doing. Now there's no such thing as a pat on the back. What was previously a matter of choice is now simply demanded from you."

"Come on Fred, it's not like you to be so glum. Is it that serious?"

"You remember old Nicholls? I used to hero-worship him. He was a marvellous old bloke, and a bloody good technician. He knew the answers. Me? I feel like I haven't got the answers any more. They've all disappeared somewhere."

The Prelude

"I know how you feel," Bob sighed. "The boffins had me totally confused today. The technology is slipping away from me – I wouldn't have a clue how to fix some of the stuff we're using now. You see these young, fresh-faced kids straight out of school, sitting around the exchanges doing nothing with wires and solder. It's all done with terminals, program languages and computer codes."

"It's partly the technology," Fred replied, taking a tug at his beer. "But that's not all people look to me for these days. They want answers to operational problems, people problems. Shit, they want me to tell them they're going to have a job next year. I don't know any more.

"And then there's all these bloody accountants in Head Office who just want more and more returns and figures. We have to make them up half the time."

"Still, it's not all bad, I guess," he smiled, trying to break out of his uncharacteristic seriousness. "There's been a lot of good changes: new equipment, new training. It's good to be out in the real world competing with other companies: showing them we can do the job and that we're not just a pack of bludgers.

"It's just that in all these changes we've lost some of the old pride and sense of direction. And there doesn't seem to be any attempt to replace it with anything that I can understand. We talk a lot about 'customer' orientation and other bullshit. It's just humming mushrooms if you ask me."

"What would make it better?" Bob asked tentatively. "How would you like things to be?"

"We can't go back to the way things were, I realise that," said Fred, pausing to drain his glass. "I'd like to see us grow; I'd like to see the quality of our work improve. God knows, most of our people try their best, but there always seem to be so many stupid things getting in the way that none of us know where we're going. Direction. That sums it up, I guess. I want a clear direction of where we're going and what we're supposed to do to get there."

Bob waved for another beer; he was starting to glow. "I've been looking for just that direction myself, mate. I haven't found it yet, but I've got a few ideas. And I've also got a proposal you might be interested in."

Dragging his sketchpad from his jacket pocket, Bob found space on the bar between the gooles of moisture made by their beer glasses.

"You talk about pride? I think you're right. It's important to people in Comlink that they can take pride in what they're doing. Let me ask you this: why are there customers who are dissatisfied with us?"

"Because we stuff it up so often. Everything seems to be disorganised. You do your best for a customer, go out of your way or stretch the rules, then it all blows up in your face. And other groups seem to let us down. Supply, maintenance, product, installation. It's no group in particular, just that we can't seem to put the whole lot together."

Bob began to sketch a rough diagram. "Is it fair to say that the quality of our service and products has deteriorated since the 'gold-plated' phone days?"

"Yeah, I suppose so. Depends what you mean by 'quality'," Fred responded. "In the past, we've sometimes overdone it, making a phone that would stand up to anything. But on the whole? Yeah, everything's so bloody pragmatic now. It's cut to the bone so you can't take any pride in what you do."

"I think you're right," Bob said, with some excitement. "We're not worrying about the quality of what we do any more, at least not as much as we used to. And one reason I'd advance is that everyone is worried about how we're going to stay in business."

"Fair enough," said the big man. "I'm bloody worried myself. What's wrong with that?"

"Nothing, provided we don't let it get us into a defensive way of thinking. At the moment, our response to threats is always the same: cutback. Cutback people, resources, charges, whatever it is. We always end up believing that the only way to survive is to become leaner, meaner, harder."

"Well, I don't agree with that. This used to be an organisation that cared for its people, and the people cared for it and for their jobs.

"At present, I've got a number of projects where we're being pressured, and the response is the same in all of them: cutback. We end up demanding more and more out of our staff, without giving them the necessary training, support or resources. You, yourself, said you were being asked to solve a whole pile of problems you're not equipped to deal with."

"So how are you going to change that?" Fred asked facetiously.

"With this. It's something I've been worrying at for a while now," Bob replied, showing Fred the sketch of a model he had been working on with Arthur Dee recently.

The Prelude

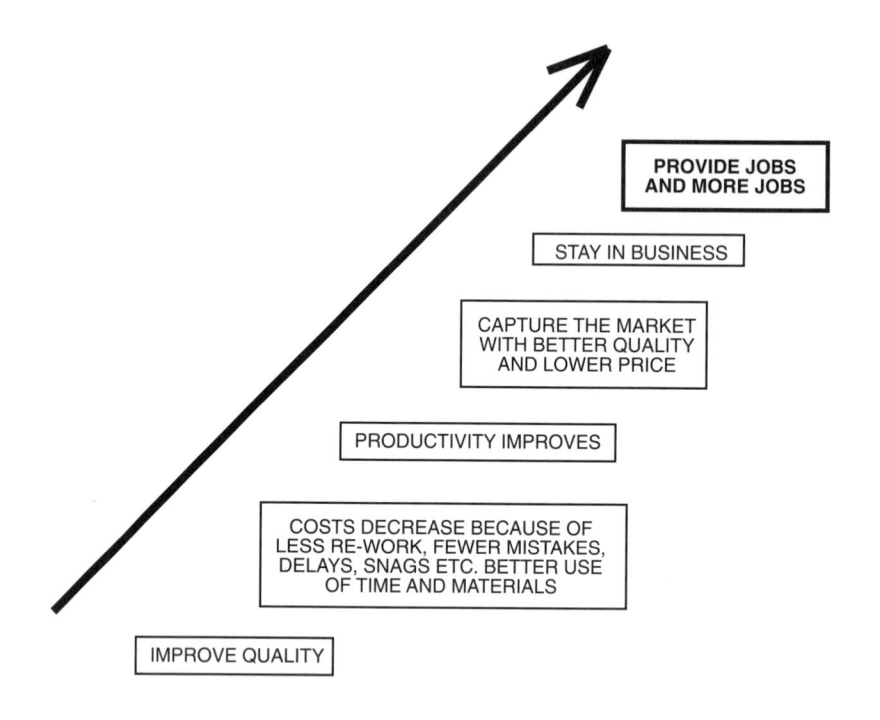

```
                    ↗
        ┌─────────────────┐
        │  PROVIDE JOBS   │
        │  AND MORE JOBS  │
        └─────────────────┘
          ┌───────────────┐
          │STAY IN BUSINESS│
          └───────────────┘
        ┌─────────────────────┐
        │ CAPTURE THE MARKET  │
        │ WITH BETTER QUALITY │
        │   AND LOWER PRICE   │
        └─────────────────────┘
       ┌──────────────────────┐
       │ PRODUCTIVITY IMPROVES│
       └──────────────────────┘
     ┌────────────────────────────┐
     │ COSTS DECREASE BECAUSE OF  │
     │LESS RE-WORK, FEWER MISTAKES,│
     │DELAYS, SNAGS ETC. BETTER USE│
     │   OF TIME AND MATERIALS    │
     └────────────────────────────┘
       ┌────────────────┐
       │ IMPROVE QUALITY│
       └────────────────┘
```

"Looks like a humming mushroom to me," Fred said disparagingly.
"Well, it's not!"
"Alright, keep your shirt on and give me a look."
He studied the diagram for some moments.
"OK," he said finally, "I'll accept the progression. If you can improve the quality of what you do, the rest might follow. Might, I said. But that doesn't help much. How am I going to improve anything when all my time's taken up in keeping the current mess going? Besides, how do I improve quality? You've just been saying you can't forever ask people for more and more effort. I've heard of quality control and it seems to me to be just more inspection and more people poking their nose over your shoulder. That I can do without!"

"You do want to improve the quality of your work?" Bob challenged.

"Sure. I'd like to give my people back some pride in what they do, so that when they do something they know it's a damn good job – and that the organisation they work for has helped instead of hindered them. If that's what you mean by 'quality', I'm all for it. But how can I improve anything? I don't make policy."

"How can you improve it? That's exactly what you're going to tell me, pal!"

Bob called to the barman.

"Let's get serious about this," he said, ordering two large 'Bundys'. "Now, Fred Winters, if I'm going to come and work for you, you'd better tell me what the problems are you're carrying on about."

"Work for me?"

"You bet. You've got the perfect set-up: a small, self-contained, multi-disciplinary group with a number of internal and external problems."

"Doesn't sound perfect to me," Fred muttered.

"It will be when we've finished with it," Bob assured him. "We're going to take a good look at the Adelaide Hills region, and we're going to improve it out of sight! And I know just the bloke who's going to help us."

"I'm all for that," replied Fred.

They clinked glasses, swigged the sweet fuming liquid, and started their schemes in earnest.

Chapter 15
Clayton's support

Janice Cheshire stood at the mirror brushing her dark hair with the ritual movements which served to wake her up each morning. There was a slight thumping in the nether regions of the house as Sandie prepared herself for uni.

Janice looked in the mirror, this time focusing on the crumpled heap under the bedclothes.

"Feeling a little duntish this morning, are we dear?" she enquired sweetly.

The mound stirred and Bob's head emerged feebly. Nine o'clock had turned into ten, and then into eleven. Eventually, he had caught the midnight flight back to Melbourne together with all the other business people who should have known better.

He groaned. His head felt like it was inside a gently roasting oven and his mouth seemed to resemble the inside of a gardener's glove. As for his eyelids, for some reason they appeared to be stuck together.

"It's no use hiding. You've got to catch Emma before she goes to school so you can arrange about this weekend," Janice said.

"I hate horses."

"Well, I'm not keen on them either, but your daughter is. And you did agree to do your fatherly duty," Janice laughed. Walking over to the bed, she sat on the edge and put her arm around his shoulders.

"Self-abuse is a terrible thing," she mocked gently.

"You're enjoying this. You should feel pity; it was a business meeting."

"Yes, of course, darling," she said, brushing her lips against his ear. Suddenly she sprang up, tearing the bedclothes away from him. Bob lay cringing on the sheet, curled up into a foetal ball to conserve the final few shreds of escaping warmth.

"How humane," he mumbled.

Bob eventually emerged from the bedroom to find Emma in the kitchen. She was throcking their archaic toaster with juvenile enthusiasm, banging the small, sliding handle up and down repeatedly, in a futile but disturbingly loud attempt to have the mechanism catch as it was designed to do.

"I think you'll have to just hold the handle down, Emma. I've got a bit of a headache this morning."

"It's called a hangover," Sandie laughed, as she entered the room. His eldest daughter was in first year biology at Melbourne University. She was a pretty girl – beautiful, Bob thought – with her mother's deep, black hair and large eyes. Dressed in a sports top, pants and runners, she looked as if she had been jogging.

The thought of all that energy expended so early in the morning made Bob a little queasy.

Sandie shook her head sorrowfully. It was an ironic gesture he, himself, used and it was depressing to see it employed against him by his own offspring.

"That will have been at least three million brain cells destroyed last night, Dad. You ought to take it easy. They don't regenerate as fast at your age."

"Whatever happened to good, old-fashioned sympathy in this household?" he moaned.

"I've got sympathy for you, Daddy," protested Emma, touching the sleeve of his robe protectively.

"Thanks, sweetheart," he said, putting an arm around her and kissing her lightly. "But there's no need to pretend. We can go to the horse show on Saturday. I'm in no condition to resist this morning."

In a second she was all over him, crying out her pleasure.

"Oh, fabulous. It's going to be the biggest show of the year. There'll be so much to see. You'll love it, Daddy! And there'll be so many people with ponies for sale. And they're such great bargains. It'll hardly cost anything, you'll see."

"Now hold on," Bob said firmly, peeling her away, "I only said we'll go. That doesn't mean we'll buy. Your mother and I aren't decided on you getting a pony yet. It's a big responsibility you know."

The Prelude

The thirteen year-old's face fell, her bottom lip preparing itself for a serious pout. But the emotion quickly passed as she realised that it would be a better tactic to get her father to the horse show, where she could stage a far more effective protest.

Bob heard the whirring cogs in her brain and held up a hand to stop her.

"Don't try and get around me. We'll think about it. That's all. We're going to the show to look, not to buy."

"Yes, Daddy," Emma said meekly. She grabbed the toast and stuffed a corner into her mouth. Suppressing a giggle, she ran out of the kitchen, pausing only to dig an elbow into her older sister's ribs.

Bob turned to the coffee machine, a mate of the solar powered one in his office. This one had never functioned properly either, and all it could manage this morning was hot water. Bob poured himself a cup and dunked a tea bag into it for a few seconds.

Turning to the window, he gazed out into the garden, trying to focus on the upcoming day. At least his meeting with Albert wasn't scheduled until after lunch. Bob's eyes came to rest on the back fence. "Couldn't fit a dog out there, let alone a horse," he muttered darkly.

* * * * *

Several hours later, Bob was seated in a low chair opposite Albert.

"I just want you to think about it," he was saying for the third time, his body tensed forward and his hands held out before him in an imploring gesture, rather as if he were holding a large, imaginary watermelon.

"You've given me no good reason, Bob. In fact, the opposite. You've told me that the interface trials are going even better than expected. We have to make the attempt."

"It's not the development phase I'm worried about, Albert. Don's teams will do it, I've got no doubt about that. And they'll give us a potentially fine product. The thing I'm worried about is that our regular maintenance, product marketing and installation processes are so disorganised we'll kill the Watch before it has a chance to make a name for itself."

Albert shook his head. "That's not good enough, Bob. If there's a problem on the horizon, I want you to fix it. I shouldn't need to be telling you your job."

"It will take time to fix it, that's just the point. We've got to create a different set of rules for the people doing the job. There has to be a different expectation of performance in the managers, the supervisors and the workers. The whole lot has to change, and we can't do that unless there's time to step back and re-consider what we're doing and why." Bob picked up a sheaf of papers from the small coffee table between them and handed Albert two sheets with graphs on them.

"In Newcastle, Alan has been able to increase the number of connections by ten percent in the past period. But the thing which really demonstrates how much room there is for improvement is the revenue figures. Revenue's risen by twenty percent, mostly as a result of alterations to our commissioning practices and improving communication between departments. And the customer satisfaction rating has gone through the roof. People are happy with our products; they only start screaming when our service isn't up to scratch."

Albert leaned back in his chair. He was not looking directly at Bob but seemed, instead, to be focusing on the tips of his shoes. Rubbing his temples with small circular motions, he raised his grey head and smiled ruefully. "One of the reasons why you're so good at your work, Bob, is that you don't give up. But this time you'll have to.

"Three things, Bob, I'll tell you three things. One is that the work you're doing on OFCAB is great. But it is only a project management issue. OFCAB is only a project. It doesn't operate in the same way as the rest of the organisation. It's relatively easy to treat it as a distinct animal, one you can adjust and tweak while life goes on around you. That's fine, but although it works there I still haven't any evidence to support the proposition that I can do the same thing you're talking about with the wider operating areas."

Bob opened his mouth to speak, but Albert forestalled him with a raised hand.

"Two. I'm responsible for the future of Comlink. You heard at the last Group meeting what sort of a position we're in. Clifford may be clinical, but his forecasts are absolutely to be relied upon. If he and his accounting people say we need the sales generated by the Watch as fast as possible, I believe him. Your job is to manage people. Clifford's is to manage finances. I'm not in a position to delay the Watch's development when its introduction can provide both the cash flow for investment and the customer base which will take us into the next century."

"I'm not saying don't introduce it," Bob interrupted, "I'm just saying we need to look at the way we'll supply, install and maintain the thing. We've got to get our house in order—"

Albert held up a hand once more.

"Three things, Bob. Then you can have your turn. I said I was responsible and I am. We are under a great deal of pressure to speed up the Watch for a variety of reasons you couldn't know anything about. Firstly, there's the Board. Their instructions to me are clear. 'Do it'. Then there's something else. I tell you this in strictest confidence.

"NetWork is on the verge of signing a deal with the New South Wales Government that will effectively destroy our monopolies. They're going to work with the Railways, stringing optical fibre along the side of the track network – cheap, easy and fast. Low maintenance, easy access. Everything they need. And with the gift rates they're getting from the state government, they can undercut us dramatically.

"On top of that, their main target is the business market, which they'll cater to with intelligent buildings built over city and suburban stations. The Dick Tracy Watch is our key to solidifying our market share in the business arena. We have to be ready before NetWork gets this proposal underway and extended into other states.

"The only option we've got is to get out into the marketplace with a new product, such as the Watch, in order to cement commitment amongst our customers."

The NetWork proposal rocked Bob. He could see immediately how it would start: small, with a series of interconnected ISDN networks, using Comlink as the overall connecting network. Then Comlink would be slowly cut out of the loop by the development of a cheap, parallel circuit dedicated to business customers.

The business world would run to NetWork's open arms. After all, they were currently being penalised by having to pay prioritisation loadings to move the mountains of data they needed to operate efficiently.

Probably the worst aspect of it all was that Comlink would have to participate in its own disembowelling. It was both an article of faith and a requirement of law that Comlink could not deny access to its network to any person or business. It might be able to charge extra for heavy users, but it could not turn them away.

Bob started to ask Albert how he knew so many details about the proposal, then thought again. Perhaps he did not want to know.

"The Board is a major problem in all this," Albert explained. "I'm working for them and with them. However, the truth is that in our industry we are affected by the political and economic pressures brought to bear from outside. For too long, we've assumed that nothing could hurt us. I'm partly responsible for that feeling. I've tried to protect Comlink from external influences rather than go out and meet them in open competition.

"Strategically, I think we've clung to the vestiges of monopoly for too long. Now we're unable to cut ourselves loose from the past. That view is also held by some members of the Board. But, whereas I would like to see us able to meet the demands of the future, there are others – including some Board members – who would prefer to see a smaller, more 'compact' Comlink: one restricted to the role of public utility, rather than a truly competitive organisation with a high degree of entrepreneurial independence."

Albert paused and looked sadly at Bob, who was leaning forward tautly. A man he had known for years, Bob had come to him seeking support; looking for a way to help the organisation. And he was going to walk away with nothing.

Albert felt tired. What had happened? Well, the buck had stopped, that was for sure.

He breathed deeply, addressing himself once more to Bob. "There are two sides to what you are talking about," he said slowly. "One is the way we communicate tasks to people. The verbal, written, sometimes unspoken rules we apply to the organisation. The other is the processes we use for doing things. The two issues are linked, as you say.

"Most people who've had any sort of formal engineering or management training have heard of development programs which address poor quality and service delivery. We tried it ourselves nearly a decade ago. It didn't work then, and I've got no reason to believe it will work now. There is always a greater need for improved communication in any organisation. Communication is based on trust, and trust develops from leadership. I'll accept that.

"But hear this, Bob," Albert said, his voice hardening. "The harsh realities of commercial life preclude the wastage of time on such efforts. There are more important problems to be considered, more important, more immediate threats.

The Prelude

"I'm not happy about the approach we are going to take, but we *are* going to take it. The Dick Tracy Watch will relieve the pressure and give us some breathing space to grow, to regroup."

Bob sprang to his feet and began to pace around the room.

"This goes beyond the Watch. That's just one project – a major one, it's true – but I'm trying to demonstrate a fundamental problem which is common to *all* of our measuring and management systems. OFCAB is where it's easy to see, but I've also found examples in R & D, the MID project, virtually everywhere.

"In general, our work systems are stable, but they're not 'capable'. We can't meet customer expectations. There's too much variation in the work systems."

"The customer satisfaction indices aren't fantastic," agreed Albert, "but they're not that bad."

Bob shook his head insistently. "If things aren't that bad, why has there been such a steady erosion of our customer base over the past decade? We never seem able to improve. The best we do is hold on so we don't slip down the spiral too quickly."

"Is that how you see it, Bob, a slow, downward spiral?" Was he nothing more than the captain of a ship being sucked deeper and deeper into a maelstrom? If that was how his senior managers saw Comlink, how must the people in the field feel?

And what had he been doing about it? Bob was right, he'd tossed the anchor out and now he was praying for something to slow down the ship. It was a long time since he had believed there was any way to reverse the decline. All his thought and energy had been channelled into a defensive frame of mind. He was trying to slow the death of his ship.

Bob sat down again, hands together, fingers interlocked tightly. He looked at Albert, meeting his eye deliberately, and answered the question with a shrug, "We'll never change anything until we start to try."

"If you had some other evidence. But all you've got is a project in Newcastle, a couple of conversations with Don Burgess and the statistician Dee – what kind of a name is that! It's not enough."

Suddenly Bob smiled. He quickly told Albert about Fred Winters.

"You see, it's a great chance. The region is isolated. It's got a variety of skills, positions and functions, a balance of managerial and supervisory positions, and a blend of different staff. It'll make the perfect test ground.

"Fred is willing to work with me for a period. We've got expertise in the form of Arthur Dee. Fred's got customer dissatisfaction – documented complaints – low morale in the depots and exchanges, high-volume requirements. It's perfect!" he concluded with mounting excitement.

Albert looked thoughtful. How much did he want to change things? He wasn't sure. He wasn't even sure he could if he wanted to. More and more it was becoming clear to him that he was just responding to pressures. Reacting. As Chief Executive, he felt isolated, unable to make decisions which ultimately would make a difference to Comlink's future. It was absurd, but throughout his career the feeling had crept up on him that the further up the ladder he went, the less in control he was. Yet surely it didn't have to be like that?

"I want development work on the Watch to continue."

Bob nodded eagerly.

"Three months. Three months only, then you drop the concept entirely if you can't prove your findings to my satisfaction. Got it?"

Bob nodded again, unwilling to speak just yet.

"Should you succeed, and you can demonstrate a better – by that I mean cheaper and faster – way of organising work systems, the decision to launch the Watch by 2001 will be reviewed. Also, we'll look at the OFCAB timelines. I have to admit that the New Year's Eve deadline exists only because of our PR people. It'd be nice to do it by then though, don't you think?"

"And MID?" Bob enquired.

"And MID," Albert agreed with a reluctant smile. "But not a word. Not one. You've got absolutely no authority to say the changes you're looking at will have any repercussions beyond Fred Winters' region."

"Apart from that, go for it."

He felt better for accepting Bob's right to try and analyse the problems, and to change them if he could. In the welter of jostling, competing problems which faced the organisation, it was so easy to gaze into the kaleidoscope, rather than focusing your attention on the ones who really mattered: the customers. After all, the customers rarely ever complained. They thought they couldn't. Most of the time you only found out about dissatisfied customers by looking at the increases your competitors were posting.

The phone on Albert's desk beeped sullenly. He stood up and walked over to answer it.

John Hunter, his personal assistant, apologised for the interruption. "I know you said you didn't want any calls, but as you've got Bob Cheshire

The Prelude

in with you now, I thought I'd better put this through. It may concern him too."

Albert took the call on his private line.

As he hung up, he turned to Bob and smiled somewhat bleakly.

"Did I say three months? I hope I can give you that much now. I might have to reconsider the time. That was John McDermott. Things have blown up in Newcastle. I don't know what Alan Dodgson has been doing up there, but you'd better find out in a hurry. I thought you said he was making headway? Seems more like he's set the cause of industrial relations back about three decades!"

"The figures I've got look alright. What's the problem?"

"Sort it out with John McDermott. It'll be better if you get it first hand. OFCAB has to go ahead, Bob. Until you can prove to me otherwise, I want you to keep it on schedule. It's your responsibility. At the moment it looks like Alan's managed to alienate the entire management team. This new approach of yours isn't called anarchism, is it?"

Bob shrugged helplessly. "I'll talk to them all immediately."

"Alright. Just be sure you fix it. I'll send someone up from IR to lend a hand. Anne might be able to make the time for it; I'd rather her than anyone else."

Reality. Albert shook his head. It always butted in at the least propitious moment.

He hoped Bob would be able to make the best use of the three months. He needed something, and soon.

Chapter 16
Twin city shuffle

She should have called him. She needed to be clear about what was happening in this god-forsaken town.

Anne Blanchard stared at the papers on her lap, not even seeing them. She hated being unprepared; there was always some bastard waiting to shoot you down if you didn't have all the answers. Anne grimaced, remembering her last encounter with Alan Dodgson. She had wanted him, with a sudden, confounding intensity. Yet it had come as a relief when she'd found a reason to be angry, to push him away. Now it dawned on her that that was exactly what she had wanted: an excuse to back away from her initial decision. Why? Fear was the only valid reason she could bring to mind.

Anne closed the folder as the taxi turned out of the airport and headed towards the western suburbs of Newcastle. There was hardly anything in it anyway, and she had read it half a dozen times. The real information was with Alan, in what he had been doing over the past three weeks. And she had been too proud – or maybe too scared – to contact him before she came here today.

* * * * *

The Prelude

Alan Dodgson stood in the middle of a bulbous, black circle of asphalt, a dead-end court which formed part of a new housing estate on the edge of Newcastle. Heavy drops of water flopped over the brim of his old felt hat as he gazed about. He was cold, wet, and miserable.

The estate resembled a section of the front at the Somme. A couple of houses were fully completed, but even those were without landscaped gardens. The rest of the sites were a glutinous swamp of churned up clay, interspersed with lumps of thin concrete and messy piles of building materials and rubbish. Here and there, the skeletons of partially completed housing dreams stuck up into the bleak sky, their steel and aluminium spars glistening with rain.

"That's the main FEUs for the estate." Bear Rinehart pointed a thick arm to where a Comlink truck was parked on the hillside about a kilometre away, next to the pit which held the main Fibre Encoder Unit.

"And that's the local unit?" Alan asked, gesturing at a smaller pit near the corner of the street in which they were standing.

The Lines Installation Manager nodded. He didn't seem to mind standing in the wet, away from the shelter of the nearby 'bug hut'. Alan sighed and trudged dejectedly after him as Bear headed over to inspect the local pit. He pulled out a pit key and slipped the long steel shaft into the cover, dragging it away.

The pit was full of muddy, evil-smelling water. Without hesitation Bear plunged his hand into the water and pulled out a small, black box. The box was attached to plastic-sheathed wires which disappeared off into the murky water. This was the Fibre Encoder Unit, the 'synapse link' of the OFCAB project. The unit linked a group of optical fibre wires together into a larger wire which, in turn, was one of a number which connected to an even larger wire, and so on.

Bear jammed a small, electronic meter with a plug at one end into a matching cavity in the black box. After a moment, he shook his head.

"This one's gone too," he intoned.

He dropped the thing back into the water with all the distaste of a man disposing of a dead spider.

Alan slid the cover back over the pit.

"That's five in this area alone. What's going on, Bear?"

The large man shrugged and stood silently. Alan was aware of the sense of tension. And hostility.

"Is there any reason why we're standing out here in the rain?" he ventured.

Bear Rinehart shrugged once more and headed off in the direction of the bug hut.

Once inside the small building, the two men took off their coats and hats, hanging them on the back of the door.

"What's wrong, Bear?" Alan said, subsiding into one of the swivel chairs spaced around a large desk. "I thought we were going to make changes to the connection procedure."

The Installation Manager glared at Alan through his thick, ginger eyebrows. He wasn't happy with what was happening, but neither was he sure how to say it.

"All this mapping and measuring you've got the blokes doing," he muttered. "It doesn't mean anything."

"How do you mean?" Alan asked.

"It's crap."

"But what about the work you've been doing with Mal Yallop and Doug Golding over the past few weeks? Haven't you been able to find anything useful there?" Alan continued, deliberately making a general, formless question in the hope of allowing Bear a wide target for his concern. In any event, Alan got more than he bargained for.

The other man heaved himself to his feet, his face flushed and angry. "Yeah, I've learnt that this whole business is nothing but a waste of time. A fucking waste of time. If you're trying to cut down on numbers, why don't you just come out and say it? Instead, you've got me running round in circles like a headless chicken, and I'm sick of it! This used to be a company where you knew what you were doing. Now I've got kids like you telling me I've got to change the way I do things. Well I've been doing this for twenty years and there's nothing – got that? – nothing wrong with the way we do things around here."

"Hang on, Bear, I'm trying to get the project moving too. We're on the same–"

"Bullshit! I'm sick of the lot of you. Who gives a damn any more?" he shouted, storming out of the room.

Alan flopped back in his chair, stunned at the violence of Bear's outburst.

* * * * *

The Prelude

Anne Blanchard sat in a chair in Vince Penmann's office, legs crossed tightly, back erect. She looked blandly at the Regional Manager while he outlined his version of the OFCAB difficulties.

Vince had never been keen on Alan's proposal to involve the work groups more directly in decision making and project planning as a result of the death of Wally Jamieson. He viewed industrial accidents as a somewhat irrelevant necessity. They happened, and that was all.

"The issues raised with me have come in via the 'back door', so to speak," Vince was saying, choosing his words with unusual care. "It's not the staff who are complaining through their supervisors, the concern is originating directly out of middle management.

"If I understand correctly what Alan has been doing, he's trying to map out and control the processes which make up OFCAB. To do this, he's had to get the foremen and workers involved in the discussion. Don't get me wrong, Anne, it's a great idea, but..." he paused weightily. "But, I think he's been moving too fast; questioning too many of the things they've been doing. Asking managers to go down to their staff and enquire how things operate will undermine their position."

Anne sat quietly, listening to the Regional Manager's concerns. She silently cursed Alan for overlooking the obvious.

"What sorts of things can I tell my men?" Vince said, jerking his thin shoulders in a spasmodic shrug. "Some of them are detailed to work with OFCAB, others aren't. I've got a set of figures which are required by Head Office, yet the blokes working for OFCAB are saying the targets don't matter – that they've been told not to worry about targets. Where does that leave me? I'll tell you. With a lot of very sloppy egg on my face."

Anne smiled soothingly. "Last month, after the accident, we worked out a plan which involved most of the staff within OFCAB. The aim is to get deadlines under control and, more importantly, to ensure that we're giving customers the product they want. Naturally, a program like that is going to take some time to get moving."

"Of course we're giving customers what they want! Jeez, if we don't know what they want we shouldn't be in this business."

Anne nodded, encouraging him to continue.

"What I'm more concerned about is that we're tossing out the old way of doing things without having anything to substitute. I can't have one lot of blokes getting involved in this stuff while others aren't getting a look in."

At that moment, Alan walked by on the way back to his office. His wet coat was clutched in one hand and his broad-brimmed hat, soaked and lifeless from the heavy rain, drooped sadly over his forehead. He glanced towards the office where Anne sat and then stalked off down the corridor. A few seconds later, the thin partitioned walls shook as a door was slammed.

"Go ahead, Vince," Anne said lightly. "You were saying that any changes involving consultation with OFCAB staff affect the whole of your work force?"

"Exactly. I don't want to speak out against Alan, but he's saying something very different to the way our policy guidelines are written." Vince shifted in his seat, like one unwillingly driven to an unpleasant truth which must be voiced for the good of humanity.

"Frankly, I don't take kindly to being told that although I've done things well for the past ten years, I've done the *wrong* things."

"I can understand that, perfectly," Anne murmured. "So there's been little consultation at the managerial level?"

"I don't hear anything," Vince protested. "All I know is when some foreman comes along and says they've found a hitch in the routine maintenance procedures. *I'll* tell him when there's to be a change in maintenance procedures. He's not paid to come and tell me what the problems are. I'm paid to tell him."

Anne stood up, holding out her hand to the Regional Manager. "I think that's enough for the moment, Vince. I should go and talk to some of the other managers involved in this. I'll come back to you after that, if I may?"

"That's fine, but they'll say the same. All Alan's managing to do is cut them off at the knees – again".

"You've been cut off at the knees before?"

"Haven't we all?" Vince snorted.

* * * * *

As she trod the few steps down the short corridor to Alan's office, Anne reflected on Vince's last comment. It probably said more than their entire conversation.

She opened the door to Alan's office without knocking.

He was sitting with his back towards her, his feet resting on the window ledge as he leaned back in the swivel chair, gazing at a mysterious point somewhere in the middle of the concrete yard.

"You've got them worried," she said simply.

"That's not what I want."

The Prelude

"You have to tell them what's going on," she said, leaning against the door jamb, watching the back of his blonde head.

"How can I? I don't know myself."

"Maybe I can help."

He swivelled around slowly, dropping his feet to the floor.

"Why would you want to?"

Anne stared at him for a moment. She shrugged expressively. "I think we can find a reason."

Alan stood up, and held out his hand. "Truce?"

"I can tolerate you if you can tolerate me," she said, advancing into the room to return his grip.

"That night, after I left you," he said hesitantly, "I had a dream. I was in a courtroom. There was some sort of arraignment and I was in the box. The charge was failure to produce a prophylactic device at the appropriate time. I was pleading innocence and the judge was laughing hysterically. It was Margaret Thatcher, remember her? 'Innocence is no protection' she was saying."

Alan paused uncomfortably, "I looked over to the jury. It was Vince Penmann, Bear Rinehart, Doug Golding, and all the others, but Ray Charles was also in there, and Mick Jagger and Kylie Minogue, scoffing at me and saying they were going to hang me for *flagrante disorganisato*. The prosecutor, Bob Cheshire, held up a packet of condoms. 'Do you recognise these?' he said. I answered 'No', at which point he turned to Maggie Thatcher and said, 'Quod erat demonstrandum. My case is proved, Your Worship'. They were dragging me away when I heard your voice in the crowd. You were yelling out, 'Let him be, he's not the messiah, he's just a naughty boy.' It was weird....."

* * * * *

While Alan and Anne were trying to rescue one experiment, Arthur Dee, Bob Cheshire and Fred Winters were in the process of planning another, some fifteen hundred kilometres away.

As a statistician, Arthur was constantly being called on to try and make sense of the world for others. In this case it was for Bob and Fred, watching closely as he clumped about in front of a whiteboard, dragging his plaster-encased leg behind him.

"He's pretty keen on these drawings, mate," Fred whispered conspiratorially, as Arthur erased one diagram and began to draw another.

For a moment Bob, considered showing Fred the results of his own work category survey – except the graph he had drawn after following Arthur's instructions for three days was not altogether flattering. Arthur grinned at them. "I've got to try and keep it simple so you two will understand."

Arthur Dee and Fred Winters had seemed to Bob to be an unlikely combination, but already a strong bond was forming between the two.

Arthur drew two simple diagrams, one labelled 'Desirable', the other 'Actual'.

"Let's look at product maintenance" he chirped. "It's one of the areas we need to address if we're going to improve customer satisfaction." He pointed to the large 'mature product' area under the diagram headed 'Desirable'.

DESIRABLE

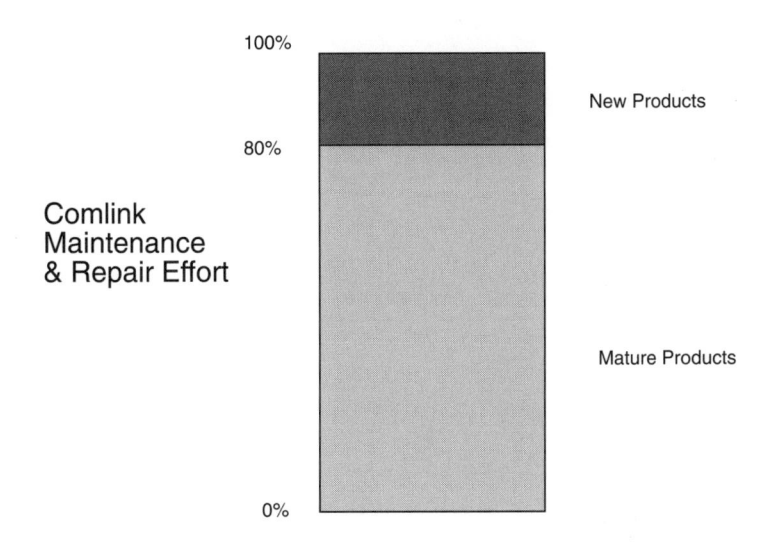

Comlink Maintenance & Repair Effort

- 100%
- 80%
- 0%

New Products

Mature Products

The Prelude

"This is where most of our maintenance resources should be expended, on the *mature* product range. They form the vast majority of our services to customers. Regular servicing of this equipment would result in less breakdowns by products which have been under strain through constant use.

"Unfortunately, we seem to be putting a lot of energy into maintaining *new* products, which shouldn't need fault repairs so early in their life. But when new products are launched without the benefit of proper installation processes, back-up resources or staff training, people in the field are forced to spend excessive time maintaining them. Resources are diverted from mature products which need them most. I suspect our current situation looks something like this." Arthur pointed to the second sketch he had drawn, a reverse of the first situation.

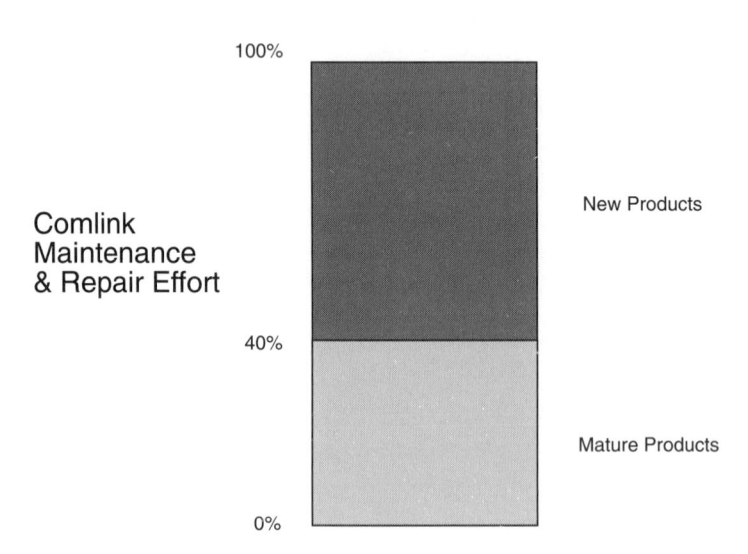

ACTUAL

Comlink Maintenance & Repair Effort

100%

New Products

40%

Mature Products

0%

"Of course, this is only a model. But it's enough to give you a picture of what we might be looking for. The next thing to do is test it. At the moment, I think it's safe to say that no-one in the region is very sure where resources are allocated with any certainty."

Bob looked at Fred Winters. The big man was leaning forward, sleeves rolled up, his huge forearms crossed and resting on the table.

"What do you say?" Bob asked.

Fred laughed derisively. "Bloody spot on! The new fax machine – the Ergofax – has been on hold in this region since before I arrived for just that reason. There simply hasn't been the breathing space to train up the installers properly, and we can't afford the problems that would cause. So we're telling people that it won't be available for at least six months. Pity too, it's a good little number: automatic pager, scanner with OCR, modem – the whole bit.

"OK," said Bob. "So we want to be able to improve maintenance resources for the mature product area so as to enable us to give a better service to existing customers. What are the sorts of things which are stopping us from doing so, Fred?"

Fred Winters lifted his large hands, palms out. "Apart from the trouble with new products, it's difficult to say. All the indicators show that we're achieving the repair and maintenance targets. So where do we go? How can I improve something that seems to be working properly already, despite the fact we know it isn't."

"Maybe something is happening to stop the maintenance people doing a good job," suggested Arthur.

Fred shrugged helplessly.

The statistician clumped back to the whiteboard and began to draw.

"You've seen one of these before? It's a 'cause and effect' diagram. It's useful for listing the various aspects of a problem you're considering. Sometimes it's called a 'fishbone' diagram. Just use any number of 'bones', there are no rules.

"All you need to do is pick out some headings you think your problem might involve. Then, under the relevant headings, list any factors which might also be involved. Again, no rules. The important thing is just to get something down which will give you a picture of the problem you're trying to address.

"Okay. The problem in this case might be, 'Unable to maintain mature products adequately'. That goes in here.

The Prelude

"Then some headings. One might be, 'Resources'. The sort of issue you'd list under that heading might be 'not enough people'.

"Another heading might be 'Administration'. Are there policies, regulations and so on which affect your ability to place resources where you want them?

"Then 'People'. Are there enough? Are they well-trained? Committed? All those sort of questions. You'll notice that some of these things might overlap but again, don't worry about it."

Fred slapped the table, "No rules! I like it. What about 'Supplies'? There's sometimes a difficulty getting spares."

"That's good," Arthur said. "Now, think of some of the other issues that might be a problem for you. For argument's sake, say you haven't got adequate storage facilities or there's too much paperwork for ordering. Put it in here. Or the cause we've just talked about, 'resources diverted by new product failures'." He marked some points on the diagram.

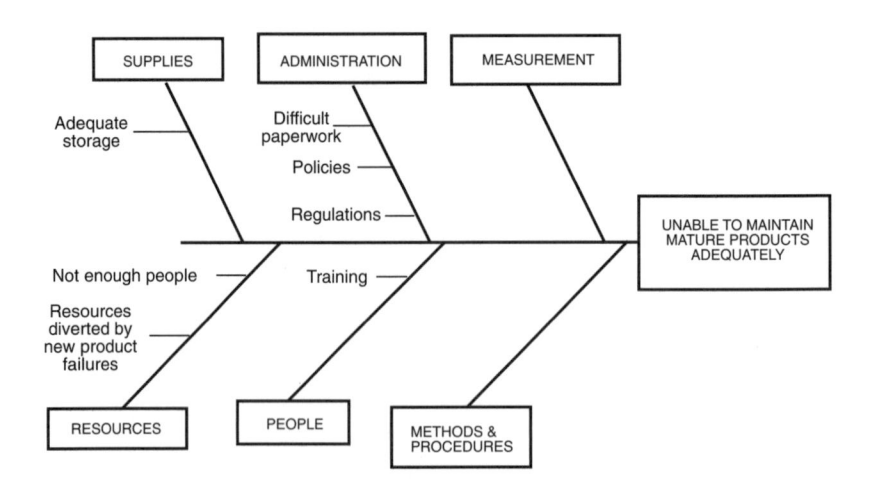

"Arthur, this is good stuff. What do you think, Fred?" Bob had seen 'fishbone' diagrams in the past, but he'd always associated them with the more boring aspects of his student years. To find a sensible use for 'fishbones' was something he'd not expected.

Fred nodded in agreement.

"I think we should hold it there for a moment," Bob said. Your managers should be involved here, Fred. They're the guys who've got the ideas and they're also the ones who are going to help make this work."

With a sardonic grin, Fred nodded. "Yeah, I suppose they ought to be in it. It's what we said at the beginning – try and let them know what we're doing."

"And *why*," added Arthur, remembering the last time he had been involved in something like this. "If we don't make it clear to people what sort of information we want, and why we want it, we may as well be spitting into the wind."

"I reckon so," Fred added. "And something else we have to make sure of is that people know it won't be a case of the messenger being shot when he turns up with bad news."

Chapter 17
Making headway

The objective was to improve performance in Fred Winters' region: to increase revenue and reduce operating costs. It wasn't a new objective, many managers had attempted it over the years with varying degrees of success. As far as most people working in the region were concerned, they'd seen it all before. And it added up to one word: retrenchments.

Bob was depressed. The first meeting with Fred's reporting managers had been reasonable, but there was an undercurrent of mistrust. The ebullient Fred had built a solid rapport with his staff and clearly most of the men working for him liked or respected their relatively new regional boss. But that wasn't enough for their plan to gain instant acceptance. The very presence of Bob and Arthur indicated that something was in the air. They were internal consultants, outsiders who were not part of the local organisation.

It had been Herb Scott, the Internal Plant Manager, who at that first meeting had come closest to saying how he felt. Bob was sure the IP manager wasn't alone in his opinion.

Herb had come into the meeting with the air of one whose every movement declares, 'What is this garbage? I've got better things to do with my time than bugger about with this touchy-feely stuff. He had taken his place late, sitting in a knotted heap with his legs planted firmly before him, spread wide like the roots of a tree. Arthur had been presenting a couple of models to illustrate the relationship between improved quality and job security when Herb interrupted.

"That's the first thing we should toss out. There's already too much job security around this place. If I could sack a few of the people I've got working for me, I'd be a lot better off," he growled.

There were mumbles of assent from the eight or so men grouped around the table.

Arthur grinned disarmingly. "The vast majority of problems in all organisations lie outside of the workers' control. Sacking them, replacing them, standing over them with a clipboard and measuring their every move cannot improve things in any way."

Herb lifted his bushy eyebrows scornfully. "You get rid of a few of 'em and it'll put the fear of God in the rest. Don't you worry about that."

It was a response Arthur had heard all over the organisation: if only I had different staff; staff who were committed, interested, capable – or whatever particular genetic strain the manager needed at the time.

"There are two things which can affect what we try to do at work," he explained. "These are the systems we work with and the people we work with. If you're not getting the right people to do the jobs, then your problem is with your selection or training system.

"It's not the fault of staff if they're put into a position where they don't have the skills or training necessary to perform well. Who controls the selection and training systems, the workers or the managers?"

Herb Scott shrugged. He wasn't buying it. He couldn't think of a way to refute Arthur on the spur of the moment, but he had no doubt that there was one. He did a quick mental review of his staff. Some of their work was appalling from time to time. When he disciplined them, the work improved. That was a simple equation, one he could relate to as a manager: you told people what to do, and if they wanted to keep their jobs, they did it.

Arthur scrawled a rectangle on the whiteboard and divided it into two uneven segments.

"I can't really expect you to accept what I say without evidence. But there's been a lot of work done by researchers both here and overseas in the past forty years, and one of the results is what we call the '85/15 rule'. It's only a rule of thumb, but it's useful for indicating where you might start to look for solutions.

"Put simply, 85% of problems can be eliminated by changing systems. It's management who control and determine systems. Only 15% of problems are under control of the workers."

The Prelude

Problems under the control of managers — 85%

SYSTEM

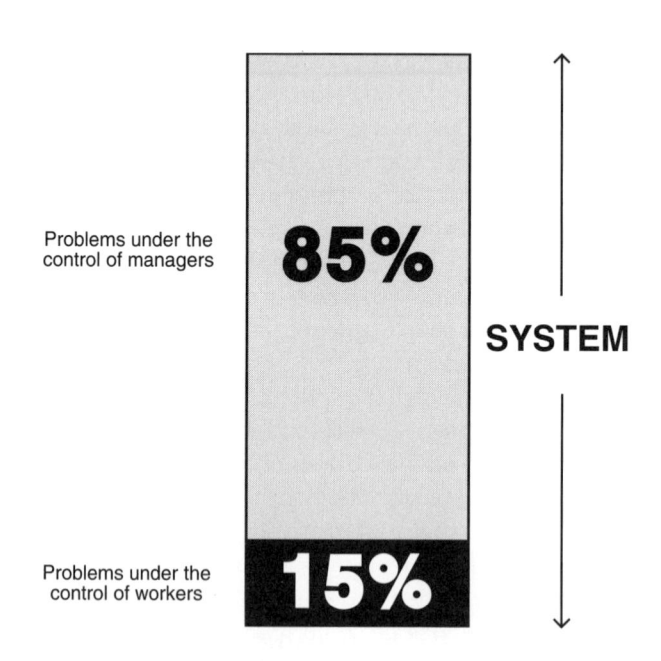

Problems under the control of workers — 15%

Herb Scott didn't look mollified. He turned to the others in the group, "Well I reckon I must have the fifteen percent belonging to you blokes!" He quipped.

When the laughter subsided Arthur continued his explanation. He had been in this position before, with tougher groups than this, and he wasn't going to allow himself to be put off by Herb's heckling.

"Let's look at an example," he suggested. "Perhaps then you'll see what I mean. Can someone tell me about a problem they've got which would be corrected by removing staff?"

There was a moment of uncomfortable silence, typical in meetings where the participants are called on to talk about a problem they have; as if those present fear that by admitting to a problem they are exposing a shortcoming before their peers.

Arthur stood his ground, a fixed smile of enquiry on his lips.

Finally, one of the men leaned forward and spoke. Morrie Levant was the Infrastructure Group Manager. He was a small man in his early forties, with a pale, shiny face and a thin carpet of sandy hair.

"We've been having a lot of trouble with broken lines when other authorities are digging near our cables," he said. "When the electricity or gas blokes want to do some maintenance, they look at the maps we supply with the locations of our cables marked on them. They start digging, and bang! They cut a cable that shouldn't have been there." Morrie clapped his hands to emphasise the sudden and absolute panic which always resulted from a cut cable.

"I've told my teams so many times: they know the rules for laying pipes and cables, but the things are never where they're supposed to be. I've got at least three ratbags who couldn't give a stuff about work. I'd be a lot better off if I could transfer them, or preferably get rid of them altogether." He sat back as a series of nods and mutters passed among the other managers.

Arthur thought for a moment. Looking at him, Bob wondered what the statistician could possibly say. The pipes were supposed to be laid in a certain place. That was clear. If they weren't, and the teams had the equipment and training necessary to do the job, then the workers were to blame. Bob could not escape the same conclusion he saw forming on other faces as his gaze flickered around the room. Morrie Levant seemed to be genuinely waiting for information which could help him, but others, Herb Scott among them, were leaning back, arms folded, with quietly knowing smiles on their faces.

Fred Winters had a go at smoothing the problem. "Who's the supervisor?"

A shrug from Morrie indicated he didn't think it was a problem with the supervisor. "Ben Aker. Good bloke, old school. Knows the ropes and can usually get things done without creating difficulties."

Fred nodded. "Yeah, Ben's good."

"With this sort of analysis," explained Arthur, "there can sometimes be a temptation to fix on the immediate supervisor. But that's not usually the answer." He paused. "Ben would be managing by results, wouldn't he?"

Morrie Levant nodded.

"Are the cable breaks which have occurred recently in any particular areas?"

The manager thought for a few moments. "Yeah, come to think of it, two of those ratbags I mentioned before work in the area where most of the breaks have been."

Several of those present smiled, waiting for Arthur's carefully constructed arguments to collapse.

"And you don't think it's anything to do with the electricity staff?" asked the statistician, hobbling over to lean casually against the wall.

"No," Morrie responded, "I don't think so. The problem's been that our cables are in the wrong place. Theirs are usually spot on."

"Do they use the same cabling procedure as Comlink?"

Heads turned towards Morrie as he answered, the tension increasing perceptibly as Arthur's questions flowed easily.

"No, they use a much heavier digger. They're often the first to put down their cables in a new development. Most of the breaks, if I remember rightly, happen when the electricity people come in after us to do some maintenance on cables they've already laid."

Herb Scott broke in. "It doesn't matter that they use a heavier machine. Our cables aren't supposed to be laid that close to their survey line. If they are, our men are doing the wrong thing."

"You're right, Herb," Arthur agreed disarmingly, "the cables shouldn't be there. Now, can you show me where the problems are occurring?"

On a wallmap of the Adelaide Hills region, Morrie indicated a rough circle centred around one of the smaller sub-exchanges. It was an area of recent development: beautiful views of city and sea with outrageous access roads and steep climbs. The kind of area which featured in real estate brochures under the title, 'Panoramic vistas, secluded rural settings'.

"Rough terrain?" Arthur asked artlessly, "Rocky, I'd guess?"

"We make an allowance for that," Morrie replied, trying to forestall what he sensed was a difficult line of reasoning. "They've got extra time to do the work if the ground is rocky."

"How much extra time?"

"A standard allowance, based on a formula determined by the Ops Directorate."

"Is it always enough?"

"Sometimes. Sometimes not."

"So, although there would be considerable variation in the time required for each job, the extra time allocated doesn't recognise this?"

"That's how it works," Morrie replied. "A standard extra amount of time – two hours or whatever – is built in to each difficult job. The assumption is that it's enough."

"Despite the obvious fact that in many cases it won't be," Arthur said. "If the time allowance is an average, there will have to be some jobs which take more, and some which take less." He scanned the group for agreement, receiving tentative nods from some.

"Such a system assumes you've got a finite work load and that it will not expand. Is that how it is, Morrie?"

"I wish it were," replied the manager drily. "The more work we get, the more we seem to get behind. We're flat out at the moment and the demand is increasing."

"So your teams have always got more work than they can finish in the allotted time. What happens if they have a good run and finish early?"

"They'll be given more jobs," Morrie replied.

"Which means the reward for quick work is an increased work load. Not very fair. Why should anyone work quickly if all they get out of it is more work?"

Most of the managers were looking at Arthur as if he'd just arrived from another planet. The concept was a new one for them, and they didn't know what to make of it.

But Arthur wasn't finished. "What about the reverse situation? The team has a terrible day and they strike ten jobs which take more than the average time. Is there any allowance for that?"

"No, they've already been given extra time to complete the work. Why would I give them more? How could I?" Morrie replied.

It was true. A decision had been taken at a senior level and it would be impossible for him to go against it without excellent reason.

Arthur nodded. "I'm not saying this is the answer to your cut cables, Morrie, but it might be worth investigating.

"It sounds like the system we employ for laying the cables is at fault. It's forcing the teams to do a bad job. If they run short of time, they can't plead difficulties, so they're forced to find some other way of catching up. The electricity company digger has already cleared a path for them. They simply have to dig a little closer to the electricity cable than they ordinarily would. They don't really have any choice if they want to get the work done."

"OK, I can accept that," said Morrie, "but it still doesn't help me solve the problem."

Others nodded, although there was new interest from them. They appeared to have accepted Arthur's reasoning and were now waiting for something they could digest and use.

"That's true, Morrie. But I hope I've shown that the reason for the problem might lie, not in the attitude of the men, but in the demands put on them by the system they work with. I'm sure we could find an appropriate way to redress the problem. I'd like to do a little research with your teams. Do you think they would agree to that?"

Morrie shrugged. "I guess so," he said with caution. "This isn't a hatchet job, is it Fred? I'll have nothing of it, if that's the case."

It was there still, thought Bob. The concern that the point of improvements was to reduce jobs. His mental shrug matched the physical one of Morrie Levant. What could you expect? It had happened so often in the past.

Later, as they discussed the results of that first meeting, Bob related his fears to Fred and Arthur.

"We need to find some way to convince people that this is serious. That what we're after is increased quality and productivity, not less jobs."

"Tell us about it, pal." Fred responded grimly. Like Bob, he saw the need but had no idea how to address it.

"I've got a few ideas which might help there," Arthur smiled.

begin mapping the fault repair process and to continue the discussions with staff which were essential for charting the complete process.

Bob had found it fairly easy to apply the first half of Arthur's equation. The 'product' was fault service, that much was clear. But the 'delivery process' was proving more difficult to define. Broadly speaking, it was the sequence of events which resulted in a technician standing on the customer's doorstep, toolbox in hand. But Bob was starting to realise that the process was a monster; a complex nightmare of paperwork, regulations, to-ing and fro-ing. And from what he'd learned so far, it seemed that the managers and supervisors in the region had – somewhat understandably – little real concept of how the process actually operated.

Froggy scowled as Bob read out the address.

"What's wrong with that?" Bob grinned, "I thought you'd be happy to do a job at a pub!"

The young technician shook his head. "Yeah, I guess it's not all bad. But I hate going back to places we've been to before. This is a place where we put in a whole switchboard about six months ago. There's been nothing but trouble since then. The thing's connected to Sky Teev and the TAB, as well as the normal lines. It's a mess."

"Well, let's fix it," Bob said, enjoying the surge of enthusiasm he felt from being back on the road after years in management.

"Fat chance! I'd love to spend an afternoon working on the whole circuit, but I can't. Get in, fix the problem, and get out. Then in another week something else will go, and we'll be back again," Froggy grumbled. "Still, as you say, it's not all bad. They serve pretty good counter lunches."

* * * * *

The pub was a noisy, bustling place with the dark, slightly dated friendliness of an outer suburban pub at lunchtime. Construction workers and contractors were leaning heavily on the laminate-covered bar whilst a couple of local businessmen in cheap shirts were resting their elbows on the gaudy, beer-soaked listowels spread along its edge.

As Froggy walked up to the bar, a taut, balding man with a huge brown moustache sprang down the length of the bar to welcome them. He clapped his hands together, rubbing them briskly.

The Prelude

"Good on you, Froggy. You know where it is, I suppose. You ought to by now."

He lifted a section of the bar top to let the two Comlink men through. Smiling encouragement, he ushered them into a back office cluttered with piles of paperwork. Several opened boxes of wine were stacked beside a desk which supported, among other things, a relatively new, highly advanced Comlink switchboard.

Froggy opened his tool box and removed a laptop computer. Placing the device gently on the desk, he plugged a thick cable into the switchboard and entered a sequence of codes. The screen filled with a neatly ordered array of numbers punctuated by an occasional line of esoteric text.

Bob shook his head. Things had changed since the late seventies when he'd done most of his work in the field.

Froggy removed a plate from the back of the switchboard and slipped a flat-ended probe into a deep cavity.

"No problem," he said. "A couple of the extensions must have been given the wrong code when they were installed. They've got an STD bar on them to prevent the staff from ringing long-distance. But these two are in the boss's flat and according to the switching diagram shouldn't have been given a bar. I'll just change a couple of DIP switches and we'll be right."

Bob scratched his chin, "I thought the de-barring could be done at the exchange now."

"No, this one's connected to an old cross-bar set-up just down the road. It's due for replacement." Froggy raised an eyebrow. "Soon, that is."

"What about the TAB and Sky Teev?"

"The TAB can go through the exchange alright, although they had to put in a special land line to carry the computer information. Most of Sky Teev comes in via the dish on the roof. It's only the Infotel services that are run through our lines. Overseas sports results, news, that sort of stuff."

A surge of noise from the direction of the public bar distracted Bob. A moment later there was a silence from outside, then a scuffling of feet as the publican ran past the doorway to the office and hurled himself up the stairs to his second-story flat.

Bob turned back to Froggy, wondering vaguely what was going on.

As he watched, Froggy withdrew the probe and replaced the cover of the switchboard. He ran a quick check before folding up the computer into a neat package. It was barely larger than the electronic meter Bob had been given by his parents when he started training.

What next?

"That's it," said Froggy, slapping down the locks on his toolbox.

They turned to the doorway, only to find it blocked by an extremely large gentleman with a blue uniform and three stripes on his sleeve.

Bob looked at him blankly, "G'day," he ventured.

"Where do you think you're going?" demanded the policeman.

Bob experienced an ely sensation, that first tiny inkling that something, somewhere, has gone terribly wrong and you're about to become involved in it.

"Umm, we're finished here and we were just going to grab a counter lunch," he mumbled.

"Finished, alright," the policeman growled. "You're under arrest. The pair of you."

Chapter 19
Caught napping

"Arrested? You're kidding!" Alan Dodgson spluttered.

Anne Blanchard smiled broadly as she eased into one of the visitor's chairs in Alan's office. The gangly Project Manager scrambled around his desk and hurled himself into the armchair opposite her.

"Tell me more," he crowed, slapping his hands on his knees.

"Soon after he was let out, Bob rang to see how we were going. You were in the team meeting, so I got the whole story."

It appeared the publican had been harbouring one of the Hills' last illegal SP bookie operations and the phones in the upstairs rooms were needed for STD calls. The past few years had seen a resurgence of SP bookies as a reaction to the computerised sterility of legal off-course gambling. With the added dimension of portable phones, it was now easy to communicate trackside information to outside confederates.

On the arrival of the police, the publican had flown upstairs to warn his partners. Thanks to the unintentional delay caused when the police cornered Bob and Froggy – whom they assumed to be in on the racket – the bulk of the evidence had been burned or flushed into limbo.

The police had been unimpressed with Bob's protestations that he and Froggy were simply doing their job. Why, the police had demanded, were there a number of unmarked extensions on the switchboard? Who had connected them? What were Bob and Froggy doing there if not assisting criminals? In short, it seemed remarkably strange that two allegedly capable Comlink technicians were in a building where an illegal telephone business was being conducted, and yet were blissfully unaware that anything was amiss. If Comlink staff were indeed capable and intelligent, how could they have gone there on no less than five occasions over the past two months and remained ignorant of what was occurring? What about the accounts, hadn't they shown up a huge volume of STD calls?

The police argument had a certain appealing logic to it – especially for the frustrated law officers who had seen their quarry walk free because of apparent obstruction by two miscreants. The pair had been arrested and taken to the local watch-house, from where Bob had hastily contacted Albert Lapin as a character reference.

But the Chief Executive's weight had proved unequal to the task of convincing the doughty officer-in-charge of their innocence, and he had insisted on holding the offenders until a magistrate could be found for a bail hearing. It was Fred Winters, brought in as the senior Comlink man in the region, who had eventually convinced the magistrate of their innocence. It was well after four o'clock when the magistrate finally released Bob and Froggy, directing the police to withdraw charges.

To refute the police argument of collusion, Fred had virtually been forced to admit that Comlink didn't know what it was doing. Attempting to defend the way his men worked by explaining work pressures and the need for speedy service, Fred had been miserably aware of a journalist lurking at the back of the courtroom. He was under no illusions as to how the episode would be written up in the local tabloid.

The magistrate had been critical in his analysis of the situation: "So, Mr Winters, you are saying these men had no idea they were assisting the activities of illegal gamblers?"

"Of course not, Your Worship."

"Yet I was under the apprehension that your modern equipment would allow you to detect problems such as unauthorised connections?"

"Well, yes, that would be the case if they were looking for it."

"But they were not looking, I take it. What, then, were they doing Mr Winters?"

"Fault repair."

"And would not a normal repair activity include a survey of the whole piece of equipment to see whether there were other, undetected faults? After all, if my washing machine breaks down I expect the technician not only to repair it, but also to look over the whole thing and tell me if there are any other problems on the horizon – problems of which I may not be aware. I am not an expert, you know, Mr Winters."

"No, Your Worship."

"I beg your pardon?" The magistrate had snapped, peering over the small, half-glasses perched on the end of his nose.

"Yes, that is, I mean, it would normally be what happens. But we are busy, very busy at the moment." Even to Fred, his truthful reply had sounded flat.

"Might I suggest, Mr Winters, that you and your organisation would have saved a considerable waste of public money and time had you been just a trifle more organised and efficient."

"If you'll excuse me, Your Worship," Fred had interrupted, tiring of the pomposity of the bench, "it's not our job to locate and detect criminals. That's why we have a police force."

"I do not attempt to turn you into vigilantes," the Magistrate had replied icily. "However, had you and your staff done your jobs correctly – by that I mean had you taken the time to observe your own policies – then this whole episode would not have been necessary. Your own staff would have been aware of the unauthorised connections, and either removed them or passed the matter on to Sergeant Wilson."

Fred had been forced to admit this was very likely what would have happened if once during those visits a full service of the equipment had been carried out. Finally satisfied by this admission of guilt, the Magistrate had concluded the proceedings.

Bob had finished off his description of events to Anne with a disheartened objection. "I can see the headlines now. 'Comlink bungle foils police action', or maybe, 'Incompetence allows racketeers off scot free'."

Anne had not been able to prevent herself laughing, and she was laughing now, while Alan lay rolling about in the chair. "I've never heard anything like it," he gasped. "And just imagine how upset old Albert must have been! To be ignored, passed over for a mere regional manager. He'd be ropeable."

Anne smirked as she imagined how the Chief Executive would have reacted. If there was a crisis, Albert always loved to be involved. He could become quite testy if no-one came to him for advice or if ignored. Anne put her hands up to her ears, bunching up her shoulder-length hair to resemble the fuzzy clumps of greyness which habitually sprouted over Albert's ears. "Really, I think you should have checked that with me first!" she said sternly, in her best Albert-voice.

* * * * *

Doug Golding, OFCAB's Product Installation Manager, was passing along the corridor on his way home for the night. He paused when he heard the laughter floating out of Alan's office. Alan waved him in, unable for the moment to speak coherently.

Doug Golding was of a serious mien, not prone to jokes at a workmate's expense, but when he heard the reason for their mirth he couldn't help laughing loudly.

"That's what happens when you go around impersonating Comlink technicians. You get slung in the can," he grinned.

Doug leaned back in a chair, relaxed. The story of Bob's plight had helped to lift the constrictive coils of formality which had characterised Alan's recent contact with his managers. Alan's first attempts to map and control the systems of OFCAB had resulted in near disaster – largely, Anne had forcefully informed him, because he had not bothered to tell his departmental managers what was going on. He had circumvented them without thinking – gone straight to the supervisors and told them how he wanted them to keep records of what they were doing. Looking back, Alan could understand why his actions had been seen as threatening by Doug and his fellow managers.

Anne had been an enormous help. Her working life had been spent communicating, negotiating, and working with groups of people at all levels of the organisation. Alan knew she did not accept everything he and Bob were trying to do – in fact she was extremely nervous that any changes made to OFCAB work processes would have ramifications throughout the whole organisation. He was grateful to her for being willing to give them assistance despite this.

Alan was keen to find out what Doug and the other managers felt about what was happening with OFCAB. "How are we doing, then, Doug?" he said, leaning forward despite himself.

Doug nodded slowly, taking his time.

"I appreciate what you're trying to do, Alan. I have from the first meeting we had after the accident. But I think Anne put her finger on the main problem when she said we aren't very good at talking to staff, or listening to their replies.

"I think there's two sides to it," he continued thoughtfully. "One is that as managers we've never been trained to do anything like that. I spend my whole time directing people, making assumptions about their abilities and my abilities. Hell, it's my job to get the job done. I need to be directive.

The Prelude

"I think the thing I've been most afraid of as a manager is not having an answer when people come to me with their problems; that I won't be able to provide solutions for them. That would make me look stupid.

"That's why the stuff you've been getting from Adelaide is useful. This 'process analysis' business helps me separate the noise from the important things. In a way, I think it will result in even more control over processes than we've had in the past. For the first time, we'll be able to predict our ability to meet customer needs . So instead of robbing us managers of authority, it will give us more."

Alan nodded with relief. Doug Golding was beginning to open up, and Alan sent a silent thank you to Bob, Froggy and the Adelaide constabulary. Perhaps it was something as simple as that, he thought. Find a link, a common piece of ground that does not threaten anyone.

Doug was smiling now, confident that he had something to offer. "Bear Rinehart has been making some headway with some of your ideas. I've just been looking over his report. You should find a copy in your Info-file."

Alan was stunned. "Last week Bear and I hardly had a consensus viewpoint about all this."

Doug smiled, "I think the Bear's seen the light. We've been looking at cable usage; trying to figure out why our supply situation is always up the spout. If we'd had a regular supply and adequate stockpile, that flat-bed wouldn't have had to deliver out to the site where Wally Jamieson was killed."

There was a silence while they each pondered the unnecessary death.

"We graphed the amount of cable used lately. You can see it on the second page," Doug said, referring to a simple chart in the data which Alan had pulled up on the screen of his Info-file.

Caught napping

30 kms

Cable used per week

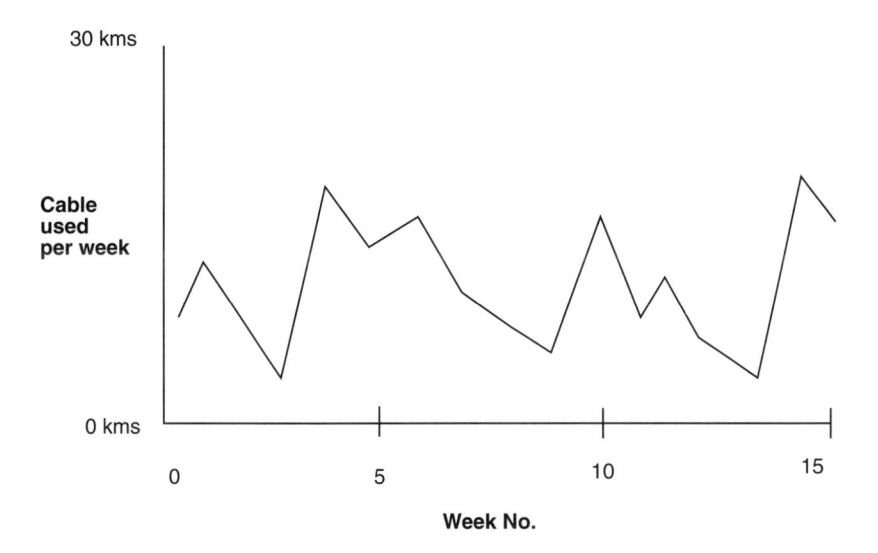

0 kms

0   5   10   15

Week No.

"See the huge variation. That was the first clue. It's what you and Bob said to start looking for. You can see here, how some weeks we'd be using five kilometres of cable, others, almost thirty."

"There would be reasons for that," Anne said, looking over Alan's shoulder at the screen. "Weather, terrain, population density. All sorts of things would have an impact on the amount of glass cable they could lay."

"Right," said Doug, "but it wasn't until Bear began to graph it that we could see a pattern develop. And that started him looking at the causes. You see how after a particularly poor week there always seems to be a peak following? When we looked at it, weather and rocky country were effects, but the main reason for the huge variation was within our control."

"So what's the main cause?" Alan prompted.

"Many of the low points are caused by lack of cable. Guys standing around leaning on their shovels. It's not their fault. It's ours," Doug said.

"And the high points?" Anne asked.

"The stock would come in, so the foremen – aware of the poor result from the week before – would put their teams on overtime to make up for it."

"So we're keeping our men standing around one moment, then whipping them into a frenzy the next? No wonder they don't know whether they're coming or going. And no wonder our costs are going through the roof," Alan mused. "I suppose I'd better contact the supplier in the morning and see if he has any specific problems that stop delivery. We might have to look at changing suppliers, or working more closely with this one."

Dropping his head, Doug smiled sheepishly. "Bear did that this morning. The only problem the supplier has is a result of our erratic ordering. Apparently we order hugely varying amounts from week to week, so he never knows what production will be required in the future. If we can standardise the ordering we can make sure we get a reasonable amount. Then there shouldn't be any need to suffer shortages and gluts. It was like you guys said – reduce variation and improve performance."

People are the weirdest things, thought Alan. One minute they're against you, the next they're with you – even ahead of you. Or perhaps they just needed the time and opportunity to take an idea on board themselves. After all, you couldn't *make* people understand an idea.

Doug Golding smiled at Anne. "You know, we've been laying cable for nearly a year now and never knew we even had a problem until we took a few simple steps to measure the process."

Anne nodded. "One thing this exercise has driven home to me is that almost everybody wants to make things better. It's just that the systems we use for getting things done stop them."

"Even me," said Alan, "I'm responsible for the overall project, but I'm beginning to realise that I've helped to create a number of systems which only make it difficult for people to do their jobs efficiently. And it's difficult to do anything about it because above me there are other people operating the same way. I wonder how far up the tree it goes?"

Anne bunched up her hair once more and leaned forward, crinkling her nose. "It's lonely at the top. I'm glad you realise that at last. But you should have checked it with me first!" she growled.

* * * * *

"I wish you'd checked it with me first," Albert Lapin said to the two men seated in his office. "It's poor warning from members of my own Board."

Neale Kale shrugged expressively, his thin lips pressed tightly together.

"Well," demanded the Comlink Chief Executive, "Can't you see a conflict of interest?"

"What about you, Leo, don't you call it collusion? Insider trading? Unfair financial advantage?"

Leo Carnic heaved his large frame out of the chair and moved over to where Albert stood. He put his arm around the smaller man's shoulder.

"We're businessmen, Albert. It's my job to advise clients of potentially profitable investments. There's nothing illegal about the deal NetWork's arranged with the New South Wales government. I'd be open to charges of negligence or professional incompetence if I refused to back the float."

Neale Kale snapped impatiently, "Whether or not Leo and myself have held positions on the Comlink Board is irrelevant. My bank holds accounts for a number of companies, some of which are your competitors. There is nothing improper in that. Why, we provide services to both the top supermarket chains in the country."

Albert regarded the merchant banker with distaste. "Does that mean you'd arrange to finance the float of one company while you were serving as a Board member of the other?"

For reply, Neale Kale pulled an envelope from his pocket and tossed it casually on the desk.

"I'm not on the Board any more, Albert."

For a moment the men's eyes locked in undisguised hatred.

"It's standard business practice, Albert. You must know that. If a company comes to us with a proposal that needs financing, one of the options is to float a public company on the Stock Exchange. What else could we do? NetWork needs an injection of funds for its future activities."

"What activities? How long has Hugh Britten been your 'client'?" Albert demanded angrily.

The other simply smiled flatly. "That's professional privilege, Albert. I'm not empowered to discuss such things without my client's consent."

"But you'd discuss Comlink's situation with your clients, wouldn't you? What about the privilege there?"

"Really, Albert." Neil Kale shrugged eloquently to emphasise his distaste.

137

Leo Carnic interrupted the pair. Unlike his associate, he wasn't particularly enjoying this interview.

"We're sorry you feel there's been some sort of conspiracy, Albert, but that's up to you." Placing an envelope similar to Neale Kale's into Albert's hand, he moved to the door.

Albert glared at their retreating backs, feeling nothing except betrayal and a sense of his own foolishness for not having seen this coming. It was what he was paid to do, to protect his organisation from threats such as this.

He walked slowly over to his chair and sat slumped in it for a long time, his eyes fixed on an invisible point somewhere outside the window, unaware of the heavy, slick drops of rain that began to splat against the glass.

The thick glass of the window was vibrating slightly from the insistent pressure of a rising wind. It would be a brutal storm when it hit. So many unseasonable storms, he thought irrelevantly. So often now, storms and heat, heat and rain. It made no sense any more.

* * * * *

The storm which was bucketting Melbourne was part of a widespread cloudbank over most of the east coast of Australia. The remains of a late tropical cyclone, it had meandered down the coast over a period of days, ducking out to sea from time to time, where it picked up fresh reserves of rain.

The downpour in Newcastle was somewhat lighter, having settled into a steady debilitating drizzle. Negotiating the Comlink sedan through the winding streets of the city, Alan looked at Anne sitting beside him, her profile occasionally sparkling as stray headlights caught the rain-spattered windscreen and threw small diamonds of light across her face.

They had left the office after Doug Golding finished his story. Alan felt reasonably hopeful about the future – that somehow it all boiled down to people. Talk to them, communicate and listen to what they had to say, and the problem was half way to being solved.

He glanced again at Anne sitting silently beside him. She had given him the most important factors, he realised, the glimmerings of an understanding that people could and would work together simply because they wanted to. And that whether they wanted to or not was largely dependent on their environment. Was there trust? Tolerance? Were people allowed to make mistakes? Were they allowed to make suggestions? Ultimately, would the organisation listen to them? He didn't have the answers yet – in fact, he doubted he ever would. But in a sense that was OK. It wasn't necessary to be right all the time.

"How do you manage to understand people?"

"Me? I don't." Anne looked vaguely puzzled.

"That's not true. All that stuff about meetings, ownership, interactions. I don't see any of that going on around me. It's all just people talking. That's all I can see."

"You're doing fine," she said, turning away from the windscreen. "A lot of the stuff we're talking about is just the names psychologists give to ordinary human conversation. We're human, we're awkward when we don't know what's happening. It doesn't take too much to figure that out."

Alan pulled the car up at the portico of the hotel.

"What are you doing for dinner?" he asked, his voice rattling with nervousness.

"The restaurant here isn't so bad. Why don't you join me?" Anne smiled.

* * * * *

It was a laughing dinner, every small movement or statement a cause for mirth. Humour was a diversion, a way of avoiding the need to place their trust in one another. The wine helped to mellow their nervousness and both indulged with an initial desperation.

For Anne, there was a need to convince herself that it was alright to trust this man, and to trust herself as well. She had shied away from that trust on the beach, where it had been easier to be angry than to face the danger of vulnerability. Gazing across the table, she thought of an old song which many years ago had formed a chorus in her personal code: *There's a time for us, someday a time for us. Time together with time to spare. Time to learn, time to care.*

But there never seemed to be the time to get to know someone well enough. It was easier to refuse them entry into your life; to remain at a distance, where even the worst threats were impersonal. In a way, the song had enabled her to avoid finding the time. While there was the fantasy, the

The Prelude

wish, there was no need to make it real. The dream was easier to live up to than the reality.

By the time the waiter came with the bill, a pleasant glow had settled over their table. Their nervousness had given way to a calmer, drifting conversation, and to more personal talk of their hopes and their past.

Alan picked up the bill, looked at it and pulled out his wallet to pay. He grabbed a plastic card and placed it on the small saucer. There was a small click as something fell out of his wallet.

Anne started to laugh. Alan stared at her for a moment, then lowered his eyes nervously to the table.

He scooped up the small plastic packages lying there, coughing and blushing furiously. "Ah, I took your advice," he mumbled. "It's best to be prepared. I mean, it's not that I planned... It's just..."

Holding up one hand, Anne stopped him in mid-sentence.

"It's OK," she said, smiling, "It's OK."

* * * * *

In the darkness of her room she repeated the benediction.

"It's OK. Very frustrating, but OK, I guess."

She cradled Alan's head in the crook of her arm, feeling the softness of his hair pressing against her breast. He was sleeping soundly.

It was funny really. After all, he'd had a difficult few days, and the wine....Still, it didn't say much for her amorous attractions. Perhaps she should just roll him out of bed; he'd probably wake up when he hit the floor. No, that wouldn't be fair. Or would it? She glanced at the small squares of plastic on the bedside table, each with its seal still intact. They looked grey in the dim room, like so many out-of-date postage stamps. She looked at Alan's head once more: probably would be out-of-date by the time she got the benefit of them. Still, there were the ones she'd put in her handbag after their last conversation, surely they'd be good. After all, she only intended to wait until morning.

Sliding further down between the sheets, Anne pressed her body softly against Alan. Her hand sought out his in the darkness and Alan's fingers curled around hers, holding her hand to the smooth, hard warmth of his chest. *Hold my hand and I'll take you there. Somehow, someday, somewhere.*

Chapter 20
Natural selection

"There's no point in being terse with me, darling," Janice Cheshire said, taking care to hold the receiver well away from her ear. "You can't blame me because you feel duntish again. I'm starting to get worried about you, Bob, you're drinking too much."

Bob ground his teeth, uncertain whether his wife was serious or just taking the opportunity for some fun at his expense.

"I wouldn't drink so much if the world wasn't out to get me," he complained, "I'm innocent."

"Yes, dear, I know. You're coming home for the weekend aren't you?"

"Nothing could keep me away. I need the rest."

"You haven't forgotten Saturday, the horse show?"

Silence.

"Emma would be heartbroken," Janice informed her husband.

"We'll talk about it tonight," Bob said, not willing to trust himself on the subject of a horse this early in the morning. How could his life be in such a mess that he hadn't even had the opportunity to speak to his wife about a simple thing like a horse for Emma? It wasn't a big deal, but it gave him pause for thought as he hung up the phone. It must have been weeks – months probably – since he'd had the chance to sit, relax and talk with Janice.

Bob staggered out of bed and headed off to drain at least half a dozen of the ridiculously small water glasses which are all that can ever be found in hotel rooms.

An hour later, he was making his way through a maze of corridors to the small office he and Arthur Dee had been given to carry out their project in the Hills region. Smiles and smirks greeted him, together with the occasional call of 'jailbird', but Bob's headache would not allow him to respond suitably.

Arriving at the sanctuary of his office, he found Simon Robertson, the Market and Consumer Research manager for the Adelaide area, already waiting for him.

"We've got a specific method of measuring perceptions amongst both staff and customers," the young man began eagerly. "It's not a method I'm particularly happy with, but I haven't been in the job long enough to suggest an alternative. I've got some ideas, but..." he paused, shrugging and smiling shyly. "You'll have seen the monthly reports on the consumer satisfaction indices. I can tell you how we approach them."

"Sure, that's a good starting point," said Bob, attempting to ignore the pulsing in his frontal lobes. "How about some coffee?"

"No, thanks," responded Simon brightly, "I don't drink coffee or tea. I've got a better idea. Why don't we get some fresh air?"

Bob glanced out the window. Burnished hard, bright and crisp, the day was an early precursor of spring. He had been too busy even to notice. "You're right," he agreed. "We can walk up to the Powerline. It starts in the next street."

The Powerline was a hundred metre-wide strip of cleared land meandering through the forest for many kilometres. It had been built originally as an access track to the high-voltage power lines which ran through the Hills on their way to the country towns of the upper valley area. The electricity towers were hidden away over on the other side of the main range and the access track had been turned into public parkland by an Electricity Commission which had become increasingly embarrassed by the presence of its inelegant power carriers.

Simon Robertson spoke quickly as he walked, firing out a description of the work he was doing and how his office operated.

"Our research should highlight the variance between what customers see as good service and what Comlink sees as good service."

"It doesn't?"

"No." Simon bent over a clump of scrubby grass. "This is Patterson's Curse."

He strolled over to Bob, holding a small weedy plant with purple flowers.

"Also known as Salvation Jane. It's a weed. Used to be in plague proportions here in South Australia."

Bob looked at it distastefully. "I've heard of it, I think. They've been killing it off haven't they? I read something about it a while back."

"That's right. Biological control. Some years ago now, the authorities released a specially imported bug, a parasite which will eat only Patterson's Curse."

He took the plant back from Bob, "Don't worry, it's not infected." He paused thoughtfully, "It's just the victim of selective customer research."

"What do you mean? You said it was a plague."

"True. But the bug will not only kill Patterson's Curse, it will also kill Salvation Jane."

"They're the same plant, aren't they?" Bob frowned.

Simon grunted.

"We usually ask our customers whether they're happy with the service they receive," he said. "That's okay, as far as it goes, but I'd like to find out more – find out whether the service we give them is what they want: if they think it's value for money."

"Why don't you?"

"Complicated," Simon responded with a smile. "Like this plant: plague in the grassland and semi-arid areas of the state, it can only colonise in open agricultural land – not in forest – so it's a problem to farmers and graziers; the cattle don't like it.

"The rub is that the cattle will eat it if there's a drought. It's a hardy little fellow, so it will survive long into a vicious drought season. Hence the name Salvation Jane. It's saved a lot of cattle in the dry north of the state.

"Stand-off. Some people say it's a good plant, a saver in times of drought. Others say it's a curse, taking over fields that could produce rich, palatable pasture."

"And in our research do we assume customers are Patterson's Curse or Salvation Jane?"

"Bit of both," Simon laughed. "There's a 'wild card' here too. The apiarists."

"The, er......?"

"Bee-keepers." Simon explained. "You see, honey made by bees which feed on Patterson's Curse is extremely tasty. People love it. The apiarists claim it provides a big yield. Here's where it gets complicated."

Bob nodded uncertainly.

"Bee-keeping in Australia is a seasonal affair. The hives are shifted around, often into areas where the bees can feed on plants like Patto's Curse.

The Prelude

In the Spring they're rented out to farmers to pollinate crops. It's a big business, and it's necessary. There are few feral bees."

"Feral bees?"

"Wild bees. There were plenty once, but we've killed them off through land clearing, fires, pollution, introduced predators. We've destroyed almost all the native bees in Australia."

Bob remembered his conversation with Alan Dodgson above the Blackbutt Reserve in Newcastle. Koalas wasn't it? All diseased, didn't he say? What had gone wrong with this country?

"What happens when you remove all the bees?" Simon asked.

"I suppose you can't pollinate the plants."

"Right. No plants, no introduced crops, fruits or vegetables – a huge proportion of which are pollinated by bees, hive bees. So figure this: if you remove the Patterson's Curse, you remove the source of honey people like most. The market will change because the honey doesn't taste as good any more so less people buy it. Some bee-keepers will go out of business, and that means even less plants are pollinated. Result? The price of honey rises as less becomes available.

"Once that happens you're into a cause and effect cycle. Price rises, people buy less: less market, more bee-keepers drop out. Not a huge effect from an economic perspective – maybe ten, fifteen percent of the total market; a few million bucks a year. But what sort of a difference will it make when there's fifteen percent less fruit and vegetables available because the bees didn't pollinate them? What will happen to food prices?"

"That's horrifying," said Bob. He looked at the spindly plant in Simon's hand. Not pretty, it was greyish-green with small, sparse leaves and a tiny purple flower which looked as though it had been added as a forlorn afterthought.

"What's even more horrifying," Simon continued, "is that the authorities did their research and they got the answers they wanted. The answers they expected. It wasn't planned, I'm not suggesting a conspiracy. It's just that they knew Patterson's Curse was a problem for many farmers and their survey procedures unconsciously reflected that assumption. More than that, their interpretation of the data was seriously at fault. It was taken out of the hands of the researchers. The people who interpreted the data were the managers and decision-makers, and they'd already made their decision, either consciously or unconsciously."

"And we have the same problem?"

"Two problems: one is corrupt data – information that doesn't reflect the way the world really is; the other is loose interpretation – seeing what you want to see in the data you've got."

Bob stopped in the middle of the track. He turned to the young man. "If that's your view, why on earth haven't you done something about it? You're responsible for our measurement processes, at least a major part of them."

Simon's smile faded. "What can I do? I'm only the local manager. I've got to go with the policy that comes from men like you."

Bob felt the heat rising within him. He was tired of hearing everyone say they couldn't do anything about the problems. All he was getting was a bunch of excuses from people. 'I can't do anything, I haven't got the power'. Well, what did they think he was doing? He was going to get shafted if he couldn't come up with some damn good evidence for making a radical change in the way they did things. It had started with the Dick Tracy Watch, but it had blown out of all proportion. The same makeshift, easy decisions were being made everywhere: from Froggy making a quick fix in the full knowledge he'd be back a week later, to Albert forcing the release of new technology they wouldn't be able to fix if something went wrong. He felt frustrated at every turn. And now this brash kid was telling him that the place was in a mess but that he didn't plan to be in the repair crew.

"For Christ's sake!" Bob shouted. "I haven't got a bloody crystal ball on my desk. How am I supposed to know what's wrong unless people like you tell me? You're supposed to be providing management with accurate, sensible data. Now you stand there and tell me you don't think the stuff you're producing is worth a pinch of shit, but that you're not going to do anything about it. God, I'm sick of people like you. I hear it all bloody day."

The built-up frustration of the past weeks poured out of Bob. He glared at Simon, angered further by the realisation that the younger man was merely taking the same line he, himself, had adopted for years. What had changed him? The thought came unbidden, holding his tongue and preventing the start of another tirade.

There was silence for a moment, then Simon spoke quietly. "Look, I talk a lot about nature, but I'm not an environmental activist. I guess it's easier for me to sit on the sidelines and knock the system rather than change it. Maybe I haven't got the balls, I don't know. Certainly, it's easier to do nothing." He tried to smile. "But I didn't come up here today with nothing to offer. Otherwise I wouldn't have told you all that stuff about the bees."

The Prelude

Bob nodded wearily. It occurred to him that he'd become so used to looking for problems it was starting to spill over into everything he did. Simon had spoken openly about his fears and that must have taken a considerable effort – particularly since he didn't know Bob from a sack of wet paper. And all he'd received in response was an attack.

"You're right," he said. "I'm sorry. I've got my share of problems, but so have you. It's never easy to talk about difficulties in the work you're doing, and what you've told me is useful. I shouldn't take my problems out on you."

Bob thrust his hands into his pockets, turned and started to walk back down the long slope of grass.

"Hang on, Bob," the other called. "Like I said, I dragged you out here because I thought I had something to offer. On the phone you said you were starting to determine customer requirements. Well, I can help there."

Bob stopped, looking back over his shoulder.

"It relates to what you were saying about the number of times people have to go back on fault calls. It's true. We do have problems in the way we're collecting data and it's affecting our service delivery.

"I had my staff do some ringing around the metropolitan area yesterday. You know we've got a policy that ninety percent of reported faults should be fixed by close of business the next day? Well, the preliminary indications are that our customers don't think that's the major criteria for good service. They're far more interested in having the phone fixed right the first time – especially private householders, who have to arrange virtually a whole day at home to wait for our tech to arrive. What they seem to be saying is that, within reason, the time taken to fix the phone is not as important as the fact that it's fixed correctly, and that they have some idea of what time the technician is likely to arrive."

"That fits," Bob acknowledged. "But the 'on-time repair' index is one of the major ways we judge our business performance."

"Well, it isn't telling us anything useful about what our customers want. We're determining our success on the basis of useless figures. And in the meantime, it seems actual customer satisfaction is dropping – not that the present data is capable of telling us that."

"Why?"

"Because we don't measure the things our customers really want, and we rarely ask people who complain whether there's been any improvement in service. We only ask a random sample of population, so we seldom hear from the ones who are really pissed off. And all the while, we're looking at that ninety percent figure and thinking we're doing great things. But the reality is that the figure forces the techs to do makeshift repairs so they can make their quotas. It's crazy."

"But we have to measure our performance. How else are we going to know how we are doing?" Bob argued.

"True. *But the problem arises when we let measurement techniques control our performance.* Under the ninety percent system, if a tech can't get to a fault on day one, he's got no incentive to get there at all because the deadline has gone. No matter what he does, he can't turn that one into a success. So he'll ignore it and concentrate on the new jobs he gets that morning. It'll drift on into oblivion or wait until work is slack enough for the guys to get some extra time to fix it."

"And the likelihood of slack time ever coming along is fairly remote," Bob added.

"Exactly. The fault repair deadline is not a system for achieving ninety percent success, it's a system for guaranteeing at least ten percent failure, probably much more."

Simon was right, Bob realised. He'd seen the same thing yesterday. Froggy Thomson had told him as much – though at the time he hadn't taken much notice. You had to hand it to Arthur Dee. He was right when he said selective deafness was rife.

Simon held up the small, green plant. "The difference between Patterson's Curse and Salvation Jane."

Chapter 21

Down and out in Adelaide Hills

Bob sat at the desk in his makeshift office. It had somehow become too personal, he thought. He was involved to an extent where he was finding it difficult to muster civility any more. His conversation with Simon that morning had shown him as much. He'd jumped down the young man's throat, boots and all, before Simon had even had a chance to say he understood what Bob was on about. The more he rummaged about in Comlink, trying to convince the organisation to take a look at the way it was operating, the more people he found with the expertise and commitment he was looking for. People wanted to help. And he was driving them away.

Bob looked down at the material Simon had given him and which he'd gathered from Froggy, Fred and others in the region. Systems and processes. A month ago, it had meant nothing to him. Now he was expecting everyone he came in contact with to see and understand his concerns.

Simon's information had highlighted the problem of imposing targets which were beyond the control of those intended to meet them. His assistance, together with that of Morrie Levant and others, had convinced Bob that it was useless to set goals based on a comparison of numerical quotas.

Yet it was important for managers to know how their business was performing. There still had to be some method of measuring the systems by which Comlink staff worked. Once a system had been mapped, its output – what it produced – could be measured. But if a Comlink manager was to make sense of that measurement, they needed to have a benchmark, something to compare it with.

Bob speculated on Arthur Dee's theory that successful improvements could only be achieved when the system itself was being 'managed' properly, and that the primary way to do this was to control the amount of variation it exhibited.

"Everything has a degree of variation," the ebullient statistician had explained. "Fingerprints, snowflakes, animals, people, the weather. Variation is built into our universe at a molecular level. Every process, every organism displays variation in the way it operates.

"Yet when humans get together in a manufacturing or service organisation, they set up – for some absurd reason – rules demanding absolute performance from everybody on every occasion.

"You've seen it with the 'fault repair' target. The way Comlink repairs faults is not aimed at actually fixing the faults or serving our customers. No way! The objective of fault repair is to get the faults out of the measurement system. If you can't see them, they aren't there!"

It was true, Bob reflected, as he looked at the range of figures on his desk. Week after week Comlink techs were turning in figures which showed they were reaching their targets. Common sense said they simply couldn't achieve such a consistent result. There had to be good weeks and bad weeks. Yet they rarely appeared on the books. The reason, Bob felt, was that those who supplied the figures and performed the repairs were forced to falsify their results. Froggy did it by performing a quick fix. Bob's own father had done it by ignoring the extra bit of work which would really have cleared a fault. Had this been happening for decades?

The phone on Bob's desk rang. It was Clifford Tate, the Services Director.

"Bob, I'm glad I found you. I've just had a call from Darren Heyden. He's worried about what you're doing there."

Something dissolved in the pit of Bob's stomach. "What's the problem, Clifford?" he asked, as ingenuously as possible.

"I don't like to interfere in these things, but I was under the impression you were working *with* Darren on the MID project," Clifford replied, in a manner designed to indicate that he was aesthetically offended by this call and expected Bob to clear the whole thing up for him as quickly as possible. "Darren tells me you've asked the MID survey team in the region to keep out of your way."

"I think their activity here at the moment would be counterproductive," Bob explained. "We're putting together a project which I hope will give us a new perspective on the way we manage and maintain our products."

The Prelude

"And will this project significantly affect the outcome of MID?" enquired Clifford cautiously, like a man who knew he was not going to like what he heard.

"I think so. That's why Darren's nose is out of joint. I think the MID survey teams are looking at the wrong things. They're just aiming to transfer existing paper systems to computer. Those systems will perpetuate errors and waste. To institutionalise them is an act of criminal neglect when we've got the chance to do something to rectify them."

There was a long pause. "I begin to understand Darren's concern," Clifford replied finally. "This project has been on the drawing board for three years, Bob. What on earth do you think you're doing by suggesting it's on entirely the wrong track? You're supposed to be in charge of the project's management. What the hell have you been doing for the past three years that you didn't say something before?"

"It hasn't been that simple...." Bob began, but Clifford cut him off.

"On top of all this, I've been getting reports from Anne Blanchard that she's knee-deep in some sort of employee participation program in Newcastle. Again, under your direction. What's going on?"

"It's not an employee participation program, Clifford, although God knows we could use some around here. It's a program to improve the efficiency of OFCAB. We're way behind target and I want to bring it up to speed. We're doing the same sort of thing here: mapping the processes, measuring their capability, checking whether what we're demanding of people is possible or if we're just picking figures out of the air at random."

"The view I hear is that OFCAB has almost come to a standstill twice in the last month through industrial action," Clifford said tersely.

"That's only indirectly the issue. We've started to get results that show up how much potential there is for improvement."

"I'm not interested in that. The reason I've rung you is not Darren's complaint, or any one thing, but a combination of factors which are proving disruptive in a number of areas. We've got to concentrate our energies on the projects in hand, not go gallivanting off in search of the holy grail. OFCAB, MID and the Dick Tracy Watch are our main priorities. The Watch particularly. We don't have the leisure or spare resources for diversions."

"Clifford, there are important things emerging from this work. It's just the tip of an iceberg which reaches down deep into Comlink. Albert has given me the go-ahead to conduct this experiment, and I feel the preliminary results are encouraging." Bob was having trouble keeping his temper. It seemed there was no shortage of people who didn't want to hear about ways of improving the quality of Comlink's service.

"Well if Albert has given you the go-ahead, I'm wasting my time speaking to you. I'll talk directly to him. I know you are doing your best, Bob, as you see it. But all you're achieving is dissent and disruption. I intend to stop it." Clifford finished sharply.

Bob sat silently for a long time, knocking his knuckles dispiritedly on the top of his desk. What was the use? he thought. He had the theory and some useful practical tools which could help managers take back control of their organisation. But what could you hope to achieve if no-one wanted to listen?

Chapter 22
One-trick pony

"In short, it hasn't been a good week," said Bob, squirming comfortably into the soft depths of his pillow.

Janice Cheshire looked at her husband sympathetically. She wondered why he tried so hard sometimes. The boy radical she had met in England in 1976 was still there, she thought, but only just. He hid in the quiet moments of Bob's life, when it was possible to be different, to be individual. Those moments seemed to be more and more rare.

Wriggling her arm around Bob's bare shoulder, Janice allowed her fingertips to trace the line of a long, thin scar, the legacy of a motorbike accident which had broken his shoulder in days when bodies could be expected to take abuse and then to repair and thrive.

She felt tired herself sometimes, tired enough to want no more.

"Even Don's upset with me," Bob was saying. "He'll probably never fix my coffee machine again.

"I tried to tell him that we could make our deadlines with the Watch by looking at where there was waste and re-work in the processes we used."

"And what did he say?" Janice asked, curling down closer to Bob in the bed.

"He wouldn't accept it. I'm afraid I didn't handle it very well. I've been very touchy these past few days, I don't know what's wrong....

"I'm worried we're not going to make it, Janice. This product has to work. It has to."

Janice held him tighter, running her hand through his hair. Bob turned towards her, lifting his lips to hers, feeling the warmth of her caress.

"He said he'd never give another idea to this company."

"Uncle Don said that?" Janice enquired, nibbling at his ear enticingly.
"Yep. And that we could whistle for his tree."
"I've missed something in the conversation."
Bob shrugged, "Something he's working on. I don't know."

Her closeness was beginning to affect him. Bob swung his arms around Janice's lithe body, stroking her back. Her slimness, her strength, never ceased to delight him, and now he felt the same sensations she could always awake in him. Bob kissed his wife deeply, pulling her close to him. As if for the first time, his hands explored the long, gentle curves of her back and thighs. Janice's breath mingled with his, her body vibrating with pleasure as she pressed against him.

"You're such a very beautiful woman," he whispered softly, his lips brushing against her ear.

"All talk," she said defiantly, "let's have some action."

They made love long and gently, he feeling comfort and strength from her nearness, she stretching herself, giving wholly in an attempt to take away the uncertainty she could sense.

* * * * *

The first thing he became aware of was the scent of the wind: the bright, cold smell that is a rumour of summer storms.

His body tingled from the small droplets of rain flung by the wind.

He was on a hillside, standing naked in a field of oat grass which sheathed his lower legs, wrapping around his calves and twining through his toes like a bed of snakes.

Further up the slope, he could distinguish the velvet crest of the hill, contrasting sharply with the darkening sky. Along the rim of the hill the curling snakes of grass rippled, stretching upwards. He knew that somewhere to his left was a tree, a huge sprawling tree, a magnificent tree borne out of dreaming legends.

As he turned towards it, the strength of the wind increased and the rain began to drive into his slitted eyes with a new fury.

It was a baobab tree: tall, grotesquely bloated, distended with water hoarded for the dry months. Its smooth limbs struck out in wide arcs,

The Prelude

radiating from the head of the tree like a crown. A crown of thorns, he felt, shuddering for the first time as he felt the grass caressing his limbs.

Suddenly, it became important for him to walk to the tree, to touch it, feel the roughness and smoothness of its bark, press his ears against its hide and stand barefoot on the mound of pebbly detritus surrounding its bole.

The storm lashed the grass, tearing at his body as he strode up the slope. He found the going harder as he neared the tree. The grass seemed thicker, able to coil more readily around his ankles, to slide between his toes and curl about his feet, dragging over his cold flesh like tiny whips.

The tree loomed larger, twisting and groaning in the ferocious storm. He was barely fifty metres distant when finally the grass stopped him, curling into a tight, knotted ball around his feet. He struggled against it, only to find its grip increasing, its thin, insistent blades growing through his flesh, sliding noiselessly, irresistibly beneath his skin, rooting him forever to the soil.

The grass dragged him to his knees, wrapping further around and through his body, searching the thin veins and rich arteries of his legs. Above him, the huge baobab tree still writhed beneath the lashing storm, twisting and squirming with the cunning of bitter experience.

Then the lightning struck. A devastating bolt split the sky, crashing into the crown of the tree, bursting the head and blasting limbs in all directions.

It took him a moment to realise that one of the broken limbs was cartwheeling towards him. He stared upward, unable to look away as it loomed closer, blotting out the burning baobab tree, the sky, the wind and the rain.

He struggled with the grass, trying to tear at it with his fingers, only to find his hands entwined, leaving him tethered like an animal for slaughter.

The limb was turning end over end, stretching to caress him, to strike him down. He looked up at it and finally found the voice he needed. He screamed. He screamed.

And woke trembling, to find Janice's arms wrapped tightly around him, her warm, soft body pressed to his. "It's alright, it's alright," she repeated, as she stroked him soothingly.

* * * * *

It was a somewhat hollow-eyed Bob Cheshire who walked through the showground gates several hours later.

Despite his endeavours, Bob was unable to rid himself of the growing oppression he had been feeling for the past couple of days, or to release his mind from the pressure of work. The sheer volume of activity he had set in motion was beginning to wear him down. In all of the projects he had been working with, particularly the one in the Adelaide Hills, they were starting to see some results, some patterns emerging. But Bob could not find encouragement even in this. There was a cost to over-reaction as well as under-reaction.

"Come on, Dad," Emma said, dragging him by the cuff of his sweatshirt.

"Okay, where to first?" he asked, trying to generate some cheerfulness in his voice.

There were crowds of people all around the shallow dirt and grass bowl of the showgrounds. Bob looked over to where a group of decidedly horsey-looking folk were gathered around a roped-off rectangle near the centre arena. Inside, a number of prim, black-helmeted, black-jacketed types were prancing around on highly strung thoroughbreds.

Emma caught his gaze and scowled.

"No way, Dad. They're dressage poons. Up themselves. Vert!" she said with eloquent disgust.

Bob blinked uncertainly, "Emma, don't say that."

She grinned at him with the exasperation of youth.

"Come on. There are the pony clubs."

Bob allowed himself to be dragged around with an attempt at good humour. It wasn't Emma's fault he had nightmares. Anyway, one thing had been cleared up that morning. The matter of the pony purchase was now a reality, although Bob had been ridiculed soundly for his old-fashioned notion that a problem existed about where the thing was to be stabled. Things had obviously changed since he was a boy in the Queensland bush. For a start, people didn't *buy* ponies any more. They bought *shares* in a pony already stabled at one of the specialist, semi-rural agistment properties within 'easy reach' of Melbourne. These Emma depicted as a sort of comfortable hotel for horses. They provided all the benefits of not having to spend your days taking care of the beast instead of riding it.

The Prelude

No, horse time-sharing was the go. For a small – *small*, Emma had emphasised – fee, you were guaranteed a certain time to see your pony. You could ride it, pet it or do whatever else you wanted. The time access simply depended on the number of shares you wanted to buy.

The concept horrified Bob. Horses were dirty, obstreperous hay-burners, but it offended his sense of pioneering to find that the past had drifted away so irrevocably and nowadays horsing was as sanitary, as easy, and possibly no more demanding than a rugged game of Monopoly.

Emma ran ahead, in amongst the stands of pony clubs and agistment 'horsetels'. The choice was wide and they spent the next hour collecting brochures and watching 3-D videos. At the end of that time, Bob found himself lying back on a bare patch of grass surrounded by colour glossies, posters and promises. The number of potential horsetels had been whittled down to about twenty when Emma spied one of her school friends on the same mission as herself.

"Becky!" she yelled, jumping up and racing over to where a skinny, non-descript girl with a Prince Valiant haircut was towing a blank-faced father around the display compound. Bob wondered if he wore the same dazed expression as Becky's parent.

After a couple of minutes Emma was back. "Becky says Fiona's here with her mum," she declared breathlessly. "Can we go find her?"

"Sure. The three of you can grab a bite to eat and compare notes on your respective campaigns. I'll meet you back here in an hour, OK?"

Emma nodded vigorously, her ponytail dancing around the sides of her face.

"Have you got any money?" Bob asked pointlessly, dipping his hand into his pocket as he spoke.

Emma pecked her father on the cheek. Taking the proffered card, she raced off to rejoin Becky. As they disappeared into the crowd in search of the missing Fiona, Bob waved sympathetically to Becky's father, quite able to understand the dispirited flutter of the man's hand in return. Picking up the scattered publications, Bob tucked them firmly out of sight under one arm and moved off through the crowd, enjoying the sensation of being alone for a change. After some meandering, he found himself at the edge of the dressage arena and paused to observe the activities which had invoked his daughter's scorn.

As Bob watched the dressage competitors, he slowly became absorbed by the unexpected beauty and strength of their performances. It was as if horse and rider became one personality in the ring, a blend of two bodies into one will. A peaceful feeling began to creep over Bob, only to be rudely shattered by a gruff, Scottish voice booming in his ear. Bob turned to see John McDermott's wide, pink face grinning at him.

"What brings you here?" demanded John jovially.

"I was hoping to get away from work for a while, but it looks like that's forbidden at the moment!" Bob joked. "What about you? Don't tell me they've let you loose from the Ops Directorate for a few hours?"

"Not much point being the boss if you can't sneak away for a while," John replied. "Besides, it's the weekend, you know. Comlink can look after itself for a couple of days. I'm here to see my niece, Pip. She's up next, the last competitor."

Bob nodded.

"Fascinating contest, this," John said enthusiastically. "Hard work. You wouldn't believe the effort young Pip puts into it. Spends hours working on that horse, teaching him small improvements, correcting the way he moves. Comportment's a lost art in our heathen world!"

Despite the self-deprecating tone he adopted, it was clear John McDermott took a great deal of pride in his niece's skills.

"I don't suppose you had a hand in her teaching?" Bob asked.

Pip's uncle nodded shyly once before bursting out with a hearty laugh. "That obvious, is it? Yes, I started with her about seven years ago. She's way beyond my scope now. You'll see."

As they spoke, a tall, glossy horse stepped into the arena bearing a slim, erect girl in her late teens. Bob watched, entranced, as the chestnut gelding glided around the arena, moving freely and willingly, without haste or disturbance. Pip McDermott, her slender form impeccably balanced, seemed to flow with the movements of the horse. She sat quietly as they performed a series of turns, half-pirouettes and collected movements, flowing from one movement to the next with supple control.

It was over too soon for both men. Horse and rider paused for a moment in the centre of the arena, a single, balanced entity, then headed gracefully to the edge of the ring.

It had been an exhibition of harmony and skill. Bob was reminded of a small Japanese poem left over in his brain from college. A haiku. An ancient, simplistic, disciplined style of writing which attempted to distil meaning into short, manicured lines.

The Prelude

> *Is it the bell that rings?*
> *Is it the hammer that rings?*
> *Or is it the meeting of the two that rings?*

"It's a lovely sport, don't you think?" John beamed proudly. "Will you be buying Emma a share in a pony?"

Bob looked around, blinking vaguely.

"Will you be buying Emma a share in a pony?" John repeated.

"Oh, I expect so. Yes, I think so."

John put his hand on his friend's sleeve. "You don't sound very definite."

Bob shook his head, "Sorry, John, I wasn't with you – I didn't get much sleep last night. Yes, yes, we'll get her some time with one."

"You ought to take it a bit easier, mate. You've been working up a storm recently, from what I hear. There's no need to go so fast. You've got time to relax."

"No, I don't think I have, John. The work we're doing in Adelaide is starting to pay dividends. We've identified major amounts of wasted effort and resources which were resulting in huge volumes of re-work. And Alan's doing really well, too."

"Don't tell me about Alan," the other said gruffly, "you might be doing OK with plenty of things, but that's not one of them."

"He's alright, he's just learning," Bob grinned. "The earlier difficulties are starting to sort themselves out now."

"Well, I wish he'd learn somewhere else. He doesn't realise the effect of what he's doing. It's all very well to be changing things on the OFCAB project, but what am I going to do when the project's over and those blokes are moved back into their old jobs? Already there are rumours going around."

"But the gains we can make are huge," Bob began, only to fall silent as he saw John shaking his head, smiling sadly.

"There are operation-wide realities, my friend. If you start radically changing things in one area, you might have to do it in another."

"What's wrong with that?"

"Well, if you had something that would make a difference....but all I'm hearing is that you've got blokes running around making graphs and charts, asking a lot of silly questions. That's not like the Bob Cheshire I know."

"It will make a difference," Bob persisted. "We can really improve the quality of the work we do in Comlink. All we have to do is look at what we do, measure the capability of our processes, then find ways of improving them."

"You've gone soft in the head," John laughed, "we *know* what we've got to do. I can appreciate we need to develop the way we talk with people, and how we involve people in the work. But all this graphing and charting, come on! These are experienced men. They know how to do their jobs."

"That's just the point, people in Comlink *don't* know what their jobs are any more. We've got to get back in control of the systems we use to run the place. They're running away."

"And how are you going to do that? The main effect I've seen seems to be even less certainty about what people are supposed to do."

"That's because we don't have the support we need from the top. You included," snapped Bob, more sharply than he'd intended.

"I stand accused," said his companion, opening his arms wide. "All I'm saying, Bob, is that you should take things a bit easier. People are saying you're becoming obsessed with all of this."

"It's worth it. I thought you of all people would be able to see that. Or don't you care what happens to us?"

Bob was sorry as soon as he said it. John McDermott was not only his friend, he was also genuinely concerned about the future of Comlink and the people who worked for it.

John held up his hand in a conciliatory gesture. "OK, Bob. Have it your way. I just wouldn't be surprised if this thing blows up in your face. Don't say I didn't warn you."

They faced each other uncertainly, as if suddenly, after so many years, they had nothing to say.

Finally, John cleared his throat. "Come on. Let's not talk about work any more. Why don't you come over and meet Pip?"

"Maybe next time," Bob said flatly, "I have to find Emma."

Chapter 23
Flight 479

Anne Blanchard stood in the executive lounge at Sydney Airport, gazing out over the flat expanses of its runways and aprons. Ink-black clouds hung threateningly over the city and pencil-thin streaks of lightning flashed out to the west, where the new Badgery's Creek airport had already been closed by the approaching storm.

Anne looked at her watch, hoping her flight would get away before the rain set in. It was already late on Monday afternoon and the small commuter plane she had taken from Newcastle had been battered by powerful winds. She did not relish the same again.

Perhaps she should have gone back to Melbourne on Friday. She could have arranged it – after all, it would be a pain to be stuck here for the night. But no, the weekend had been worth it. The project was well in hand and they were beginning to make up lost ground. A new, lively spirit was puttering around the corridors of the OFCAB offices, as managers began to feel more secure, more confident in their ability to manage their programs rather than simply respond to various crisis pressures, as they had so far been doing.

But that hadn't been her only achievement over the past week. Anne smiled to herself, strolling away from the window to settle in an easy chair. She'd see him again in two weeks time. That was good. They'd have the interim to figure out where they stood, and where they were going. She didn't know at the moment. And for once she didn't care.

Anne lounged back to await her flight, extracting the personalised headphones from the arm-rest of her chair. She flicked through to the 'Electric Eighties'. It was an old song, light-hearted, self-mocking:–

*I took off for a weekend last month
just to try and recall the whole year.
All of the faces and all of the places
wondering where they all disappear?*

*I didn't ponder the question too long,
I was hungry and went out for a bite.
Ran into a chum with a bottle of rum
and we wound up drinking all night.*

*It's those changes in latitudes,
changes in attitudes.
Nothing remains quite the same.
With all of our running and all of our cunning
If we didn't laugh we would all go insane.*

"Hello, Anne," a high female voice intruded through the music.

Anne opened her eyes to see a small, be-spectacled woman in her late fifties with a large carry bag and a hefty briefcase clutched to her side. Anne wondered idly whether these bulky items would pass muster as cabin baggage. Probably not, she decided. She peered at the woman, trying to fit the face to a name and a set of experiences.

"Hello Olive," she said after a few seconds, smiling at the CAWPS representative.

CAWPS – the Council Against Wasted Public Spending – was a vocal interest group, heavily involved in the continuing debate about expenditure of public funds by government and semi-government bodies. At times, its activities extended to cover organisations such as Comlink which were now independent of their public service past. In the aftermath of Wally Jamieson's death, CAWPS had publicly questioned the value of OFCAB, but with little result. The locals of Newcastle were genuinely interested in any project which was going to put their city back on the map.

Olive Wetherby was a senior regional co-ordinator for CAWPS. Notwithstanding her dedication to the tenacious style of local politics, she was known to Anne as an honest dissenter rather than an opportunist.

Anne removed her headphones and shook the other woman's hand. "Heading to Melbourne, too?" she enquired.

The Prelude

Olive Wetherby nodded. "If we get off the ground tonight."

"At least we'll be delayed by natural forces. I won't have to negotiate a position between the parties," Anne joked, as the crumpled, older woman eased into a chair next to her.

"Forces – yes. Natural? No. A storm we're responsible for."

It was true, Anne thought. The effects of Greenhouse had become too much of a problem to simply ignore. Now, when it had finally become obvious that the problem was real, that something should be done, consensus positively oozed out of the woodwork. But it was years too late.

Anne looked out the window. The heavy, black clouds were swinging closer now. Low to the west, in the narrow band between the lightning storm and the mountains, a final slash of orange sun spread in a wedge across the city. Smiling at Olive, the formalities over, Anne closed her eyes again and settled back once more. She was glad to be on her way home.

* * * * *

Flight 479 from Perth, due into Sydney's new Badgery's Creek airport at 4.20 pm, was approaching its destination. Captain Harris cursed as the obtuse ground-radar operator confirmed that the airport, not yet fully operational, was still closed by the storm now raging over most of the city area. His crew began the necessary procedures and the jet altered course, heading for the alternative Sydney airport at Mascot.

Thick, dark clouds shouldered the plane and a spiderweb of light criss-crossed the sky, narrowing visibility to a couple of thousand metres. Despite this, the storm was not something Captain Harris was especially concerned with. It was an inconvenience, a hazard, but hardly a danger.

As the plane began its approach into Sydney Airport, a white charge of lightning crashed across the nose of the jet. The bolt splattered across the front of the plane, creating a corona of eerie blue light that hummed around the cockpit. In a fraction of a second, it curved through the metal fuselage and was directed away to the wings, which were designed to dissipate it harmlessly into the atmosphere.

But the charge ignored the hopes of yesteryear's designers. The jet had been built almost thirty years ago, when Greenhouse storms had been the ravings of misguided ecologists. A strike of such magnitude was not within the bounds of the original manufacturer's imagination. The special 'leak circuit' built into the plane's electrics and its paint and metal surfaces, treated to leach the charge away from the fuselage slowly, could not cope. The massive bolt of lightning speared through the plane, tearing away half the wing as it exited.

The disabled jet was thrown into an erratic dive through the sky. It slewed away from its flight path, flattening into a southward trajectory as Captain Harris struggled to control its wild descent. Visibility was less than two kilometres; no more than twenty seconds. With the surrounding air space crammed with traffic and his plane's radio useless from the electromagnetic disturbance around it, all Captain Harris could hope for was that no aircraft were heading south at that moment.

The crew and passengers of Flight 479 never saw the Melbourne-bound jet plane looming up on their left. With all communication down in the immediate area, neither pilot was aware they were on a collision course. As the two planes converged in the poor light, the already-broken wing of Flight 479 crashed into the side of the on-coming jet, tearing a huge gap in its fuselage and splitting the thin aluminium tube in half.

Flight 479 spun away through the gloom, plummeting from the sky. It burst like rotten fruit across the Southern Freeway, spewing burning fuel across the eight-lane motorway in a wall of destruction which engulfed hundreds of cars crammed bumper to bumper in the peak-hour traffic. The Melbourne-bound plane broke up in the air, raining out of the sky and splattering obscenely across the outer suburbs in a wide arc, its main body coming down in a large housing development just north of Liverpool.

If it suddenly ended tomorrow,
I could somehow adjust to the fall.
Good times and riches, and son of a bitches.
I've seen more than I can recall.

With these changes in latitudes,
changes in attitudes.
Nothing remains quite the same.
Through all of the islands
and all of the highlands
If we didn't laugh we would all go insane.
If we weren't all crazy, we would all go insane.

Chapter 24
Waiting

There are those rumours which have to be true: by their strangeness, their unexpectedness, and the overwhelming strength of their presence. True rumours are instant, appearing with shocking, hasteful indecency. Several million people knew of the collision between Flights 479 and 24 within moments of its occurrence.

Bob was in his office, catching up on some of the tasks which seemed to have reproduced themselves while he was in Adelaide, when he received an urgent message from Albert's secretary. He made his way hurriedly to the twenty-fourth floor, where Clifford Tate and John McDermott were already present. Norm Sanders, the head of Network Operations, and Mark Rowlands, the Business Division Manager arrived shortly after.

Albert spoke briefly. "Whatever you're on at the moment, I want you to forget it. John will fill you in. I'm on to Network Monitoring now; I'll be with you in a moment." He turned his attention back to the phone call he had been engrossed in when they entered the room.

John McDermott gave the others the news in short, sharp sentences.

"About thirty minutes ago two commercial flights went down in the southern suburbs of Sydney. Not much known yet. Mid-air collision. A lot of dead. Ground casualties will probably be large. For the next few hours the network is going to be at bursting point."

Mark Rowlands spoke up. "Right about now, the major computer down-loading activities are happening between Sydney and Melbourne. That takes up to twenty percent of available circuits for about two hours every day."

"Well get on to your people and tell them to shut down the transfers," John McDermott snapped. "Upwards of ten million people will be trying to ring their relatives in Sydney in the next couple of hours."

"But if we cut the lines during transmission a lot of data might be lost. Some of the Financials' equipment might be damaged too. We've got a damages contract."

"I don't give a damn, do it!"

John McDermott turned his attention to the head of Network operations.

"Norm, you'd better get over to the Operations Monitoring Centre. Tony Fields will be having a nervous breakdown. Albert's on to him now. You'd better wait 'til he's finished."

The engineer moved to one of the office phones to order a car.

Albert finished his call. "Network Monitoring is into red already. Tony's got them organising the other shift to come in early – if they can be contacted. I think you'd better be with him, Norm. He could use your experience."

Norm Sanders nodded. "We're down on console operators already – you know the absenteeism level we've got."

"Well, do your best. Pull staff in from wherever you can get them. A lot of faults are going to start showing up when the system becomes overloaded."

Albert felt cool and in control. The organisation had a comprehensive plan in place for a variety of disaster scenarios. The demands on the network over the next twenty-four hours would be enormous, but he was confident it would hold together.

"What can you do about the Public Assistance Numbers, Clifford? When people can't get through to Sydney, they're going to start ringing PAN to find out what's wrong. It'll put a lot more traffic into the system."

"I'll get extra shifts into all the PAN Centres straight away. Our local Area Co-ordinators can work with Network Monitoring to channel inquiry traffic away from Sydney. We should get up to hundred percent operation within an hour," Clifford said crisply, moving towards a nearby phone.

"Bob–" Albert began, but was interrupted by the entry of his personal assistant, John Hunter.

"Walter Minogue on two."

They all fell silent. Albert picked up the phone and began to speak with the Sydney Regional Manager.

The Prelude

John Hunter walked over to the television in a corner of the room. Keeping the sound low, he flicked across a number of channels, pausing at a newsbreak. "The first pictures are coming through."

The footage, taken from a helicopter circling the crash site on the Southern Freeway, was graphic. A stretch of the freeway, perhaps a kilometre in length, was strewn with twisted, indefinable shapes which must have been cars, buses, trucks or pieces of the destroyed airliner. It was impossible to tell. Much of the heaped-up metal was still burning, the flames rich and red. Palls of smoke hung above the shattered expanse of debris and bodies. It was still raining heavily and the whole scene shone with a dark, wet slickness that seemed to blend metal, plastic, flesh and blood into a thick, grey paste.

As the managers gazed at the scene of absolute destruction, the telecast cut to the station studio, where a pale young woman was reading a bulletin.

"These exclusive shots from our Channel Eight Eye reveal the tragic disaster which struck Sydney a short time ago. Details at this stage are sketchy, but we do know that two commercial planes, one incoming from Perth, the other southbound to Melbourne, collided in the skies over southern Sydney approximately forty minutes ago. At this point, there appear to be no survivors from either plane."

The newscaster's eyes flickered to a point off-camera. She turned back to her audience.

"We'll take you now to the second crash site, near suburban Liverpool, where police and rescuers have already begun the heart-breaking task of sifting through the remains of the wreckage."

The announcer's well-modulated tones were replaced by a shaky, male voice, broadcasting from a second helicopter.

"All that's left of four suburban blocks is about a dozen houses untouched. I'd guess maybe fifty homes have been shattered, walls pushed in by lumps of aircraft debris, roofs caved in. Thank God there's no fire....Thank God? It's more like the devil's playground down there. Rubbish, scrap, people. I can see....Oh, God....the ambulances can't even get through....You don't need me....Let's get this thing down there, Barry, and do something."

The commentator was right. Words were unnecessary. The images spoke for themselves as the restless camera panned across the suburb, flitting from one gruesome image to the next. Dispassionately, it focused on a small child squatting in the gutter. The child's hand was resting on a rain-soaked sheet, stroking the contours beneath it.

Huge sections of the plane had hit the ground, sliding through houses, trees, anything in their path, carving ugly swathes through people's lives. The ambulance and emergency workers who had made it into the area were working feverishly. One ambulance officer stood in a circle of rain-spattered body bags; they lay at his feet like bloated cocoons.

Albert put down the phone and stared at the screen in fascinated horror. Finally, he gathered himself. "It's going to be worse than we could've imagined. Walter is already inundated with breakdowns. The combination of system overload and the storm in Sydney is playing havoc with the network. In some areas, lightning's causing disturbance to the microwave circuitry. Our back-up systems have cut-in, but Walter says he's got no idea what's going to happen next.

"Jesus...it's awful," he said, staring at the screen.

* * * * *

Half an hour later, Bob was on the phone to Janice. Once the first shock of disbelief had dissipated, almost everyone's thoughts had turned to their personal problems. Most people had a relative in Sydney, many of them living on the south side. Darren Heyden, for one, had an estranged wife and two young sons living in the suburb where flight 24 had come down. So far, he had been unable to contact them.

Bob was trying to quiet Janice's concerns for her sister, Linda, who lived with her husband and children in a suburb near Liverpool, barely three kilometres from the second crash site. Bob could not give her any information or any assistance. "Just keep trying, darling. Everyone's wanting to get through right now. There's nothing you can do except keep trying."

"When will you be back? I'm so worried, Bob," Janice asked, clearly as shocked as he by the disaster.

"I don't know. I've got no idea what's going to happen in the next few hours."

He rang off and tried once more to get through to Newcastle. He wanted to put Alan's staff on stand-by in case they needed to shift some resources to Sydney on short notice. By some miracle, he managed to get a line through, uttering a prayer of thanks for the extended ISDN network which facilitated calls to other Comlink regions.

The Prelude

"Alan. It's Bob Cheshire. What's going on up there."

Alan Dodgson's voice sounded brittle over the line. "It's unbelievable," he said simply.

"I know. Look, how are you situated for labour resources? If we need to get some technical and lines support for Walter Minogue, can you do it?"

"Yes, I guess so."

The flat note in Alan's voice rang an alarm bell in Bob's head.

"Alan, is everything alright there? Have you got relatives in Sydney or something?"

There was a long silence on the other end of the phone.

"Anne Blanchard left here about three this afternoon," Alan said finally. "She was on the way back to Melbourne. On Flight 24," he said in a remote voice. "She's dead, Bob. Anne's dead."

Both men held on in silence, saying nothing.

After some moments Bob said softly, "Are you sure she was on the plane? She might have missed it, taken another. Anything."

He could almost feel Alan shaking his head as he began to cry quietly.

Chapter 25
The ties that bind

The network began to fall apart about seven o'clock.

In an unmarked city building, Clifford Tate stood behind the glass wall of the observer's room, looking into the Network Monitoring Centre. Several dozen Comlink technicians were seated at consoles arranged in a sweeping arc. The room functioned like a NASA Mission Control Centre, providing an instant computer analysis of any point in the Comlink network.

In the centre of the wall opposite the technicians was a large computer-generated map of Australia. Large cities were highlighted on it by yellow dots. Between the cities, lines ran across the map showing the network links between various population centres. In ordinary circumstances these lines shone green. But when the traffic became busy in certain areas, the relevant lines would glow a warm yellow. In peak times, such as a Monday morning on the eastern seaboard, some of the lines turned an angry red, denoting significant overload. In addition to the screen of Australia, there were a number of smaller projections detailing sub-systems such as the Melbourne and Sydney metropolitan networks.

The function of the technicians in the Monitoring Centre was to direct the flow of traffic through the system. When business trading started between Melbourne and Sydney around nine each morning, the lines would usually become congested. When this happened, some of the traffic would be switched through the network in the opposite direction. The effect of this was that callers in Melbourne who were trying to ring Sydney might have their call directed through a circuit in Adelaide or even Perth, where the three hour time difference meant that most people had not yet started their morning

169

The Prelude

calls. The person in Melbourne never knew their call had been on a six thousand kilometre journey. Call re-direction was simple and effective. Once the network infrastructure existed, the cost of operating it was not the major consideration.

Clifford stared at the central screen. The inter-connecting web of lines shone with a sullen, red glow. The sub-screens showed the same: a clogged, over-loaded lattice of almost inoperative lines. To make matters worse, in the past half-hour the lines themselves had begun to drop out. On the sub-screen representing Sydney's network status, a large black spot covered the crash sites. Lines of black radiated out from them in a thin web.

The black lines meant complete area systems not functioning. Dead. They had expected to see a certain number of inoperative lines in the crash areas, but for some inexplicable reason the lines were wandering away from the site, still stretching and growing long after the event. Even as Clifford watched, another section of red went down, to be replaced by a black streak. It was a section linked to one of the medium-sized exchanges. The failure would put extra pressure on the remaining lines, increasing the likelihood of a snow-balling failure.

And no-one knew why.

"They want you back upstairs, Mr Tate, at PAN."

Clifford nodded. He rubbed his eyes wearily as he looked at the array of projected maps. God, he'd known it would be hectic, but no-one had expected so many malfunctions, so many system failures in back-up equipment. What on earth was wrong?

And Anne.

Clifford realised that for many years he had cultivated an aloof image, and that now he was a victim of that image. No-one spoke words of sympathy and loss to him, and he could not bring himself to say the words to anyone else. No-one assumed for a moment that he would be affected. He was Clifford Tate, calm, controlled and dispassionate. But Anne had been his senior personnel manager. They had worked closely together for a number of years, each respecting the other's skills and abilities. It didn't make sense that she wasn't here now, throwing her weight into the battle to control what was about to become a major technical – and social – problem.

Clifford reflected grimly on the effect a failure of the Comlink system would generate. At present the nation was stunned. But after the shock would come the anger and outrage. You couldn't blame a storm. You couldn't blame

The ties that bind

a dead pilot. But if the communication system failed, you could blame that. Despite its enormous complexity, the telecommunications system came down to a very simple issue: when you picked up that handset, it either worked or it didn't. There were no excuses. And no shortage of people were waiting for Comlink to fail.

Clifford watched as another tendril of black appeared on the screen. Turning away, he headed up to the PAN room.

* * * * *

The Public Assistance Number room was in chaos: the noise of alarms, section leaders running to boards with lists of people available, operators calling across the room to supervisors, all blended into a frenetic, disordered tapestry. Above it all, the Status Board whined loudly.

Nearly a hundred telephone operators were frantically answering public enquiries. The operators, mostly women, were seated in clusters of four, facing inwards around oddly-designed work stations.

Like so many four-leaf clovers, Clifford thought, narrowing his eyes to avoid the harsh overhead lighting. Only there was nothing lucky about it.

Maggie Campbell, the PAN manager, stood next to Clifford. She held out a sheaf of papers to him.

"We're almost up to full strength. I've doubled the supervisors and we've got a commitment from most of the people here to stay as long as necessary."

"We'll probably need them the whole night," Clifford said, taking the list of meaningless names. It never ceased to amaze him how Comlink people committed themselves to help in a crisis. Calls for overtime and allowances would come later. Right now, the immediate concern was to maintain the network integrity.

"What about the other centres?"

Maggie Campbell directed his attention to an electronic map showing the various PAN facilities around Australia. Many of the centres were in country locations. In these days of electronic 'phone books', it was irrelevant whether the operator who answered public enquiries worked in Brisbane, Wagga Wagga or Canberra. They all had access to the same databases.

The Prelude

"The country localities have worked out well," Maggie explained. "Many of the people live close, so we've been able to pull them in quickly. Normally, they shut down at midnight. But not tonight."

Clifford nodded. The pressure on the network was intense, and conditions in the central PAN room were becoming increasingly stressed.

Under ordinary conditions, an enquiry call would come into the switchboard on a common circuit and be answered by one of the operators. If the caller was kept waiting for more than ten seconds, a buzzer would ring and the unanswered call would appear on the Status Board. If a call went unanswered for thirty seconds, another, sharper, tone would ring insistently until it was answered. The Status Board showed almost a thousand backed-up calls waiting to be answered. The number had been climbing steadily for the past hour and showed no sign of abating. Many more callers had given up waiting and dropped off the queue.

The lines to Sydney were jammed with people attempting to contact relatives and friends. When a caller had tried to ring Sydney continually but could not get through, the chances were they would ring PAN. When this happened, their call remained on the larger network. Multiplied by tens of thousands, the effect was disastrous. Lines which should have been used to channel traffic to Sydney were being pressed into service to answer the calls of irate customers unable to get through. It was a dangerous spiral which kept escalating, eating up valuable resources.

The problem was being aggravated by the failure of parts of the microwave network. No one knew why yet, but a sizeable percentage of the system which carried signals from mobile telephone equipment to the underground transmission wires had shorted out in the inner Sydney region, despite the fact it was supposed to be protected against the electronic disturbances created by large lightning strikes. The most worrying complication of all, however, was the unexplained failure of the in-ground network around the crash site.

The Status Board had settled into a continuous, pervasive whine. The alarm system wailed continuously, telling the operators they were not working fast enough, reinforcing what they already knew: that they were not coping with the huge influx of calls.

Clifford turned to Maggie Campbell.

"Can't we turn off that noise?" he demanded irritably. "Surely they can't work with it!"

A women at the nearest desk turned to him. Clifford met her eyes: about thirty-five, probably casual, probably with a family; straggly, blonde hair and rounded shoulders. "It's OK, you get used to it," she smiled, shrugging her shoulders.

Clifford felt ashamed. How could these people maintain their equilibrium in this chaos?

"You shouldn't have to get used to it. Maggie, get some electricians in here to disconnect that thing, so people can get their work done without interruption. Have we arranged food and drinks for everyone?"

The PAN manager nodded. "In an hour we'll have enough staff in here to arrange for breaks for some people. The canteen's open; it'll be working all night."

Clifford felt a surge of appreciation for the short, middle-aged woman beside him. Maggie Campbell was an excellent manager, doughty and resilient. A former operator herself, she understood the pressures facing her staff.

"OK. You don't need me for a while."

Clifford moved to the doorway, pausing to gaze once more over the chaotic dance of activity. "Thanks Maggie," he said. Realising he was still holding the roster list, he handed it back to her.

"And Maggie, if you need to do anything out of the ordinary tonight, do it. You've got my authority and support. Let's just get the job done."

Chapter 26
Aftermath

The night dragged on for Clifford in a series of conferences with Comlink's Public Relations unit and, when they could get hold of him, Albert. There would be considerable flak directed at Comlink over the coming days and Clifford was determined to deflect as much of it as possible.

Around eleven o'clock, news came through from Sydney that they had found the cause of the network failures around the crash site.

Through a bizarre set of circumstances, the failures related to the Halon scare of the mid-eighties. Halon had been a major chemical propellant used in electrical and fuel fire extinguishers, but its release into the atmosphere caused almost thirty times more damage to the ozone layer than the same amount of fluorocarbon emission. Eventually, Halon was banned and new chemical propellants were substituted for it.

When Flight 24 came down it did not burst into flames. Instead, fuel from its ruptured tanks – 35,000 litres in all – flowed into the streets, the sewers and drains and, disastrously, into the underground pits which housed the Comlink cables. Many of the drains and sewers in the area were already backed-up with the huge volume of water dumped by the storm. When fire teams hosed down the area, spraying foam over the crash sites, the combination of Jet-fuel and the chemicals used in the fire-fighters' foam flowed into the Comlink pits, where it began to react with the plastic cable-coatings. Small, thin cable coverings dissolved quickly, disrupting the local area communications. As the night progressed, larger cables were apparently being stripped by the caustic mixture and were dropping out of the network.

Although the techs had discovered what they thought was the cause, they could not halt the slow, corrosive effect. No-one knew how much of the larger cabling would eventually be affected before they could clean up the mess.

※　※　※　※　※

While Clifford worked with the PR people, Bob was with Don Burgess in a spare office further down the corridor of the twenty-fourth floor. The scientist had covered a whiteboard with a series of diagrams depicting the network, and what he guessed would be the effect of the chemical cocktail eating into it.

"The absurd thing is that this shouldn't be happening. The mixture created by blending Jet-fuel and the new foam constituents shouldn't affect our cable coating this way. Our specifications take into account the action of chemicals such as these," said Don, tapping a felt-tipped pen against the board distractedly.

"Could it be something like the Dick Tracy splitters? You know, what we found in Adelaide. A contract awarded on a cheap price so that the product isn't any use?" Bob asked.

"No, I doubt it. And even if that were the case, this still shouldn't happen. I don't know of any plastic which would act in the way described. Tell me again: what did Walter say when you spoke to him?"

Bob glanced at the notes he had jotted down when talking to the Sydney Regional Manager.

"Pits in the area full of a mixture of Jet-fuel and foam; techs found the coverings slimy and soft, apparently dissolving at the ends where they were connected to the cable joints." Bob shrugged. "The small ones are going first, indicating the stuff's taking time to get inside the cable through the covering."

"It might seem to indicate the covering is dissolving, but the polymer structure *doesn't* dissolve like that," Don said.

"It must," Bob countered. "Look at what we've got: Jet-fuel, foam and plastic. That, and an increasing rate of failure we've got to try and counter. There are large cables running through the area connecting major parts of the network. If they go down, we'll be in even more serious trouble."

The Prelude

Don Burgess turned once more to the whiteboard. "Are all the cables failing in sequence? All the two-pair, then all the ten-pairs and so on?"

"No, that's exactly why I'm inclined to think it's something to do with a particular batch of cable which was cheap and shonky. Sometimes it's the ten-pair, sometimes it's the two. But on the whole, it seems to be the smaller ones first."

"We've got the symptoms fourth hand." Don slammed his fist against the board. "I wish I could see what was really happening."

The two men lapsed into silence, both staring at the web of failed cables he had sketched.

"Could you try it yourself?" Bob asked uncertainly.

"Sure. At eleven o'clock at night. Just where do you figure we'd get cable joints from at this hour – not to mention Jet-fuel? We've got fire extinguishers in plenty, but the rest? Come on, Bob."

Bob paused for a moment, then sat forward, his eyes widening. "The tech school! Tonnes of it. Cable of all sorts. Joints, practice joints that have been put together by the students."

"The place is closed.....Isn't it?" Don asked, catching Bob's excitement.

"We'll soon fix that!" Bob punched up Comlink's internal phone directory on a nearby console. He entered the name of the Training School manager, Jake Kennedy, thankful that the directory listed the home phone numbers of senior executives. "Make a list of what you'll need, Don."

The phone seemed to ring interminably before it was picked up. With a sigh of relief, Bob found himself speaking to the head of the training school. He swiftly outlined the position with the network. As he completed the briefing, Don shoved a list of hastily scrawled demands under his nose.

"Jake, we need to try and figure out what's happening in Sydney with these cables. Can we open the training school? I want to set up a test with some cable and joints."

"Yes, sure. I can be out there in about half an hour to open up. There's a nightwatch service, but you'd never find them. What do you need?"

Bob rattled out the list.

"Jet-fuel? This is a phone company, not an airline. You're out of luck there."

"OK, don't worry about that, I'll get it organised. Can you get the rest together?" Bob said.

"See you in half an hour," came the reply.

Bob scanned the phone directory again. In a moment he had the number he wanted.

Ashley Thomas, the Supply Group manager, was still in his office on the eighth floor of the building. His response was more or less what Bob had expected. "Jet-fuel? This is a phone company, not an airline."

"We need it, Ashley," Bob persisted.

"I'll see what I can do. I'll get on to my counterpart in Civil Aviation. No doubt he's still at his desk for the same reason we're still here. If I can get some, I'll have it ferried out for you."

"Let's go, Don," said Bob, leaping out of his seat.

* * * * *

It took them about forty minutes to reach the training school. The empty building was ablaze with lights as they drove up and Jake Kennedy was waiting for them at the entrance. The deserted halls were eerie as the trio hurried to the test lab which Jake had already set up with the tubs and cables Don Burgess had called for.

In less than ten minutes they were disturbed by the raucous intrusion of a siren. Bob peered through the blinds of the lab to see a small van with a swirling orange light on top making its way across the parking area to the main building.

"I think we've got the fuel," he yelled, dropping the blind and racing off towards the front entrance.

He reappeared a few minutes later with a gangling youth in the blue and white uniform of the Civil Aviation Department. Each of them was staggering under the weight of two jerry cans of Jet-fuel.

While they went out to get another four, Don poured several litres of Jet-fuel over the cable sections lying in each tub. Once these were covered, he took a foam fire extinguisher and emptied its contents into the tubs.

"Alright," he said as Bob reappeared. "Now we wait. The concentration is higher than they would have experienced in Sydney because there's no water mixed in. At least twenty minutes, I should think."

* * * * *

The Prelude

Don Burgess plunged a gloved hand into one of the tubs and extracted two cables. They were ten-pair cables with a joint at both ends. The joint was a lump of fibreglass a little smaller in size than a beer can. It contained the connections to join the cable to the next section in line.

The cables were slimy, cold and hard.

"No damage," Don said, frowning. He passed the cables to Bob and tried another tub. This one contained several smaller cables, used for connecting single houses or groups of houses to a larger ten-pair cable.

"No damage here either."

He dipped into the third tub. This time, he held out two cables, both ten-pair again. On each cable the covering had shrunk away from the jointed ends, opening up like a flower. It had the same slimy feel but, whereas the others were hard, these ones were soft.

"Eureka!" he cried, brandishing the cables. He held them out to Jake. "What's the difference between these and the ones in the other tubs?" he queried.

"Nothing," Jake said blankly, "same materials, same connector joints, same inside."

"Damn. What about age?"

"They've all been around for years. They came from the practice classes. There's a stack of them in the storeroom."

Don's shoulders slumped.

He tried once more. "How about construction?"

Jake laughed. "I think those were probably put together by a gorilla wearing boxing gloves."

"That's it!" Don exclaimed, waving the cables triumphantly. "I'll bet these undamaged ones were made by either the head of the class or one of the best students. Those others are bad joints, made by someone without much experience.

"With the poorly constructed joints, the fibreglass has not bonded around the cable covering properly, allowing the cover to shrink away from its anchor point when it comes in contact with the Jet-fuel mix. The plastic shrinks under the effect of the mixture, but it doesn't dissolve. The cover goes baggy and soft as it shrinks away, letting the mixture into the sensitive inner wiring.

"That's why it's only some of the cables going out of action. It's not a bad batch of coating, it's poor jointing over the years that won't become evident until it's put under stress like tonight."

Jake Kennedy grumbled his disgust at all linesmen. "Slack buggers," he muttered.

"It's not that," Bob responded. "You know how well our people are trained."

"So what to do?" Don demanded.

"Re-covering the cable joint should help," Jake suggested. "In the areas where Walter Minogue is worried he might have a major breakdown, he can have his linies put an extra fibreglass sheath around the existing joints, making sure it bonds effectively to the coating. That ought to give them an edge."

"It's enough for Walter to go with," urged Don.

Bob picked up the nearest phone and called Albert's office. It took him a couple of tries to get through, but when he did he relayed the information to Albert, so that he could get it through to Walter Minogue in Sydney.

As he hung up, Bob looked to his companions. "Why so many poor joints?" he said.

"Why indeed?" answered the scientist.

Chapter 27
The king must die

The violent deaths of eleven hundred citizens caused an enormous tremor in communities all over Australia. The country seemed caught in a spasm of introspection as people looked inwards to their own mortality.

The skills learned by the media in past decades – the presentation of processions of sorrow, the comprehensive intrusions, the expressions of shock, outrage and sympathy – were applied relentlessly. Here was a disaster worthy of the exercise of raw technology.

In the past, attention had been limited to the trauma of the individual or 'the victim's family'. Here, the victim's family was an entire country. And the family watched spellbound as images of horror and tragedy were replayed and relived, until finally sorrow and tears gave way to fear, and then anger.

The findings of the aviation researchers showed Flight 479 had been struck by lightning. "Not much you can do about that," the family said. "A huge strike. Totally unexpected in size."

The cause of such a large lightning strike was consigned conveniently to Greenhouse. Everyone knew storms nowadays were larger, more violent. Rainfall had increased in the past decade; tropical storms came further south. It was easy to accept the explanation because, whether it was true or not, Greenhouse was a useful way of avoiding responsibility. It was so big, so close, so out of control, that it was no longer anyone's problem. Governments could handle it. And if they couldn't, well, that wasn't the fault of the individual.

The king must die

The aviation authorities promised a review of the design of 'leak' circuitry and lightning protection for all aircraft. The air traffic controllers were blameless, since they had been unable to contact Flight 479. The rescue authorities had performed Herculean tasks in black, driving rain. Their performance had been hampered by the storm and the poor communications, but everyone knew they had worked hard and well. Even the government had come to the party, setting up a disaster relief fund and promising compensation for victims and their families.

So where was the emotion to be directed? Who was to carry the blame, the guilt?

Albert Lapin knew.

He stepped forward to the side of the grave, bent and tossed into it a handful of dry, dusty soil. He found difficulty in looking into the deep cavity.

It had been a bleak valediction from the priest, matching the atmosphere of profound grief in the large congregation.

The dead tree gives no shelter. Albert remembered the previous year's advertising campaign: Comlink, the tree of life, spreading its branches over the entire country in a twisting network of communication. *The dead tree gives no shelter.* He brushed the few remaining specks of dust from his palms.

Anne Blanchard's father stood silently, one arm held protectively around his wife's shoulders. Behind them stood her brother, his arms reaching out to encompass and shield them in their grief. Layers of protection, layers of hurt.

"I'm sorry, so very sorry," Albert repeated with nervousness born of the universal fear of intrusion on the bereaved.

Awkwardly, he turned and walked away from the graveside to where Bob and Janice Cheshire were standing with Alan Dodgson. The tall, young man was standing stiffly, his long, angular face creased with pain.

"Alan, if you want any time...."

Alan's blue eyes were grey and flat in the overcast light. He shook his head. "A few days. Then I think I'll get back to it. It'll be best if I keep busy."

Albert nodded, wondering why death reduced everything to clichés. There didn't seem to be any way to reach through, to say how one really felt.

He walked away from the small group towards the waiting limousine.

The censure had begun to sheet home to Comlink. The gaze of the media had shifted from the fruitless aviation investigations to an issue which provided promises of excitement and vindication.

The Prelude

Comlink had failed. There was no doubt about that in Albert's mind. The most powerful myth of the organisation was its unswerving public service, the notion that it would come through for the community: that when there was an emergency, Comlink would be there.

Well, there had been an emergency, and Comlink had been conspicuous by its absence. There had been large scale failures from ineffective wiring and maintenance; exchange failures; a quarter of the microwave network had gone down, apparently through the effects of an electromagnetic pulse. Even the emergency sub-systems, designed to cope with the needs of rescue teams in a situation like the crash, had disintegrated.

There had been plans, practices and disaster simulations with emergency authorities. Dozens of scenarios had been considered in the past – some of them so similar it was frightening. Yet when the crunch came, Comlink had failed. All it could offer was a clogged network which prevented any sort of information getting out to millions of relatives and friends.

And the failure could not be pushed back to the lower levels of the organisation. It wasn't unskilled, lazy, militant, stupid, bloody-minded, lax, uncommitted workers. The blame for failure could go nowhere but to the top – the Board had made that clear in the emergency meeting last night.

Worse than the mounting external censure was the dull, inescapable sense of failure which appeared to be incapacitating the organisation from inside.

Too many people realised now that their promises had been false. The rhetoric of the PR staff and the advertising agencies had not resembled the reality of their situation. Already, it was emerging that spare parts had been in short supply and that lines designated for emergency use had been cannibalized over the years. In the exchanges, blocks of lines which should have been protected against the effects of electromagnetic disturbances had either not been maintained adequately, or had never been proofed.

The people of Comlink had coped remarkably. They had given their time and their effort, many around the crash site risking physical danger. There was no problem with the people. The problem was with the organisation itself.

The titan had not been prepared, despite the great strengths of the organisation: the depth of its resources, its infrastructure and its technological skills.

For Albert, the bitter truth related to what Bob Cheshire had said: Comlink was so stretched there had been no time or resources to spend on maintaining or improving its own systems. When the facade was put under stress it began to crumble, exposing those behind it.

Luke was waiting. He held the door open for Albert to slide into the back of the limousine.

"Let's go, Luke," Albert said quietly.

Chapter 28
What future?

First there were the 'Letters to the Editor'. Then the 'FOI' requests from journalists and opposition politicians began to pour in. Finally, as editorial comment around the country shifted towards an indictment of the nation's communications system, the current affairs programs turned up to do their 'public interest' exposés.

Against this background, it was pointless to direct public scrutiny to the virtues or successes of Comlink. The community did not want solutions yet; it was still seeking an outlet for pain.

Under the media's focus, a distorted picture began to emerge of a disorganised and defensive organisation which produced inadequate products, managed them badly, and maintained them even worse. The problems which the Sydney crash had thrust into the headlines clearly went beyond the simple disruption caused by unprecedented demand. While the situation was not as discreditable as many commentators made out, it was nonetheless true that on the night of the crash in Sydney, the nation's communication system had caused unnecessary and prolonged distress to millions across the country.

Bob Cheshire sat in the outer office of the Chief Executive's suite. So much had happened in the ten days since the crash, he thought. The network had finally settled down to what approximated a reasonable operational level, but only after a massive amount of work on the part of those associated with the provision of Comlink services.

A buzzer sounded on John Hunter's desk.

"You can go in now," he said.

Clifford Tate was sitting behind the desk which had previously been occupied by Albert Lapin. He motioned Bob to a chair.

What future

In the midst of all the chaos, Clifford had somehow managed to retain his sartorial distinction. His shirt was a hard, flat white, his suit a perfect, featureless black. But the strain of the past week had taken its toll on most of the Comlink managers, Clifford Tate included. He looked tired, colourless and hollow-eyed.

"As you're aware, Albert felt it prudent to resign, rather than wait for the Board to decide the issue for him. He felt that way he would at least have some control in nominating his successor."

"Congratulations," Bob said uncertainly.

"Looking around me, I can't see that much I should be celebrating," the new Chief Executive responded grimly.

"The one positive event in this disastrous mess is the way our people have coped. We're in trouble, Bob. Deep trouble. And we don't have the answers."

Clifford was facing urgency and uncertainty. He needed some sort of action, something to quiet the still escalating criticism which was threatening the organisation. He looked speculatively at Bob. Maybe there was something in what Bob was proposing. Maybe there wasn't.

"It will be months before the fallout is over," Clifford said crisply. "In the meantime, one thing has become clear to me. We need to drastically improve our service delivery. Last week, people wanted a service. We couldn't deliver it.

"Two things have come out of the last week which I want to discuss with you. Both relate to systems failures: the problems with cable joints around the crash site, and the failure of the microwave network."

Sitting silently for a minute, Bob gathered his thoughts before speaking. It seemed almost unbelievable that only two weeks ago he and Clifford had been arguing about the MID project. Now the tall, thin Services Director was the acting head of an organisation of more than sixty thousand people. And he seemed willing to consider the possibilities Bob's work offered.

Bob took a deep breath. "We believe, as a result of work we've been doing in Adelaide and Newcastle..." A small catch in his throat betrayed the extent of emotions he thought were firmly controlled. "...We believe that the percentage of faults in the area around the crash is probably not greatly different from that of the whole network."

"You mean the entire cable network is in danger of falling apart?" Clifford demanded.

Bob thought for a moment. "Try this," he said. "Connecting a pair of cables with a fibreglass joint is a relatively simple job. You open the pit, check the wiring, put a shaped mould over the joint, apply the resin and hardener, and that's it. Simple. Then you come back later when the joint has set and check it for integrity and soundness. The outcome is a strong, working joint. At least that's the plan. It's a system: a chain of events or processes beginning with the ordering and supply people and ending with the lines staff who make and check the joint.

"Ordinarily, we should be able to arrange things so that variation in the job is kept to a minimum. By this I mean that the number of points at which we deviate from the desired outcome – a solid cable joint – are kept to as few as possible.

"But we've got too much variation in the system, so when conditions change there's greater potential for a poor result. For instance: parts might be unavailable, but because faults are still occurring and lines still need to be commissioned, a liney who doesn't have a joint mould might use a substitute, such as an aluminium drink can with the end cut out.

"It's true! And other things might happen: like the worker has so many jobs backed up he can't afford the time to go back and check the joints, so he just hopes they'll be alright when they dry. Or any of a zillion things. The thing is that each of these problems is beyond the control of the bloke who actually does the work. The system he works with exhibits variation, but he has no way of controlling it."

Bob produced a folder. He stood up and walked around the side of the large desk.

"These are the results of some of the work we've been doing in Adelaide," he said, handing a chart to Clifford. "This is a graph of phone installations in the Hills region over the last six months. Throughout that period demand was high, so our installers always had more than enough to do."

"What has this to do with Sydney?" Clifford interrupted.

"I think you'll understand shortly," Bob responded, trying not to sound anxious. "You can see that at some points the level of installations was high, but that at other times it was low. Yet throughout the whole period the demand from customers for phone installations remained at a steady level.

What future

"You'll notice that the mean, or average, number of installations throughout the period is slightly above seventy-five. The target established for this area, by the way, also happens to be seventy-five.

"What we found out is that the local area managers, under pressure to achieve their targets, were pushing their demands down to the supervisors and lines staff.

"These points here," Bob said, putting a cross next to several of the peaks on the graph, "coincide with the times when it was coming up to the end of the two-monthly accounting period and a quick result had to be shown. So the men worked harder, faster, and with high overtime costs. The result was that the quality of their work suffered: more breakdowns, more poor installations, more unhappy customers."

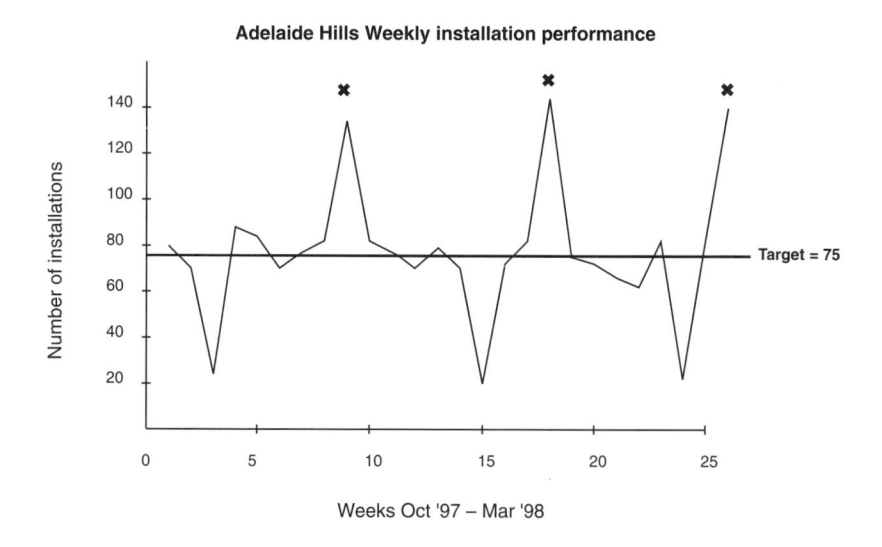

Adelaide Hills Weekly installation performance

Weeks Oct '97 – Mar '98

'A quick result', thought Clifford. Wasn't that exactly what he was asking for right now. And why not? He wasn't going to last long in the chair if he couldn't achieve some rapid improvement.

He looked up at Bob. "I appreciate your concern. But if we're going to achieve things we have to have targets. And if we are behind target, we have to work harder. It's up to local management to ensure that the work's done properly."

"There's a problem with that," Bob countered. He was conscious that here was an opportunity to reach Clifford and he was determined not to let it slide away.

"Two problems, in fact. First, the local manager is being judged by quantity. His performance-pay rests on him achieving the targets set by Head Office. And Head Office has let him know it wants x-many installations and is not overly fussed about how long they hold together.

"The second problem is that we force our staff to do quick and dirty work. The impact of that is felt not only by the customer, but also by other sections – namely the maintenance people who have to go out and fix the fault which wouldn't have occurred in the first place if the original installer had had the time, equipment and resources to do the job properly. So our costs go up and no-one is happy: the installer is dissatisfied with the quality of the work he's doing; the maintainer is equally dissatisfied with the huge volume of unnecessary repairs required, and the customers are really pissed off because their new phones don't work."

Clifford's expression was veiled as Bob continued his explanation.

"That's one area where the variation comes in. The other area is here, at these low troughs denoting poor performance." Bob indicated a couple of the lower points on the graph.

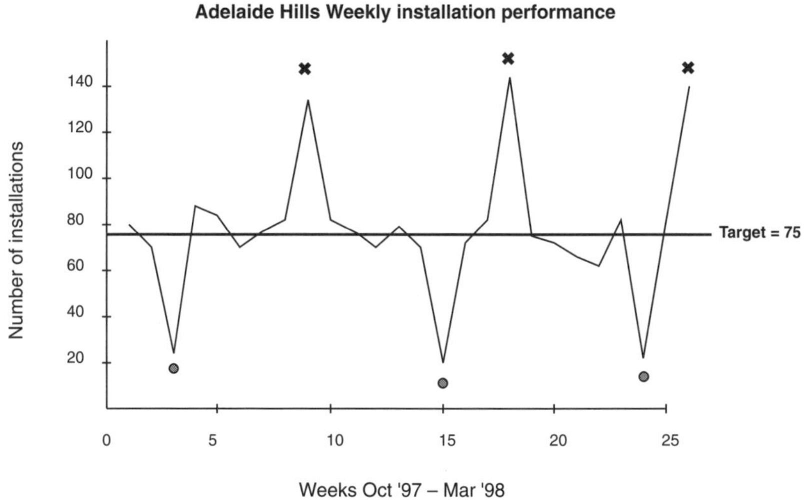
Adelaide Hills Weekly installation performance
Number of installations
140
120
100
80
60
40
20
Target = 75
0
5
10
15
20
25
Weeks Oct '97 – Mar '98

"When we started to research these we found they were mostly the result of erratic supply, poor quality tools, rostering problems caused by absenteeism, department re-organisations, introduction of new products which the men didn't know well enough, and other similar problems – none of which are within the control of the individual installer who is called on to meet the targets of Head Office.

"What that means is that although we continue to demand a fixed rate of performance from staff, there are so many causes of variation affecting what they do that it's nothing more than mere chance when they meet our expectations."

The Prelude

Bob pulled out another chart, a copy of the first but with two lines drawn on it which ran above and below most of the points on the graph.

"These lines represent the 'control limits' of this particular system. There's a very simple formula for working them out.

"The control limits tell you what a 'fair' result is. Within any stable system a good result is just as likely as a bad result, provided they both fall within the control limits. Just where exactly in that range the result falls is a completely random event, because the people doing the work in the system – the installers – have no control over it.

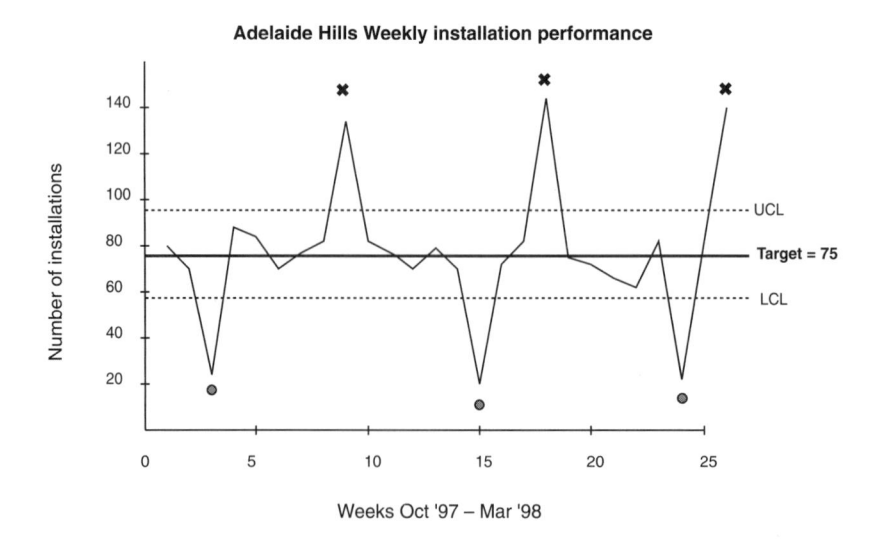

Adelaide Hills Weekly installation performance

Weeks Oct '97 – Mar '98

"That's why it's useless to demand people work to a particular target. Rather, we should recognise that *work within the control limits is acceptable*, because the system we make people work with forces them to produce results which could be anywhere within that range."

Clifford was still silent, waiting.

Bob took a deep breath and continued. "Instead of setting arbitrary targets, what we should be doing is asking staff to work within the limits set by the variation in the system. *And reducing the variation in that system.*

"If we can reduce variation, we can get a better result for everyone: the customers, the installers, maintainers, and ourselves. All we have to do is reduce the variation."

"And of course you're going to tell me how we can do that?"

"In the case of the installers," Bob offered, "we could start with efficient parts supply, product training, and good installation equipment. These would enable the installers to do a better job.

"There are probably other issues which need addressing, but the only way to be sure is to talk to the people themselves.

"It looks like there might be a problem with the information which is being put onto the installation forms at the clerical end, and there's difficulty with installers turning up to places only to find there's no-one home. All of these things add variation to the system and that places everyone under greater pressure than need be. Excess pressure makes people perform poorly: mistakes, re-work, wastage."

Clifford stared at the simple graphs. "You're suggesting the installation process is similar everywhere? Peaks and troughs; times when the people are forced to cut corners?"

Bob nodded. "And the only way to change it is to reduce the variation in the systems we work with. They're out of control. I think the last week has shown us that all of us – not just the senior management – have to get back control of the systems in this organisation."

Two days in Albert's chair had been enough to show Clifford the distorted reality with which his predecessor had been living. He did not fully accept Bob's view of the problems – had never accepted it, not from that first moment when Bob had spoken out at the management meeting against the proposal to speed up the Dick Tracy Watch. God, that seemed so long ago. It was....how long? Three months? Less? Yet the reality of it was that he wasn't in a position to ignore Bob's work or his conclusions.

The need for change was critical. Public outrage was intensifying and government pressure increasing. The situation was being fanned by community interest groups, such as CAWPS, and Hugh Britten, the Managing Director of NetWork, was taking full advantage of the situation to mobilise opposition to Comlink. Clifford faced stern direction from the Board. He had to do something. More than that, he had to be seen to be doing something. And quickly.

From where he stood, only one factor held out any hope. At this point in its history, Comlink *could* change. The airline crash, despite its disastrous and tragic nature, had resulted in a climate which was conducive to change – not because of external forces, but because of the mood within the organisation itself. The crash had not created an instant desire for improvement within Comlink, but it had uncovered deep-seated concerns among many in the organisation.

If Bob was right, the work in Adelaide and Newcastle had begun to generate a groundswell of acceptance. In the light of the Sydney disaster, it was important to nurture positive changes. Clifford felt himself drawn to Bob's conclusion. Perhaps there was something to work with after all.

Another factor was the people of Comlink. They had performed miraculously. No-one in the wider community or media wanted to recognise the value of their contribution yet, but that didn't mean it hadn't happened. He remembered something Bob had said on another occasion: it wasn't the people in the organisation who were the problem, it was the systems they worked with. It was clear that on this occasion the people of Comlink had filled in the gaps left by deficiencies in the systems. And responsibility for deficient systems resided only with those who managed them.

Clifford became aware that he was tapping his pen rhythmically on the plastic cover of Bob's folder.

"I want you to continue the work you're doing, Bob. Two weeks ago I said you were to keep away from the MID project. Cancel that. MID is the development which is going to fix our capacity to interpret data over the next twenty years. If it's on the wrong track, I want to know. As well, I want you to work with John McDermott's people on the problems we've had with the microwave network in Sydney." He stole a quick glance at the diary on his desk, an old-fashioned hand-written one. "Can you give me a report on Thursday?"

Bob nodded soberly.

"Let me know if you need anything in the way of resources," Clifford said, standing up. He held out his hand to Bob. "This crash has highlighted serious deficiencies in the quality of our service. Let's see if we can fix that."

Bob walked out of the office buoyed by Clifford's decision. As he walked through the outer office he saw a delegation of officials waiting to meet with the new Chief Executive. He recognised two of them as a senior UCWU official and the Secretary of CAWPS.

Outside in the hallway, a film crew was lounging against the wall. The reporter, a neatly-tailored, Angry Young Man, well-known for his investigative tenacity, stood briefing his cameraman in low tones.

Chapter 29
Wednesday morning 7 a.m.

"Another pancake, Bob?" John McDermott enquired heartily, dropping another of the flurpy, butter-soaked circles onto Bob's plate without waiting for an answer.

Bob looked to the others around the small breakfast table: Norm Sanders, the Network Operations Manager; Mark Rowlands, manager of Comlink's Business Division, and David Hamilton, the Consumer Division Manager. Norm stared up into the air, eloquently ignoring the plaintive look from Bob. Dave Hamilton appeared to be engrossed in his coffee, although a slight smile creased the corners of his mouth.

"Does he always eat enough for ten men at breakfast?" Bob asked the group at large.

John McDermott laughed, helping himself to another pancake. "I'm a growing lad, Cheshire."

Bob smiled back. The Operations Directorate had given him a fair hearing. Norm Sanders, in particular, was interested in the work he was doing. In fact, when the issue of OFCAB had come up and John had been ready to dispute the need for haste in developing the programs which Alan and Anne had set in motion, Norm had come to Bob's aid, disagreeing vocally with his boss.

He had supported Bob's argument that through a combination of increasing technical complexity and 'paper' accountability, he and many other managers had lost touch with, and control of, the systems they were intended to manage.

"Bob's right," he declared, "we should be working with people and improving things with their help."

Wednesday morning

Dave Hamilton disagreed. "We need to manage people," he insisted, "it's our job. People are the variable. They've got individual, unique problems that need to be answered by their managers."

Norm shook his head. Bob suspected these two were long-time sparring partners, used to challenging each other's assumptions.

"We've got to provide the system that enables them to solve their problems," Norm countered.

Bob was both gratified and surprised at the support he was getting.

They had been talking for about half an hour when he finally struck on an analogy which awakened John McDermott's interest.

"Think about the dressage competition we saw the other weekend. Your niece Pip.

"Imagine that the horse and the range of movements it is expected to perform make up a system.

"Pip's job is to get the best outcome possible from that system. In other words, to win the competition. She does that by guiding and controlling the horse in order to create the perfect performance the judges expect.

"Pip doesn't do the work of the horse, it functions as a result of her guidance. A poorly-trained horse will exhibit huge variation in the way it performs the dressage movements; it might never do the same thing twice. On the other hand, a well-trained horse will act with less variation, placing its feet just so, each and every time.

"Pip's coach is like a manager. In order to improve the outcome, the coach gives her direction and advice, trusting in her intelligence, skill and commitment to control the horse. If the coach simply stands on the sidelines and shouts to her, 'Do it this way and no other, you're here to ride, not to think,' both of them are wasting their time.

"To achieve the kind of high-quality result which will win an event, coach and rider must work together to improve the horse's performance through further training, closer analysis of what horse and rider are doing wrong, and better riding equipment. They need to sit down together, look at what's happening and then do something about it.

"And the truth is that while the coach might be able to see what the problem is, it will more often than not be the rider who supplies the solution.

"That's how we should operate: our task as managers should be to support our staff, to enable them to have as much control as possible."

"Fair enough," John McDermott acknowledged. "Let's look at the microwave network problem for a while. I'll yield to you on the matter of quality improvement, but I want to see some results."

Bob settled back into his chair. The shadow which had come between he and John at the horse show had faded as they talked through the breakfast meeting. He had come to the realisation that John was not an enemy, he simply wasn't sure what Bob was trying to do. The onus for communication surely lay with the one who was trying to instigate any change, Bob decided, just as the responsibility to respond lay with those who would be affected.

John McDermott poked the few escaped fragments on his plate with his fork. Bob's view was a challenge – a challenge which would work to upset the delicate balance of forces which had been constructed through years of negotiation with governments, unions and community groups. That balance was, at best, a patchwork of fluctuating and unreliable alliances, but it was all any of them had had until now.

"What do you say, Bob?" he asked thoughtfully. "What would you expect to find as reasons for the failure of the microwave system in Sydney – a system we know was designed to cope with just such situations?"

"The same sort of things we found with the cable joints," Bob replied. "Hurried installation which left the system vulnerable to stress; inadequate preventive maintenance due to work pressures. And no record of either in the regular reports.

"I'll bet if you dig out the fault repair records for the area you'll find that a number of faults have been repaired at the same location two, three, even more times in a short period."

John looked uncertain.

"That's exactly what we found on a small scale sample in Adelaide. Hell, I even got arrested trying to prove it."

"Then why don't the recurrent faults show up as problems?" Norm Sanders asked. "The blokes who do the work should be screaming."

Bob shrugged. "They probably do mention it to their supervisors. But we don't measure re-calls, we never have. In the system we use for measuring things, it's never been important to us whether we're going back to the same place time and again. Besides, as with a lot of the things we do, we manage to make sure it's no-one's responsibility to uncover and fix problems."

Wednesday morning 7.a.m.

He turned to Mark Rowlands and Dave Hamilton. "You guys are responsible for installation. When something goes wrong with a product your staff have installed, how do you get to know about it?"

"We have overall fault repair figures from the maintenance departments," Dave Hamilton replied. "But no, I take your point. There's no way of telling if it's a product we've just installed."

"How about asking some of the clerical people what sort of patterns there are with fault calls?" Bob ventured. "Get them to keep some simple records and you'll soon have a pretty good idea of what's occurring. The people you've got repairing phones are an entirely different group to those installing them. Unless you compare the effect one process has on the other, you can't get a real picture of what's happening."

John McDermott shifted in his seat. His strong voice rumbled as he spoke. "You were right about the cause of the cable joint failures in Sydney, Bob. And I think you're probably right when you say that the cause of those poor joints is as much our responsibility as that of the people who put them together. But you're talking about a major shift in the way we operate. It's not something you can contain in a small enclave of the organisation."

"I need help, that's certain," Bob said quietly.

John sat silently for a moment before speaking again.

"Norm?"

The greying operations engineer was definite. "I'll go for it. We need to change the way we do things. The crash in Sydney didn't create the problem, it only brought out into the open something which has been there for a long time."

"Mark?"

The Business Division Manager paused thoughtfully before he eventually nodded. "Count me in."

"What about you, Dave?"

"Sounds good to me."

John McDermott turned back to Bob. "Well, my friend, let's go take a look at the horse!"

Chapter 30
Slow dancing

By late morning Bob was in Sydney, sitting opposite Walter Minogue, the area's regional manager. The man looked tired, more tired than anyone Bob had seen in the past two weeks. And he had seen some extremely worn out people.

Walter's already thin face had taken on a grey hue, almost as pallid as the thin strands of hair which stretched across his scalp. He sat slouched in a navy blue suit that seemed fractionally too large for him.

The manager was not in a good mood. He had done an excellent job, yet the system had failed. A system for which he was ultimately responsible. And now Bob Cheshire had turned up, directly from Clifford – snotty, cold Clifford Tate – wanting to know what was the story with the microwave network.

Even before this bloody mess, Alan Dodgson had inadvertently been causing problems through his demands to adjust the Stores and Supply systems which underpinned the OFCAB effort.

And Alan worked for Bob Cheshire. Ipso facto, Cheshire was an asshole.

Walter closed his eyes for a moment. So much had happened since the night, two weeks ago, when Albert Lapin had been virtually his only contact outside the swirling, storm-tossed maelstrom that was Sydney. As the night had dragged on and he had been forced to report more and greater equipment failures, he had sometimes felt that Albert was the only sane person in a world of madness and destruction. Now Albert was gone. But the memories weren't, and Walter didn't appreciate Bob Cheshire's presence in his office now, particularly when a lot still needed to be done.

Besides, he had barely finished burying his brother, Chris, who had been caught in the flaming hell of the southern freeway when Flight 479 splashed a burning sheet of fuel and wreckage over hundreds of home-bound commuters.

Walter ran his hands through his thin hair, scratching his fingernails over his scalp in an effort to relieve the tension which had become so constant he barely recognised it. What would happen when he did slow down, finally did stop?

"We have to know what the problems were, Walter," Bob was saying. "More than that, we've got to find something we can do about them. There are a lot of people out there who want nothing more than to see us fail in our first attempt to pick up the pieces from this thing. If we fail once, it's probable we won't get another chance."

"That's an old one," Walter replied, flipping a hand dismissively. "Put the fear of God into the troops. Tell them the place will close down if they don't pull up their socks. Well, it's not going to work. Not just me, but every Comlink employee in this city has their socks pulled up so high they're having trouble breathing."

"That's why I'm here, Walter. To help find answers. I'm not asking you to give me resources, you're already stretched too thin, we know that. But the failure of the microwave network is too important and too unexpected for us not to determine the cause. Our test and construction specs, our intuitive knowledge, our maintenance program – everything we thought we knew – told us that in a severe storm like the one on the evening of the crash we might expect a failure rate of about one percent. More than *twenty* percent of the portable phone network failed that night."

"You're not telling me anything I don't know," Walter bridled. "What do you suggest? You're going to sit around for a week, draw some pretty graphs and pictures, tell me I need to be more organised, and then bugger off back to your cosy little cubicle in Bullshit Castle!

"Well it's real life here. I've got people after my blood. I've spent half a year's overtime allocation in two weeks and already the bloody accountants are after me. Absenteeism is about twelve percent instead of the usual four. We can't get parts. The residents' action groups and politicians are after us; NetWork and the Government are as thick as thieves up here, and my people are copping a lot of abuse. We had six employees killed by those planes. Six. And God knows how many of our people have lost someone they love. You'll just have to stand in line if you want to make trouble for me!"

Walter Minogue stared at Bob through a haze of frustration and anger. He needed to let Head Office know just how he felt. His people were handling the abusive calls, the undirected bitterness, the political point-scoring and the futile, seemingly-endless stream of accusation. He needed support, not some bloody witch-hunt which would inevitably find him to be the responsible – and removable – link in the chain. He could see it coming. God, he only had another three years to go. Couldn't they get off his back for a while?

"I'm not here to conduct a witch-hunt," Bob said, as if reading the Regional Manager's mind. "We need to know why so many microwave links failed so we can stop it happening again. And because it's vital for the work we're doing on the Dick Tracy Watch."

Walter Minogue didn't buy it for one moment. He thought of the old joke about the world's three most often used lies: the cheque's in the mail; I'll respect you in the morning; I'm from Head Office, I'm here to help.

* * * * *

The next two days were slow dancing for Bob – two steps forward, one step back.

What could he say to Walter and his staff? That the organisation had suddenly changed? That it was not a crime to take risks? That it was okay to toss out the pointless measurement systems, the futile exhortations to work harder? That by focusing your energy on the customers you could make life a lot easier for yourself and your organisation?

He couldn't say those things. And even if he could, who would believe him? People would not trust the organisation until the organisation trusted them. It was a perfect circle, and he had no way to break it – no way to gain the trust of people like Walter Minogue, whose experience of the years told them that nothing would be different this time; that the organisation was still looking for scapegoats.

But Clifford had been clear. He expected results. A report which could form the basis of action.

After days of frustration a small victory was granted to Bob on the Friday afternoon. He had been working with 'Taffy' Jones, the ex-patriate Welshman who headed up the Microwave Maintenance Section. They were concentrating on the HSF 43s, the repair docket completed by workers sent to repair a fault in one of the 'black box' transmission units of the microwave network.

The black boxes needed a certain amount of periodical maintenance. At the bottom of each repair docket, following the section where the tech listed the fault repairs carried out, were two small boxes with the notation: 'Preventive maintenance carried out. Yes or No'. Bob was concerned. He had noticed that although the box marked 'Yes' was invariably ticked on the forms, the space reserved below it for details of what parts had been replaced during the preventive maintenance check was almost always blank.

He pointed to the bottom of the form. "Why aren't there any comments down here, Taffy? They never put anything in here. 'Yes' is always ticked, but there's never any comments about what they did."

Bob spoke casually, but a small warning light was burning brightly in his mind. He remembered a story which Arthur Dee had told him a few weeks earlier:

The photocopier division of a large company was concerned about the number of service calls they were getting. Machines were breaking down all over the place. Customers were drifting away. They had an army of servicemen out on repair calls, but nothing ever seemed to get better.

Then, one day, someone decided to do a process survey to see how the maintenance and service activities worked.

They found that because of the large number of repairs and the resultant pressure on the service staff, the repairers were only fixing what was wrong at the time. Even if a machine was due for its six-monthly service shortly after the repairer called, he still wouldn't do a full service. He'd just fix the obvious fault. So the thing would probably break down again a few days later. Had a full service been done at the time of the original repair call, it would have uncovered the hidden faults. The job would have taken longer, but there would have been only one call, not two or three.

The company decided to instigate a program of preventive maintenance. When a service call brought a technician to a customer's machine, he would always complete a regular service, no matter whether it was yet due. It took time, and in the first six months the company lost many customers through being unable to respond quickly – the servicemen were doing a full service,

201

The Prelude

so they were unable to do as many calls each day. That sent their performance figures tumbling, and the photocopier division came under extreme pressure to revert to the old method of working.

But after about a year things began to improve. The machines stopped breaking down because they had been maintained well and regularly. Customers realised they could buy a reliable, hassle-free machine from the company, so they came back. Sales increased, overall costs were cut back, and the technicians found they were deriving greater satisfaction from their work because they weren't called back to an increasingly belligerent customer three times in the space of a few weeks.

* * * * *

It took only two hours to find out that in most cases the technicians ticked the 'Yes' box on the HSF 43 form regardless of whether they had done a major service or not.

The reason was simple. The techs were so busy repairing sudden faults there was no opportunity to complete the regular maintenance procedures. They were locked into a disastrous spiral of wasted effort. The more they responded to fire-fighting repair work, the more faults surfaced because the equipment was not being adequately maintained.

Part of the regular maintenance procedure was to check and repair the seals on the black boxes. If this was not done then, although the units might function with no problems for a long period, a storm the size of the one which had struck Sydney on the night of the crash would test the worn seals beyond their limits. And this was exactly what had occurred. As a result, a substantial proportion of the microwave network had failed when it was needed most, leaving Comlink open to charges of incompetence.

The fault reports, Bob realised, had been providing management with a false picture of what was happening. Because service staff had needed to use all their time to keep the system patched together, they had been forced to provide corrupt data about maintenance checks. The corrupt data had been sent up the line and nobody had questioned it. After all, performance indicators were used to determine the effectiveness of a manager. If the indicators said everything was fine, who was going to argue?

Contacting Clifford, Bob argued the case for increasing the maintenance staff available to Walter Minogue. The only way to get out of the cycle which had caused the failure of the microwave system was to turn resources from crisis repair on to preventive maintenance: to enable maintenance work to be done, rather than just being a tick in a box.

Initially, Clifford had been unwilling to endorse Bob's proposal, but in the end he had to accept it. It was essential that the problems which had been highlighted by the crash were rectified. As Bob argued, a demonstrably successful maintenance program would go a long way to ensuring the Dick Tracy Watch could be introduced without risk of failure.

Bob watched the scepticism on Walter's face as he told him of the extra resources which Clifford had approved to build an effective preventive maintenance system.

"The extra techs will only be on a temporary basis. Your performance figures will probably be shot to bits for a few months, but the extra people will hopefully alleviate that aspect of the problem. Clifford has agreed that the region should not be penalised for attempting to remedy a long-standing problem which it didn't cause. The situation, no doubt, exists all around the country. Now, thanks to your people, we know what needs to be done about it."

It was clear to Bob that the Regional Manager would not believe his promises until they became fact. Perhaps that was the way it had to be. It was ridiculous to imagine that everything changed automatically. Each step was just that, a small step in a slow dance to achieve trust and co-operation. And Bob had learned that the dance could not commence until the partners introduced themselves and began to talk.

Chapter 31
Commitment

Clifford Tate peered into the mirror which hung in the small en-suite of his office. He shrugged his thin shoulders, settling his jacket before buttoning it carefully. For a moment, caught by his own gaze, he stood stiff-backed, replaying the crowding problems, requests and demands which suddenly seemed to have become part of his life.

"Ready when you are, Boss," said John Hunter through the en-suite door.

Clifford held one hand out, palm down, defying it to shake. He looked into the mirror once more. Touching two fingers to his thin navy and silver tie, he turned and walked out into the main office.

John Hunter handed him a sheaf of papers. "These are the in-depth reports, plus a hard-copy of the speech. It's for back-up, in case there's a failure with the auto-cue."

Clifford nodded distantly, taking the papers. He mentally rehearsed the position of the lectern, the salient points of the speech, the operation of the controls, the list of attending journalists.

Walking to the connecting door at the side of his office, he stepped through, moving quickly and silently to the platform. A small pop escaped the sound system as he dumped the bundle of papers onto the lectern.

Clifford looked out over the assembled crowd. Several of the senior executive group were sitting in the front rows, ready if a figure, statement or policy was needed on the spot. Behind and around the managers were rows of media representatives. A good turnout, Clifford thought. They want to force failure down our throats.

At the front of the auditorium were the video cameras, their battery-powered spotlights blazing brightly. Photographers, leaning forward, elbowed their way between their electronic counterparts. Behind these ranks were the journalists, portable tape recorders ticking over, electronic notepads out. While the photographers were eager, pushing, this latter group cultivated an air of relaxed indifference.

Looking to the sides of the auditorium, Clifford noted that John McDermott's people had done an excellent job. A number of displays had been set up showing the most advanced products Comlink had to offer. If he was to present a picture of the future, Clifford wanted his audience to see and understand the depth of skill and creative ability in the organisation.

The audience was expectantly quiet as Clifford began: "The purpose of this press conference, ladies and gentlemen, is to look forward to the future.

"But first, I'd like to reflect for a moment on the past. For that is where we learn the lessons which enable us to shape and change the future.

"Comlink has been around in one form or another, under one name or another, since 1809. Historian Geoffrey Blainey once wrote that our story is the story of an Australian miracle: the story of how people who were far away came closer together.

"Our country has been shaped, powerfully and irrefutably, by the spread of telecommunications. Where we were once distant and isolated, we are now closely linked. Our identity rests on our ability to communicate. Our freedom rests on our ability to communicate freely and openly.

"To ensure that identity and freedom, we must manage our communications industry effectively."

Clifford paused, nervously aware that his next comments were a departure from the standard corporate speech.

"An organisation which commands, which dictates, which rules by fear, anger or confusion will never be truly effective. Management which threatens, cajoles and bribes, blames people instead of systems, will not ultimately succeed.

"At Comlink, we didn't start out to build a system like the one I've just described, but build it we did. It happens easily. Consider your own newsrooms and editorial desks. Is individual effort and commitment invariably rewarded, or do you go farthest, get highest, through your ability to play the game?

"Maybe the truth is somewhere in between. Studies we have conducted over the past few weeks have shown me – forcibly – that very often we've left our employees and our managers with no choice but to 'play the game'.

The Prelude

"Through hidden injunctions and regulations, unconscious values and beliefs, we've conspired to stop our people using the skills and capabilities they possess. Instead, we've locked them into boring, repetitive and non-productive tasks because it was easier than trying to figure out a way to improve things.

"The result of that stifling and over-control was that, on the night when our country most needed the ability and freedom to communicate, communication was denied."

"Communication was denied through a combination of failed electronic systems and failed management systems. *That must never happen again.*

"But there are no convenient sacrifices today. No Judas-goats. The failure, the confusion, the problems within Comlink have been caused by systems – by the way we do things – not by the people who do them.

"The things which are going to change as a result of the problems brought into the open by the disaster in Sydney are *systems*.

"There are some of you who will say, 'Big deal, he's just trying to shift the blame, trying to protect his own position when he should be kicking behinds and laying his own head on the block'. I can't stop you thinking that. But if that is the way you think, you are wrong. Hopelessly wrong.

"It would be easy for me to follow the old path: to find a few convenient heads to remove; produce a status report which showed that everything was suddenly different; discipline some of the workers so that I could get into a fight with the union and show everyone how tough I was as a boss.

"But the truth is, that would change nothing. *Real* change will only come when we change the *systems* we use to get our work done.

"And that means changing the reason why we do our work.

"In the past, Comlink has looked inwards for solutions. We've turned a shoulder to our customers and their needs, concentrating instead on technological solutions and arbitrary targets.

"All that must change if Comlink is to retain its place in the telecommunications future of Australia.

"Now, at the risk of depriving you of some expected blood, I'll tell you how we're going to do this ....."

Clifford punched the control panel on the lectern and one wall of the auditorium dissolved into a holographic display.

* * * * *

Bob Cheshire sat in the Chief Scientist's office, watching the broadcast of Clifford's speech. Beside him, Don Burgess toyed sporadically with a lump of electronic equipment resting in his lap, his long nose quivering as he poked at the device's entrails.

Don's people were making good progress with the Watch, but the scientist remained unconvinced of Comlink's ability to produce a good-quality product for consumers within the timelines set by management.

"I'll believe it when I see it," he sniffed.

Bob looked over at his incorrigible associate. Don's scepticism, although widely aired, was matched by his dedication to his work. The scientist wanted to see changes to the way Comlink worked. He believed strongly in the need to develop a better approach to customer service and to improve the quality of Comlink products.

"You're seeing it now, if you'd only look," Bob said. "This is a live transmission. Clifford wanted it that way so everyone in Comlink had the opportunity to hear what he said, rather than getting a second-hand, bowdlerised version in a ninety-second news story tonight. It's a big risk."

Don was silent. Bob had rarely seen him so preoccupied. He seemed to be questioning so many things lately; questioning motives and reasons. Like a man who wanted to prove that what he was doing was right.

"We're starting to take a long-term view, Don. At least that's something. You're the one who felt we were watering down the impact of new projects in order to make them suit short-term expediencies."

"That is something," Don admitted. "But when I *see* the change instead of hearing about it, then I'll believe it. Risks are a step forward, but we need more. We have to start anticipating and focusing on our customers' needs. And then we have to meet and exceed those needs.

"I believe you're on the right track with what you're doing, Bob. But there's got to be so much more before...." Don's voice trailed away as he turned his attention back to the equipment in his lap.

Bob felt a stirring of resentment. After all, he had been doing his damnedest over the past six months to make a difference to the way Comlink operated. It bothered him that Don wouldn't accept that work – and the support from Clifford – at face value. But perhaps, like Walter Minogue, he'd heard it all before.

How could he make people realise that change was possible, if only they would accept that what made it different this time was the commitment

207

The Prelude

and leadership from the top? And the need, the undeniable need, to do something for an organisation which was worth saving.

He turned to his companion. "Greg Porter will have a preliminary report in two weeks. We'll know where we're going with the Watch soon after that."

Greg Porter was one of Bob's senior project officers. Until recently, he had been working on the MID project. Like Bob, he had felt some difficult-to-articulate concerns about the direction of the program. When Bob had asked him to spend some time with Arthur Dee looking at the processes they had started to apply in the Hills Region, Greg had been glad of the opportunity to participate in a project which might give him a fresh perspective.

Over the last two weeks, under Arthur's guidance, Greg had been looking at the processes surrounding the production of the Dick Tracy Watch.

Ordinarily, the development of a new product by Comlink was treated as a series of separate responsibilities: marketing would assess the need for a new product; R & D would design, construct and test it; the operations staff would install it, then later, much later, the repair and maintenance people would become involved.

The situation was similar to a car assembly plant: each group in the chain operated independently; each contributed a special skill once only. When the job moved on to the next person, responsibility and influence shifted. In Comlink, Don Burgess was unusual in that he worried about what happened to his product when it moved on in the chain of events.

Greg Porter and Bob were contemplating applying a variation of the car-manufacturing analogy to the development of the Dick Tracy Watch. From the late eighties, Scandinavian car-makers had been experimenting with alternatives to assembly-line production. They had found that giving a team of people responsibility for the construction of individual cars resulted in significant improvements in efficiency.

The model recognised the principle that different activities did not have different overall functions. They were all intended to give the customer a sound product which would be backed up by good service. It was a fallacy to think the various jobs could be separated and compartmentalised. They were all part of a continuum which resulted in good quality service.

Bob hoped that such an approach would help to ensure the success of the Watch.

Clifford's speech drew to a close and the clamour of questions from the media began.

"Just when are we going to see all this change?" Don Burgess demanded.

Bob shook his head tiredly. "It takes time," he sighed, hearing himself voice the well-worn phrase of so many years. Don wanted a promise that everything would be alright from now on. Well, he couldn't give that promise. No-one could. Inevitably, some people would see a threat in the approach to which Clifford had now lent his support. Others would see it as positive, refreshing and exciting. It was up to them, Bob thought. He could not *force* people to change the way they thought. Nor did he have the right to. It would be a very long time before any large-scale change would be brought about. And it wouldn't happen until people were convinced that it could.

Chapter 32
Orpheus with his lute

Don Burgess sat staring blissfully at the screen of his computer. At times like this, he knew, the approved behaviour was to leap up, waving your fists at the sky and shouting to wake the dead.

After all, two thousand years ago, when Archimedes discovered the theory of displacement, he'd leapt out of the bath, slopping water everywhere and hollering 'eureka! – I've got it!'. Archimedes' work had been one of the first steps in mathematics' slow march towards the understanding of space and time which was still emerging from Einsteinian physics.

Yet now, when his own time had come, Don Burgess did not feel like crying it from the rooftops. Instead, he felt curiously warm and alert; acutely aware of everything around him, yet filled with a marvellous stillness.

Archimedes was right to be enthusiastic when the moment of discovery had come. Discovery was beautiful. Mathematics was beautiful. A perfect blend of form and content, like the chemical building blocks which determined the shape of life itself. There may be music of the spheres, but equally, Don reflected, there was music of the trees. Music of the trees to be played across the world.

The screen of Don's computer held graphic images: a central tree, thin, tall, few branches at its lower levels, a canopy at its peak, like a living sombrero; to the sides of the tree were complex spirals and honeycomb diagrams, perhaps representing cellular or molecular possibilities.

The scientist smiled into the screen, focusing for a moment on his reflection distorted by the curve of the glass. He leaned in towards the screen, watching his nose grow, sliding widely across the face of the glass. His smile broadened out, drifting to the edge of his vision.

He typed in a short command to save the material. For a brief moment a message appeared on the screen asking if he would like it saved under restricted access.

Don Burgess entered the password, grinning as he looked at it. 'Orpheus with his Lute' he typed, waiting a few seconds for the machine to store its data.

With a sharp click, he shut the lid of the computer and lifted it off the desk. He looked at the old-fashioned Grandfather clock against the wall of his study. It was three a.m. He'd done enough for today. Enough for a lifetime. He needed time to think about what should come next.

Chapter 33
The gods themselves

The announcement of a deal signed between the New South Wales Government and NetWork Ltd was made two months later.

It came as no surprise to many managers within Comlink. No-one was ever certain how Albert Lapin had gained early warning of the proposal agreed to by Hugh Britten and the Minister for Transport, but his information had been accurate, and the advance notice had served to provide Comlink with a chance to plan for the future.

Bob Cheshire had not been involved in that planning directly, but its chances of success rested largely on the results of the work he was doing.

Over the period following Clifford's announcement that Comlink would strive to adopt a 'service' philosophy, Bob continued to work with Fred Winters and Arthur Dee in the Adelaide Hills region. The project proved invaluable, highlighting uncontrolled variation in a range of systems with which Comlink people worked.

Uncontrolled variation resulted in wastage of time, effort and resources. Comlink's historical response to wastage had been to increase targets and quotas. As a result, workers had often been compelled to submit false returns and figures. Eventually, the picture had become so clouded that no-one – manager, supervisor, technician, clerk, engineer or linesperson – had any idea of the real position.

Yet decisions were still needed, so Comlink managers were forced to respond with what data they had, often unaware that they were using information which presented a false view of the way things were happening.

The gods themselves

In response to this problem, Fred and Arthur, Comlink's 'odd couple', had set up simple 'process mapping' studies in all the areas under Fred's control. Once these studies began to generate data, they were handed back to the people who worked in the areas so that those people could suggest the methods of improvement themselves.

Arthur Dee's statistical methods proved easy to use and easy to pass on to the various people involved in a system. For the first time, the managers and supervisors in Fred's region began to have a clear picture of how the systems they managed were operating. A wealth of information was generated, to be utilised and interpreted at the level where it originated (rather than being sent back to Head Office to disappear into a futile report that no-one would ever read).

But, while the information obtained was crucial, it didn't necessarily remove the old pressures, nor did it tell a manager what he or she should do differently in the future. But Arthur's 'WOI' did.

The WOI was a simple problem-solving model, the 'Wheel of Improvement'. The idea behind the WOI was so simple that it quickly became a standard point of reference for managers working on the project.

Even Fred, who had no time for clever diagrams (which he termed 'humming mushrooms'), found the WOI an easy tool to use and applied it in the search for solutions to the problems laid bare by data collected from the region's PAN exchange.

The WOI — or, as it was often termed, the PDCA cycle — was a four step process: *plan* what you're going to do; *do* it; *check* to see if the results match what you planned; then, if there are any differences, *act* on them.

213

The Prelude

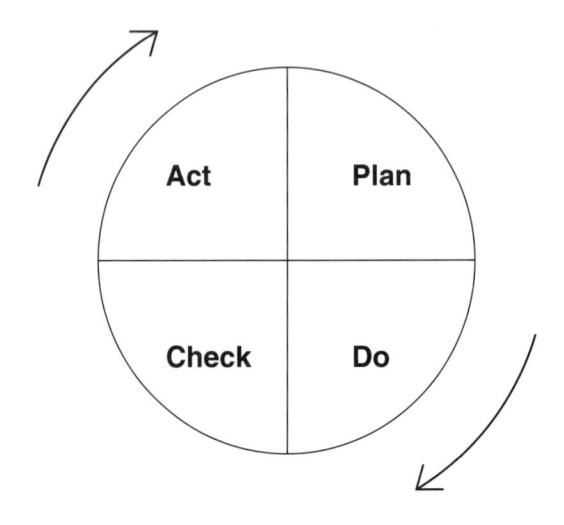

```
        Act  |  Plan
       ------+------
       Check |  Do
```

The effect of the WOI approach was considerable for people working in the Public Assistance Number department. Alarms attached to the PAN status boards were removed. For the first time in Comlink history, there were no sirens screaming to telephonists that they were doing a poor job. Instead, telephonists were invited to greet the caller and to supply a name if they wished. In the past, these measures had been frowned upon for reasons of speed and workers had been restricted to a terse 'Number?' or 'What's the problem?'

The telephonists were encouraged to keep a simple log of faults reported to them by customers. It quickly emerged that more than 30% of fault visits were repeat jobs.

Fred put the matter to the technicians – they were the ones who spent all their time going back to places they had only visited a few days or weeks earlier. The techs agreed to carry out a maintenance check each time they were called to a fault repair and to fix any obvious problems the check revealed.

The process was initially time consuming but after some weeks work pressure began to ease off to the point where it was possible to start scheduling jobs, rather than simply rushing from one to another.

Once a degree of scheduling became possible, it was easier to provide customers with a time at which a technician would call. This, in turn, began to reduce the wasted effort which occurred when a tech turned up at a house where no-one was home.

Gradually, benefits of this reduction in wastage began to show: the techs started to feel they were doing a better job and achieving a lot more in their working day; the PAN telephonists began to receive less abusive phone calls; stress levels began to lower, and absenteeism dropped.

In addition to these gains, Fred's discussions with the various groups involved in the fault repair process produced a number of suggestions from the PAN floor, one of which enabled Comlink to gain considerable improvement in customer satisfaction for very little cost. In the past, when a fault was repaired external to the customer's premises, the customer usually had no idea when the job was done. Occasionally, a tech who had just completed a job might ring the customer back to inform them the work was completed, but if the customer was out – as was often the case – the matter simply stopped there. As a result, people might have a perfectly functioning phone or switchboard, yet it could be hours or even days before they were aware that Comlink had done its duty.

At the PAN staff's suggestion, Fred and Arthur rigged up a computer which enabled PAN to advise customers when their phone had been repaired. When the repair job was done, the tech would enter the customer's phone number into the computer, which was programmed to call the number at regular intervals until the customer answered. The call would then immediately be switched through to a waiting PAN operator, who would inform the customer that the fault had been repaired and enquire about other aspects of Comlink service: directories, billing, and so on.

The computerised call-backs were an improvement which benefited both customers and staff. They gave PAN operators the opportunity to give good news to their customers – something which hadn't happened much until now.

It was slow going at first, as this and other changes were made and started to have an effect, but eventually the surveys began to show customer satisfaction levels increasing steadily. Also of importance, customer confidence

The Prelude

started to mount. Customers began to feel the organisation was giving them a good service, and were prepared to say so.

At the quarterly Regional Management Meeting, Fred Winters was able to present the preliminary results: customer service indices up 15%; sales up 5%; operating costs down 18%.

The Senior Regional Manager, Doug Evans, nodded slowly, "Maybe I'd better meet your Arthur Dee. You might have something here."

"You bet your ass we have," Fred smirked.

*　*　*　*　*

In Newcastle, similar gains were being achieved with the OFCAB project. The news from there was good, although Bob worried about the extent to which Alan Dodgson was concentrating so single-mindedly on his work.

Variation was the key, Bob reflected, as he sat in his Melbourne office reading Alan's report. Reduce variation and you would reduce wastage. The system's performance would improve.

But to reduce variation, you had to be clear where it was occurring. That's why it was so important to map out the performance of the system. The fault lay there, with the systems, not with the people.

Simple graphs and models like the WOI could help to identify and deal with problems such as the way different departments affected each other. If the next department or person in line was not recognised as a customer, the system would often be working away furiously to no purpose.

Alan and his people appeared to have taken the idea to heart. Their performance, measured in terms of customer satisfaction, had improved drastically. Confusion and alienation in the community had lessened, political pressure and industrial relations concerns had been reduced, and installations were proceeding adequately. But the icing on the cake was that commissioning rates were vastly improved. People were having their phones connected faster, and when the phones were commissioned, they worked.

The gods themselves

Bob tossed the report onto his desk. He rubbed the bridge of his nose firmly, massaging away some of the tension.

It seemed absurd, somehow unreasonable, that so much could have happened in the less than six months since he'd returned from holidays to find a hostile management meeting chaired by Albert.

Albert was gone. So was Anne. And it would take Alan a long time to recover from his personal hurt. In that time, Bob realised, he, too, had changed. What had begun simply as formless concern over the hasty decision to speed up the release of the Dick Tracy Watch had snowballed. It was now an organisation-wide issue, with others such as Alan, Fred and Arthur Dee involved. They had given shape and substance to Bob's original misgivings – shared, expanded and articulated them. And Clifford, Clifford of all people, had openly supported him. It was remarkable enough that Clifford should be sitting in the Chief Executive's chair, but that he had publicly and forcefully given his commitment was startling beyond Bob's normal understanding of corporate life.

Somehow they had managed to catch the flavour of the moment. Their work had provided a focus for ideas which had long been unspoken. Bob remembered a slogan used by one of the Green parties which had flourished a few years ago: There is no resistance to an idea whose time has come.

That was true to some extent, Bob decided, but an idea was not something which could be displayed in the window at K-Mart. An idea resided in people. It was a collective, sometimes unconscious, response to a set of circumstances. Ideas did not force themselves on people, people forced ideas on their environment. For better or worse.

Bob's thoughts flickered briefly over the MID project. Things seemed to be going well with that also. Contrary to his earlier fears, there had not been a need to change radically the project description. It had proved relatively simple to devise ways of biasing the data collection systems towards customer service. All the measurements were there, they simply needed to be aligned to the twin tenets of customer service: the consumer is your customer and so is the next person in line between you and them; and the only one who can determine the effectiveness of your service is the customer.

Bob thought back to a distant conversation with Simon Robertson. It was the Patterson's Curse/Salvation Jane riddle again. At the end of the day, if your customers were treated like Patterson's Curse, you'd be out of business quickly.

Bob hoped that would turn out to be the case with NetWork. He looked at the morning paper which lay on his desk. Hugh Britten was grinning from the front page. But the problem for Hugh Britten, as Bob saw it, was that he had taken a short-term solution. He might be able to make it work in the long-term, but Bob was betting that by then Comlink would be well ahead.

The NetWork move to concentrate on the business market was a risk. The creation of intelligent buildings was a high capital investment. Britten was betting on two things: that there would be no radical changes in technology – otherwise his constructions would be outdated – and that the NetWork organisation would be able to retain its efficiency as it expanded.

Bob doubted the second of these possibilities. Size increased complexity. At present, NetWork was a small, aggressive and vital organisation. As it expanded, it would inevitably become more sluggish; communication would become more difficult and responses slower.

It was an easy scenario to describe – Comlink was the same. Yet now the monolith was trying to claw its way back to its roots; to rekindle the close, service-oriented relationship it had with its customers in a distant past. The distant past was possibly a myth, but that didn't matter. A myth could give more purpose and clarity to those inside an organisation than a thousand official memos.

Bob could sense the movement. It was just beginning and it was yet faint: a few people in Newcastle and Adelaide; others in Sydney, where Walter Minogue had become interested; even Perth and some of the smaller Western Australian centres had somehow heard what was going on and were looking for some direction. But most importantly, the push for improvement would live or die on the threshold of Clifford's office. If the leader of the organisation showed his or her commitment, change was possible. If the leader withheld support, everyone would withhold support.

Bob felt certain NetWork's ties with the government, its heavy investment in long-term building projects and its reliance on a fixed technological base would slow it down. And the cardinal sin in a business marketplace was slow reactions.

At the same time as Comlink was discovering a measure of freedom and an ability to re-gain control of its destiny, its main competitor was willingly selling the same freedom. It would take NetWork years to discover the future it was constructing. By then, Bob hoped, it would be too late.

The gods themselves

And as for the first of Hugh Britten's problems – future developments in technology – Bob felt fairly safe that one would come home to roost as well.

The ultimate reality of the telecommunications industry was constant, irreversible change. When Bob had been born, computers in industry or the home were a fanciful dream. The smallest hearing aid was the size of a cigarette pack. The moon was a lump of unassailable cheese. Now, a shoe-box full of electronic equipment could carry more traffic than a five-story mechanical exchange. A hair-like optical fibre allowed more people to talk over a greater distance than a wire cable the thickness of Fred Winters' arm.

A camel could fit through the eye of a needle.

Chapter 34
The song begins

Don Burgess sat on the Orpheus data for almost seven months. Even he was not sure why.

It had something to do with anger and uncertainty. So many projects over the years had been taken and watered down; twisted to suit short-term opportunism when they should have been developed strategically and nurtured to strength and vitality.

There was risk too. Orpheus would change a great deal. It would have to, otherwise he would have failed. But it would only change things if it was accepted, its virtues fostered. The scale of change implied by Orpheus was staggering. Its impact would shock and frighten many. Who knew what would happen? He certainly didn't. Not in any complete sense.

Don wanted to open the Orpheus data to Comlink, but he held back, distanced by the continual demands the organisation had made for compromise and speedy results.

He had in his computer a product which would shake the world of telecommunications to its roots. What happened to that product – how it was used, how it was nurtured and developed – were all deeply personal issues. At the moment he had control, but once he released the Orpheus data there would be no going back.

Bob Cheshire's work had crystallised his concern. An organisation tolerant of waste, which controlled its people and suppliers by imposing targets and threats, which did not listen to its customers or stakeholders and which did not direct its technology and service to the task of meeting customers' needs – in short, an unhealthy organisation was one which would somehow corrupt the creativity of Orpheus.

Don wanted assurances that Comlink could accept and embrace the changes promised by what he could offer.

Entering Bob Cheshire's office on a hard, bright afternoon in late May, Don thought for a moment about a lecturer he had once had at university, a crusty old gentleman of Germanic background, given to wearing limp, grey cardigans and smoking a pipe (when the law still permitted such acts of social pollution).

The professor had written his personal motto across the top of the lecture-hall blackboard. It had stayed there throughout the year. No-one it appeared, was game to clean it away. *Mit der Dummheit kampfen Gotter selbst vergebens.* Against stupidity the Gods themselves contend in vain.

In some senses, Don thought, organisations were victims of their own in-built stupidity; a stupidity stemming from the false assumption that systems and structures are designed to control the individual.

Don Burgess had fought against that assumption over the years, creating its contradiction through his work. He believed passionately that the task of any system of work or society was to support people in their endeavours, not to hinder them. The concept that people were almost powerless in the face of the organisations they had created – that organisations somehow took charge, absorbing personal creativity and controlling the individuals who worked within their boundaries – was unacceptable to him.

"Thanks for coming, Don," Bob welcomed the scientist. "I've got some news which will affect the Watch."

Don sat stiffly, the small carry-case of his portable computer clutched tightly across his knees.

The past months had taken a toll on both of them, Bob thought. Don looked strained, and he, himself, had been working virtually non-stop on MID, OFCAB, the Hills project and a host of others. With Clifford's backing, he and the team of people working with him had wandered into areas and problems they had not dreamed of before. In every area of Comlink activity they were finding people who could contribute, people who could demonstrate ways to improve the systems with which they worked.

For Bob, it was both an exhilarating and an enervating time. There seemed no end to the opportunities for improvement within Comlink and no end to the desire they were discovering among Comlink people to try and make things better.

That desire was what made change possible. It had existed for as long as the organisation but, until now, it had been stifled and silenced by years of neglect; buried beneath mistrust, lack of information, suspicion and insecurity. In some areas, it would take years to break through those layers and establish a degree of trust between the various groups and levels.

The belief that he was involved in a process of empowerment was vital to Bob. People needed to be in control of their work systems. Improvement could not emerge in a work community stultified by fear, insecurity or powerlessness. And although empowerment frightened some people, there were many others who more than made up for those constrained by their own fear.

Bob looked at Don Burgess, seeing the changes in the research scientist also. The work with the Watch had been going well. It had been hard, but it was a product which was worth the investment of time and effort to get it right. A shared belief in the value of the Watch was probably all that had saved their friendship over the past months. They both wanted it to have the opportunity to become a worthwhile product.

And so, it turned out, did Clifford.

On his desk, Bob had a folder containing the report which had gone to Clifford earlier that day. In the terse, narrow script characteristic of the Chief Executive were written two words: "Do it".

Bob smiled at the scientist, keen to tell him that they now had the go-ahead to treat the development of the Watch as a single, integrated process. The work which was proceeding now would continue, but the commercial realities of marketing, installation, repair and maintenance would be addressed concurrently with the scientific development. Not as an afterthought.

The Dick Tracy Watch was to be Comlink's first attempt to control an overall system and manage its outcome for the benefit of the customer.

How they would achieve the task depended more on the people involved than it did on Bob and his staff. The main point was that Clifford had agreed to let those people decide their capabilities. Instead of determining the Watch's time-line in the Board Room or as a response to a newspaper article, the various groups involved would analyse their capabilities and set a schedule which would achieve their objective. Once they were able to work within the capabilities of their system, they would be able to fine-tune it for improvement.

"He accepted my report," Bob said, smiling widely.

"That's good," Don paused a for moment. "What report?"

Bob shook his head in mock despair. Picking up the report from his desk, he held it out towards the scientist and began to explain. But Don interrupted him.

"Bob, I need to talk to you."

Bob sat back and waited. Whenever Don had a problem it built up inside him until some oral release valve was tripped and everything spurted out. The process usually left the listener stunned and drained. Bob had been at the receiving end of enough Burgess outpourings to know that well.

Much to Bob's surprise, Don did not take up the invitation to release his verbal frustrations. Instead, he sat tensely, his face pale and his jaw held tightly. Finally, he shifted the laptop computer from his knees, placed it on the desk and opened it silently. He keyed in the password and waited. The Orpheus file appeared on the screen.

Bob looked at it, wanting to understand, but failing to see its significance. "It's a tree," he prompted, "like the one you showed me on the way to Adelaide that day."

The scientist nodded. "It's crazy," he said uncertainly. "But I think I can do it. The initial results are more than promising, they're wonderful."

"What results?" Bob asked, puzzled by the expressive fusion of joy and uncertainty on his friend's face.

"I've had them for some months, but I didn't show you before. I'm not certain why. It was just that I wanted to be sure. Sure it was alright. To show you, I mean." Don hesitated, looking closely at Bob and running his fingers slowly through his hair.

A sudden tension pricked Bob's mind. Something strange was happening here.

"It was this morning," Don explained. "For some reason, I felt I had to do something about it. It's been on my mind for months. There's that old saying, 'If you're not helping with the solution, you're part of the problem.' I've been refusing to help."

"Slow down, Don. Take it easy. You've been helping us with the solution for years. What's makes you think you haven't?"

"It's true, Bob. I've just been sitting back, waiting for you and Comlink to make everything right for me; to make me feel I could show you Orpheus and that you'd understand what should be done. I've wanted the organisation to fix things first: to fix the waste, the mistrust, the problems it has. Well, those problems are mine too."

He smiled and gripped Bob's arm earnestly.

"I've got the solution, Bob. It's important. So important it seems almost like a fantasy to me - as though the next time I open my computer the file won't be there and the dream will be over. But it's real. It's the solution."

Bob transferred his gaze to the screen. "What's special about the tree, Don?"

"Orpheus. It's called Orpheus," chided its inventor. "I was going to call it Prometheus at first, but the name's been used."

"What does Orpheus do?" Bob asked uncertainly.

Don turned away from the screen. It seemed to take him several seconds to focus on Bob. "Using the genetic engineering techniques developed in the past ten years, allied with current electronic processing technology, I believe we can develop a method of using specialised biological organisms – plants and trees – to facilitate the transmission of electromagnetic frequencies.

"It's a 'tree phone', Bob," he said rapturously. "It will send and receive signals in the same way a microwave dish or a hand-held transmitter works to move electromagnetic signals from one location to another. Instead of poles, wires, steel dishes and de-coder stations, all we'll need is trees – custom-designed trees, perfectly normal in every other respect apart from the fact that their electromagnetic emissions are made to operate on a given wavelength. Thousands of trees. Millions of trees. Billions of trees – all over the bloody place."

"And trees photosynthesise," Bob said, unsure whether what he was hearing was a joke, a dream or a potential truth. "More trees, more carbon dioxide converted to oxygen."

"Exactly! We've never had a solid commercial reason to plant trees before. All we've been able to use them for is chopping down and processing. Orpheus will give us a way to use trees in a natural context.

"It will take years, about thirty years by my guess. And a lot more skill than I've got. But this is the theoretical groundwork which will enable us to create plants and trees which can be programmed to convert and transmit electromagnetic radiation. It's a crude analogy, but it will be something like the way plants photosynthesise energy and use solar radiation to convert carbon dioxide and water into oxygen and organic matter.

"If I'm right, within thirty years solid-state electronics, cabling and switching, pits, wires, poles, microwave dishes, will all be totally unnecessary in a communications network."

They both remained silent for some moments, staring at the odd-shaped tree in the centre of the computer screen. Bob felt a cold touch in his stomach. It was a quantum leap in technological applications. Organic transmission. The tree phone. It was bizarre – improbable, Don had said.

Yet there it was. And if Don Burgess said that it was theoretically possible, Bob felt a comforting certainty that he might even see the results in his own lifetime. But the scale of it. He felt stunned. Unable even to try and contemplate what it might mean.

The genie was out of the bottle, Bob realised. Even if this went no further, it would only be a matter of time before someone else discovered the principle, or Don himself took the idea elsewhere. Where? NetWork? A concept like this belonged to a community, not to a single company driven by share-holder interests and the same materialistic ethic which had contributed to the current state of the environment. 'Greenhouse' was a word which had come to represent an amorphous threat hanging over the earth. Maybe this wouldn't mean the end of it, but it was a beginning. The beginning of a way to remedy the collected abuse of the past century.

But what to do next? Was Comlink ready for it? Hell, he couldn't even testify to his own readiness. It was too much.

Or was it?

Don's words rang in his head. Was he part of the problem, or part of the solution? An hour ago it had all been clear and simple. There was plenty of work to do, plenty of direction and a comfortable knowledge that things were going along a predicted path. Now that was gone, and Bob felt he was standing alone on a wind-swept hill. A flash of a past dream blurred across his mind: a tree, huge, crowned, ageless, standing before the wind. A bolt of lightning had thrust out of the sky to tear it apart.

Don shook his head. "What should I do? It's such a huge concept, yet so fragile. How do I bring it out into the open?"

In response, Bob picked up the phone. He punched in the number for the Chief Executive's direct line.

"Clifford we have to talk. It's something important."

The voice at the other end was terse, "I've got people with me, Bob. Can't it wait?"

Bob caught Don's eye and winked. "No."

The Prelude

"Alright, be here in fifteen minutes. But I can only spare a moment, Bob. I've got a major meeting at four." The phone clunked down, transmitting a burst of silent chagrin down the line.

"Will your tree phones be able to transmit emotion as well?" Bob joked.

Don took the question seriously. "Not yet," he replied quietly, pondering the possibilities.

"That's good, I'm safe!"

"Will Clifford see us?"

"Yep! He says he's got a meeting at four, but I think we can convince him this is more important. Now tell me more, we've only got fifteen minutes."

* * * * *

Fourteen and a half minutes later, Bob Cheshire and Don Burgess were standing in the outer office of Comlink's Chief Executive suite.

"There will be difficulties. Not just with the technical management of a project this size, but with community involvement, scientific pressure, political input and social impact. The whole thing is probably a Pandora's Box," Don rattled nervously.

"You're the scholar of Greek myths," Bob responded, "What was left in Pandora's box after she opened it?"

The scientist thought for a moment. "Hope," he said finally.

Bob looked at his watch. Fifteen minutes was up. He gestured Don to follow him.

John Hunter saw them moving towards the door, "You can't go in yet he's still busy."

Bob, feeling enthusiastic, grinned at the personal assistant and ignored his warning.

He turned to Don. "Ready?"

"Let's do it," said the scientist.

They exchanged a smile as Bob reached for the door handle.

The song begins

As they entered the Chief Executive's office, both men felt a sense that the horizon was opening up for them, providing possibilities rather than problems and barriers. Perhaps it was a shift in the way they saw things, or perhaps a more fundamental difference. Certainly, in the past months Comlink had seen a gradual development of confidence in its people and a related willingness to trust.

Bob felt fresh, awake. He was still frightened by the potential of Orpheus. But the future was no longer a threat. It was an opportunity.

Bob smiled once more at Don, knowing somehow that for them, the prelude was over.

Glossary

Like American English, the Australian version of our shared tongue is full of curiously-turned phrases and quirky descriptions.

We took a decision not to remove or "Americanise" these expressions, partly because they add to the flavour of the novel, and partly because they are a whole lot of fun to roll off the tongue.

For those who require translation, we have put together the following list of terms used in *The Prelude*. We hope it is useful.

agistment	Agreement to look after and feed horses/cattle in return for payment.
bloody	Mild swear word. Not usually regarded as profane in Australia. May be likened to American use of "damn".
bloody-minded	Difficult person, stubborn intransigent, one who displays obstructive behaviour.
boffins	People involved in scientific (esp. technical) research.
bowdlerised	Of books, censored, emasculated, abridged.
brace of ports	Two glasses of wine.
bug hut	Small, pre-fabricated huts inhabited by construction workers; notoriously uncomfortable, flea-ridden and noisome.
bugger	Rarely used as a term of endearment.

Bundys	Dark rum; classic Queensland rum made in the town of Bundaberg.
bushland	Countryside in a natural state. May apply to forest, plains, desert or a variety of environments.
butcher's paper	Flip-chart. Before the proliferation of plastic bags, butchers used to wrap meat in large sheets of similar weight and texture.
duntish	The unpleasant, thick-headed, vaguely squishy feeling one has the morning after (q.v. Douglas Adams and Peter Jones, *The Meaning of Liff*)
en-suite	Hotel/motel room with its own bathroom.
flash fire	Bush fire.
flat out	To work with as much energy and commitment as one can muster.
fussed	Miffed or irritated.
galumphing	Horses gallop; elephants galumph.
go; the go	The right thing to do, as in, "Wearing purple flares and love beads was the go in the mid-Sixties".
going out the door backwards	From the card game "Five hundred", in which the winner is the first to score five hundred points. The expression applies to a player who plays so poorly he/she ends up with minus 500 points.
good on you	To compliment someone on a job well done.
gooles	Small, circular puddles of moisture left on a bar or table when a cold glass of beer is picked up (Douglas Adams and Peter Jones, *The Meaning of Liff*).

Glossary

Green Party	Environmentally-based political group.
humming mushrooms	Derogatory term encompassing the stranger experiential activities sometimes perpetrated upon managers by organisational psychologists.
Judas-goat	A sacrifice, tendered in order to expurgate sin.
Kylie Minogue	Highly-successful singer/actor of Australian origin.
lift	Elevator.
lollop	The sprawling, blundering cuteness of a large, hairy, and overly friendly animal.
mate/s	Friend, companion, fellow worker. Used as a form of address amongst equals, more often between males.
mud crabs	Tasty crustaceans which live in the mud of coastal mangrove swamps.
pit key	Steel rod used for lifting the concrete lid from the underground pits in which telephone wires are concealed.
poons	Unpleasant people.
pottering	The sort of comfortable, aimless meanderings, often accompanied by indefinite hand movements, made by one who is in search lost keys, a screwdriver they have put somewhere, or any other class of domestic items which have a habit of disappearing as soon as you turn away.
rang off	Of phones; hung up.
ratepayer	Taxpayer.
runners	Gym shoes.
shop front	Store front.

skittles	Nine-pins, bowling pins.
spot on	Absolutely correct in every detail.
story	Storey (as in "two storey" telephone exchange).
stuffed it up	Made a mistake of major proportions.
tender	To bid for a contract for the supply of goods or services.
throcking	repeatedly banging the handle of an old toaster up and down in the forlorn hope that it might catch (q.v. Douglas Adams and Peter Jones, *The Meaning of Liff*).
tonnes	Metric tons (1,000 kilograms or 2,200 lbs).
touting	Pestering customers, soliciting business through promises which are unlikely to be filled once the contract is agreed upon.
twopenny bunger	A large, highly-explosive firecracker. The term dates from the time when a bunger (so called because it was lit and thrown) cost twopence.
uni	University or college.
up themselves (oneself)	Snobbish, conceited.
vert	Expression of disgust.
wallies	Nerds.
watch-house	Police station.
we'll be right	Don't worry, everything will be alright.
windscreen	Windshield.

About the Author

Stephen Bright is a communications expert and writer who specialises in organisational change and development.

Stephen works in Australia and the United States on a consultancy basis. He has worked extensively with many organisations to facilitate the implementation of Quality Management and Continuous Improvement practises.

His work focuses on 'internal' communications — helping management and staff to understand *how* and *why* their organisation needs to change and the benefits that change can bring to the organisation, its customers, *and* to people who work in the organisation themselves.

Stephen's work has received numerous awards. In 1992, he was awarded the Australian Institute of Professional Communicator's highest award, the Diamond Serif, for 'Best All Round Communication Achievement in Australia'. He also received the 1992 Gold Serifs for 'Best Special Purpose Writing' and 'Best Special Purpose Design'.

For *The Prelude,* Stephen was awarded a Gold Serif for the 'Best Employee Communication Project in Australia'. *The Prelude* was also a finalist in two categories of the International Association of Business Communicator's Gold Quill Awards.

Fax or mail to:

Somerset Consulting Group Inc.
1208A Somerset Ave, Austin, Texas 78753
Phone: (512) 834 0076
Fax: (512) 835 4998

Order Form

Additional copies of *The Prelude*:

Please send me .... copies of *The Prelude* @ $12.95 per copy.	
SHIPPING, HANDLING & INSURANCE	
$3.00 basic charge **plus**	$3.00
$1.00 per copy	
Sales Tax (TX residents only — call for tax rates)	
TOTAL COST	

Enquiries welcome about quantity discounts.

Cut here

PAYMENT
☐ Payment Enclosed
☐ Purchase Order # ....

☐ Visa   ☐ MasterCard
Card #   ....
Exp. Date ....
Signature ....
(We will add 5% handling fee)

Name:

Title:

Organisation:

Mailing Address:

Phone: **Fax:**

Other Quality Resources:

Please send me information about:—

☐   *a diagnostic* that will help me determine my support requirements;

☐   the *resources available* from Somerset Consulting Group Inc.;

☐   how my organisation can obtain materials *customised to suit our specific needs*;

☐   how my organisation could use *purpose written literature* to articulate its vision for the future.

Fax or mail to:

Somerset Consulting Group Inc.
1208A Somerset Ave, Austin, Texas 78753
Phone: (512) 834 0076
Fax: (512) 835 4998

Order Form

Cut here ✂

Additional copies of *The Prelude*:

Please send me ………. copies of *The Prelude* @ $12.95 per copy.	
SHIPPING, HANDLING & INSURANCE	
$3.00 basic charge **plus**	$3.00
$1.00 per copy	
Sales Tax (TX residents only — call for tax rates)	
TOTAL COST	

Enquiries welcome about quantity discounts.

PAYMENT
☐ Payment Enclosed
☐ Purchase Order # ……….

☐ Visa   ☐ MasterCard
Card # ....
Exp. Date ....
Signature ....
(We will add 5% handling fee)

Name:

Title:

Organisation:

Mailing Address:

Phone: **Fax:**

Other Quality Resources:

Please send me information about:—

☐ a *diagnostic* that will help me determine my support requirements;

☐ the *resources available* from Somerset Consulting Group Inc.;

☐ how my organisation can obtain materials *customised to suit our specific needs*;

☐ how my organisation could use *purpose written literature* to articulate its vision for the future.